PLATINUM RUST

ANDREW GNIADEK

Warning: *Platinum Rust* is a work of violent fiction with no relation to anyone living or dead. All characters are fictional created by the psychosis of the writer.

Copyright © 2021 by Andrew Gniadek

All rights reserved.

No part of this book may be reproduced in any form or by any electronic or mechanical means, including information storage and retrieval systems, without written permission from the author, except for the use of brief quotations in a book review.

CONTENTS

CHAPTER 1
BUSTED

"Ehhm, what's that burning smell? Oh, damn my popcorn!" Reaching for the microwave door a split-second instinct to stop blazes across my mind and just as many others do, I brush it off. Then all of a sudden a light clang, bang, and metal dropping on the ground sound.

"Dammit my arm fell off again!"

All of a sudden the sound of my motel room window breaking.

"Police! Open up!!"

As I go to open my mouth to say 'wait' I see a small metal canister. BANG!! Followed by a crashing blackness.

"Jeez Sam, a concussion grenade!?" Reba exclaimed.

"Hey Reba, this guy is very dangerous and we don't have a swat team. Me, you, and Hector ain't exactly a thirty man swat team. A mass murderin' crap stick like this needs to be taken down quick!" Sam shouted.

They entered the motel room to take the suspect into custody.

"Weird that a guy with one arm is able to kill four large

dudes. Umm, Sam,, Reba, how do I cuff a guy with one arm?" Hector asked.

Reba took a deep breath and sighed.

"Go grab the chain shackle from the trunk of one of the cars and wrap it around his waist, then cuff his one arm to his waist. Or maybe I should call your mom and tell her to give him a loving hug!"

"Reba, be easy on the guy he is all the muscle we brought, even if he isn't the brightest tool in our shed here." Sam said defensively.

Hector being the muscle with an imposing stature, six foot seven and 280 pounds of pure dumb Texas beef. Not all muscle but enough to intimidate most suspects. Hector the youngest at 24 with 2 years in the department. Sam an 18-year police veteran 5'10" at 46 years old and about a hamburger away from type 3 diabetes. Reba a year younger than Sam at 45 years old and about a pack of cigarettes away from terminal lung cancer. Even though Sam and Reba were both detectives Reba held the higher rank as an officer due to being with the department 2 more years than Sam. They pulled Hector out of regular patrol to help with special arrests like this one.

"Hey, Hector grab everything from the room and make sure to wear gloves this time! We don't need another case thrown out because of mishandled evidence." Sam said.

"BZZT" all of their radios went off at the same time, dispatch.

"Hey guys, we got a call about a possible body down by the old oil refinery." said a voice over the radio.

"Give me about an hour and I can come down there." Hector said.

"Roger that." The radio voice said.

Once back at the station Hector held the suspect up in his arms while Reba un-cuffed the suspects right arm from his hip. Hector held him tightly as Reba pulled the suspects hand out to take finger prints on a pad with markings for each finger. The suspect moved his fingers in and out and let Reba roll his fingers onto the ink pad then onto the white cardboard pad. Reba shackled the suspect again as Hector held him up.

"Let me get some time in the interrogation room for a little while with this guy and I will head over to give Hector a hand with whatever the hell is going on over there." Sam said.

Interrogation rooms in small police departments don't have a one way mirror like in TV shows. Usually only one or two cameras in a janitors closet they claim is an interrogation room, but this police station used only one camera. The suspect was 6 feet tall, light skinned, medium build, short dirty blonde hair, with a five-day unshaven face. Wearing an un-tucked black t-shirt with a faded rock band logo on it with a pair of blue jeans and some worn black sneakers. Looking up into the camera the suspect says:

"Ughh, where am...oh yeah police. Umm, can I get some coffee or a beer?"

As an interrogation technique police tend to wait several hours with a suspect in a room to loosen them up to giving incriminating information.

"C'mon I'll tell you everything, I'm too drunk to sit here and not fall asleep." The suspect said, looking straight at the camera.

Being one of the rarer ones and willing to give up all the information he had in exchange for one of his cans of chewing tobacco. Hector dropped off a white file box with the items he recovered from the suspect's motel room on Sam's desk to review.

The following recovered items:

6 cans of Yak Chewing tobacco (1 opened)

1 box of popcorn

1 burnt bag of popcorn from the microwave

1 Pair of Jeans

1 Rock n' Roll T-shirt

1 pair of socks

1 pair of underwear

1 Zip up plain black hoodie

1 Modified Magnum revolver handgun

1 Gun belt

6 Boxes of 50 count .44 Magnum ammunition

32 Rounds of Magnum ammo

3 Modified revolver speed loaders

27 small pieces of silver metal

2 long pieces of silver metal

1 trucker style baseball cap

"Come on! Just bring me a can of my Yak green chew or if you don't trust it, buy me a new one and I will tell you everything you want to hear!" The suspect yelled out to the camera above.

Both Reba and Sam were watching the interrogation room from a closed-circuit screen in a room behind the interrogation room. Sam and Reba glanced at each other, and then dug through the evidence gathered from the motel room. Six cans of Yak wintergreen long cut chewing tobacco, 1 opened. They decided to open up a closed can. Inspected it and determined it was indeed chewing tobacco. Sam entered the interrogation room with Reba following closing the door behind them, giving the suspect the can of Yak watching him eagerly attempt to peel it open.

"Now time for you to explain who you are and then explain to us what happened. Or, just confess for killin' four guys, shit bag, so we can go home!" Sam said, slamming his fist on the table.

"Oh hell yeah, my name is James Hawthorne from California. I am exactly 6 feet tall and weigh 220 somewhat fit pounds. I can bench press 100 pounds more than I weigh making me above average for my weight. Oh, and I can run really fast for a little while." James said.

Reba and Sam both gave an exhausted deep breath out.

"What is up with this guy did we obtain any info?" Sam asked, looking at Reba.

"Prints are going out for processing in a few hours, but besides white, dirty blonde hair, blue eyes, and no left arm we ain't got much else."

"Well hell, got that statement from the bartender that describes him as such."

"Sam you dumb ass that is about most of the men in Texas except for the arm. The bartender said he had some sort of robotic arm and I don't see one in the crap we picked up from this guy's room."

Both Sam and Reba stepped out of the interrogation room to come up with a plan for getting answers. James thought about his best tactic for getting out of any situation where you are trapped is to give yourself up right away. At least that is the explanation given to James when he learned how to be one of the best at what he does.

"Well, are you just going to slide me the can of chew then hide behind a monitor!?" James yelled, questioning the camera.

Just then Sam stepped in with a giant greasy burger dripping with some sort of orange slime while Reba watched on the monitor. Sitting in front of him this thing, an overweight mustache with a food stained light blue shirt appearing like a bad Rorschach test.

"MMgrumph, quesh, quesh, yeah we are listening and I will be sitting right here for whatever story ya got to yammer on about." Sam said.

"Huh!? All I got was your heart screaming for you to stop eating that slime, you banana slug!"

"Hrght mermah nggh, you better watch your mouth or you can plan on getting another grenade thrown at you in this tiny room!"

"Oh okay, so it was you that threw that one through my window at the motel. Well, that is going to cost you some teeth. Let me be straight with you I do not make threats, just promises of pain to come. Let's stop playing the tough guy game and I will tell you a story that will make you wonder what is real in this world."

Tap, tap, tap coming from the guy with one arm tapping on the can of chewing tobacco on the table looking up at Sam to ask him something.

"Can you give me a hand opening this and put a pinch in for me?" James asked.

Pointing to the can then to his mouth wanting some help with the opening the can of Yak. Sam stared at him and opened the can and took out a pinch of chewing tobacco and let the can with the rest fall to the ground as his meaty fingers shoved the tobacco into the suspect's mouth. Then Sam kicked the open can with his right foot spreading the chewing tobacco all over the floor of the interrogation room. He grinned as he plopped down on the chair opposite of James chewing his greasy hamburger with an open mouth.

"Here ya go buckaroo." Sam said.

"What the hell? You wasted the rest of it on the ground?!"

"This ain't no relaxation spa bud and only one of us gets what they want here. News flash, it isn't going to be you."

"Alright, I see how it is and now I am wondering why I am still here? Didn't my prints get run through the system yet? Usually I am released by now."

"Buddy, I don't think the President would let you go for what you did tonight. Besides our system is down and you're lucky little finger prints are going to be processed in another county tomorrow morning."

"Ah crap on a stick. Tomorrow, how many more hours until then?" James asked.

"Eight or nine more hours since it is almost midnight. So, what is this mysterious story you have that is gonna let you out of killing three civilians and one of our local city council members?"

"Aw what the heck no one will believe you if you try to tell them my story anyway."

"I don't need your story I just need to know what happened last night!" Sam yelled.

As James gave a blank stare to the detective thinking to himself with the inner voice saying "well, I guess Fred would make me move me off world for a while for this one."

"Well, Sam Grey, who lives at 1546 Sycamore Ave by himself, I am a bit of an over indulgent employee, studying not only my targets, but also all possible incoming threats to a situation. I had to know everyone in your small department's backgrounds to be safe. It also looks like if I did break loose you or your partner would not be able to run fast enough to catch me. In my line of work I try not to complicate things and the only reason I looked into this department was because I am after a former case you and your partner processed about three months ago." James said.

Sam gorped down the last bites of his burger not budging as James told him his personal address. Standing up to walk to the door not saying anything he left the interrogation room. Reba stood in front of the monitor waiting for anything they could use. Both Reba and James scoffed when he left the room without even trying to interrogate him.

"Reba, do you want to take over and listen to this nut

jobs story? Sorry, it is too much and I would like to go home."

Astonished Sam left her alone with a killer to interview. Everyone thinks all detectives are good at their job, but it isn't the case for Sam who is on the border of corrupt cop. The only reason he isn't corrupt is he is too lazy to be corrupt. Taking bribes takes extra effort and the FBI has already had to remove three cops from this small department because of it. Sam lied leaving to meet up with Hector to try to find out what he found down by the old oil refinery.

The pudgy cop left and a woman that appeared closer to 65 than 45 and smelled of cigarettes came into the room. Wearing a light blue button up shirt a little too big for her with some black slacks. Stating Reba as her name. Smaller than the last cop by a few hundred pounds. They would only give their first names to James, but he knew them from the background information he had on each.

"So, are you going to tell me my address as well to try to scare me too?" Reba asked.

"Na, I just tried to see if I could make the stupid cop to leave and entertain an intelligent conversation with a real cop."

Reba reeked of cigarettes from outside the room, but now she smelt like a burning cigarette blowing in your face even without one in her hands.

"Okay, so let us begin with last night and a little background and I will determine if I want to hear any more of this long-winded story you are set to tell."

"You are a smart person and have got a lot of gusto going for you. The only problem you show is you are too soft on getting your cases to trial. Someone's mom calls or another family member of the person and poof evidence seems to disappear. One of these times' someone's promises they won't do it again will come back and bite your face off." James said.

"Before you begin to judge me, let's nail down to what we need to know. For now look forward to a night in our holding cell, and we will continue this conversation tomorrow unless your prints come back with something the Feds may want you for. When you speak keep in mind you are in some pretty deep shit and getting out will take more than a good story to pull you out of it. So, we will see if anything changes in the morning when we start again. It is late, and I am not pulling an all-nighter for some drifter dirt bag."

"Well, a place to sleep sounds damn good right now since I am still drunk."

Reba took James by the right arm and led him down a set of stairs to the left of the interrogation room. A metal bed with a paper thin mattress, a toilet, and a sink all sat in a room smaller than the interrogation room above it. Reba locked James in the cell then had him turn around as she reached through the bars and unlocked the shackle from his right arm and hip. James went to the metal bed and passed out for the night.

CHAPTER 2
WELCOME TO TOWN

As the sun rose a sudden clatter of the single holding cell door opening to a familiar face. Sam wearing another Rorschach button up shirt, this time a light yellow. With a doughnut in one hand while making a waving motion with the other to head up and go to the interrogation room. Clock on the wall showed the time at 6:15. Sam appeared to pull the all-nighter Reba had refused to do. More haggard than the day before Sam did not chat at all.

"Sit down and wait until Reba gets here." Sam said.

No offers of coffee or doughnuts for the suspect. By the looks of Sam's mustache he already had at least a dozen to himself. Three hours later Reba showed up with a fresh light blue shirt and a less strong cigarette aroma to her. At least one of them had showered in the past 24 hours. She had a bowl of plain oatmeal and a coffee.

"Mornin' James, I received some news on your prints. They did show up in the database and the Feds want you to stay here for three days and await transport. Told us to keep getting as much out of you as we could in the time you are in our custody. Here ya go, eat some oats and a coffee then let's begin with what happened when you got to town last night. From the beginning of you arriving in town of course." She said, then rolled a fresh can of chewing tobacco across the table.

"Wow do you guys do bad cop one day then good cop the next? I do appreciate it and I will give you everything in my recollection of what happened last night. Just so you know no one died or was dead when I went back to my motel room. What happened to those guys happened right after I left." James said.

James took a brief pause to think to himself looking into the bowl of oatmeal. It is weird that my prints didn't allow me an escort out of here the same day. What the hell are you up to Fred? What could be keeping you from sending someone?

"I got to town about 6:30pm last night and checked myself into the roach coach motel. Unloaded my night bag in the room and went to go find something to eat. Walking across the street to the Bandelero restaurant and bar. I ordered up a burger and had about four cold beers when someone walked over to me and asked where I got such a nice trucker hat. It seemed kind of random for someone to ask a stranger. He said his name is George and also passing through. Some guy just trying to make conversation. George bought me another beer then he said he is a refrigeration repair man on his way to some sort of HVAC training in Austin. Texas is a big state and a lot of people travel for this and that, no big deal. Heck free beer why would anybody turn that down?

George stood about the same height as me, in a little better shape than you would expect a guy that fixes your air conditioning to be in. All types of red flags buzzing from the sight of him. He had some military tattoos on his neck giving him away as Special Forces. Wearing a black suit seemingly out of character for someone claiming to fix air conditioners. I told him I am in town going to Austin for an auto show to show off my van's audio system when it broke down. I figured since he lied to me it seemed okay to lie to him.

Getting close to 10pm when I went to bid him good night when I realized he followed me out of the bar. I thought whatever, the guy probably is going to go back to his room as well. Being the only other person at the bar with me. Then two more guys appeared standing in front of me almost like they came out of the shadows. It turned into an "oh great" type of situation. I kindly said "hi" and tried to walk away. Then I got shoved by George from behind and they all three tried to jump me.

You know how in movies all the guys try to fight the main person one at a time? Well, that's not how real life happens with three people punching and kicking all at once. They never attempted to attack someone with the type of advanced prosthetic that I possess. My left arm is designed to release my hand at will up to ten feet and retract back to my wrist with a thousand pounds of pressure holding everything together. Luckily when George shoved me I purposely dropped my hand on the ground in a fist. Sorry, but I really feel like an idiot trying to show my movements with a nub for a left arm flailing around." James said.

"It's okay keep on goin'." Reba said.

"So, I swung my hand up in the air like a whip and knocked one of the guys punching me to the ground then released and retracted my hand once again pulling it into one of the guy's backs. The first guy I hit had a busted out cheek with bone showing and the other guy began to scramble to his feet again when I sent his teeth crashing together with a swift right upper cut.

George locked around my waist and I could see him

reaching for something when crunch went his shoulder as I punched down on the arm reaching for the weapon with my solid metal left arm like a baseball bat. A broken shoulder is something to slow down most people, but he went down going for his ankle with his other arm. At the same instance I pivoted on my right foot moving backwards away from George to gather some distance. Now preparing to go for a kill or be killed move. With my left hand now back retracted I removed the silicone tips from my fingers exposing the needle like tips. Putting my hand in a full flat five-finger extension I readied to throw my left hand like a ninja star.

That's when George pulling out a knife from his ankle decided to fight another day and took off running away. Right when I am trying to wake up one of the guys to find out who they are all I hear is gurgling and "They will kill me if I talk" says the one that is semi-conscious. Then wouldn't you know it a damn air-conditioning van comes flying back towards me and George says "I don't need this, I will take my friends and leave. It wasn't supposed to be like this." He loads up his buddies and is gone in a blur. I go back into the bar and grab a shot of whiskey and go back to my room.

Of course, I am amped up for a little bit but also I am a bit drunk and tired. I take a dip of my tobacco load my gun up and prepare for something bad. I call my friend who doesn't answer and go grab some popcorn and finish off the three beers I brought with me. Drinking the beers before the popcorn as it goes. Then I do what any drunk does and twist the dial all the way and throw the popcorn into the ancient microwave. I pass out and forget all about it until the scent of burning popcorn hits my nostrils. Then we end up here in this luxurious police station without a left arm." James finished.

CHAPTER 3
WHO I AM

"Well, that seems very amusing James but what makes you so special to take down three trained men? Would it be you may have been on something other than alcohol and it was a drug deal gone bad? Leaving out one other man in your account of the story would make sense if you were on something other than alcohol and chewing tobacco. Besides three of them were found wearing white cleaning outfits with a carpet cleaning van parked in the parking lot not an air conditioning van. The other one in street clothes and appeared to be an innocent victim in your shooting rampage. Are you sure you were not buying meth from the carpet cleaners? They had about two pounds of it in the van with a pay/owe list with your name right on it." Reba said.

"Wow, someone is really out to get me and I thought I was paranoid. Sometimes I wish it was a drug deal gone bad, at least then I could get the hell out of this place. Besides all of my ammo comes from home base where it gets a little radiation treatment to make it easier to identify if one of my co-workers has gone rogue. Of course, it is not enough radiation to harm anyone, but a little bit kinda like a modern x-ray machine."

"So, just who are you and what is this quote profession you proclaim to be doing?" Reba asked.

"Well, to put it in the simplest terms I am a government bounty hunter handling assigned special cases. In the classification of special bounty hunters I am part of the "B Squad" and work closely with the "Enhanced Squad." The term "B" in "B Squad" refers to me and six others that blend in with normal people to retrieve our bounties. Being "Enhanced" means you are part of enhancement experiments with an altered your physical condition. The Enhanced definitely make a roid hound look like baby seals. Each group is assigned a target and an anticipated completion time before the "Extermination Crew" arrives. The Extermination crew has it easy and just eliminates targets with extreme prejudice. The B Squad and the Enhanced Squad are tasked with bringing targets back in alive.

So you understand the B Squad is interchangeable with the Enhanced squad as far as missions go. A lot of the time we end up working together, so we can stay ahead of the Extermination Squad. Our tasks are to bring in enhanced soldiers that ran off for whatever reason and try to pull them back into the military for re-conditioning. A lot of them end up in the rehabilitation center, which is basically a prison for super soldiers. Most of the ones that run off once served in the military for a good time and acquired severe PTSD.

Imagine you are the line that is sent in to kill an entire group of people for no reason other than your government orders you too. About 80% of the time they go with me peacefully without any issues. The other 20% make things a lot more interesting for my team. Each person whom is enhanced is assigned a termination timer once they receive their enhancement. The timer is set high for compliant enhanced soldiers and goes low for the dangerous ones. It is one of those things where if the public knew we had a group of soldiers with the ability to do what superheroes do they would expect there to be no conflict.

The truth is that most other countries grow their own enhanced soldiers with abilities equal to the soldiers here in America. Some of the secret war agreements are that enhanced soldiers could only be in involved if other enhanced soldiers are being used by the opposition. The same setup is set in all other countries with enhanced soldiers for recovery. B squad, an Enhanced squad, and a Termination squad is required to exist if a country wishes to possess enhanced soldiers. The rules are set by a group from far beyond our time here.

If the public saw a person jumping over a three story building or lifting a bus, there might be a panic. For an example I brought back a guy only 5'7" and 140 pounds with enhancements. Capable of bench pressing 800 pounds and could squat 1200 pounds with his enhancements. It is a major concern when this person runs away from his squad and starts popping up at public weight lifting competitions.

Now this fresh Enhanced ran away before deployment for his first mission. When I went to retrieve him he said he did not belong to the military. The guy only had about 15 minutes left until being made into pavement hamburger. This is one of the times trying to reason with the guy to go with me to keep him alive did not work. Guess what I did, trying to make sure this jackass was not eliminated by the Termination squad?

Left with no choice, while he bragged he would take out the Termination squad with no effort. I pressed my unsheathed left-hand index finger into the middle of his heart. Blood gushed all over my hand and I went into the zone of numbness to this guy. Funny how someone is gutsy until they are dying. All of a sudden tears began flowing and he started begging to live. I contacted the retrieval crew with news I retrieved my target and they kept him alive before he bled out.

A lot of these guys go with the simple make me tough enhancement and it ends up being the easiest type to take down. The formula will only allow a person to be made about five times stronger than their current physical limit with no side effects. The tougher ones go all out for the 8 times stronger than their physical abilities. At the higher level they need to be enhanced at a slower rate taking several years to complete physical enhancement. Usually they become much taller and skin along with hair colors change with the enhancements. One reason most avoid this is during the second phase there is about a 50% death rate and if you stop before going on with the four phases you will die.

They recruited me about ten years ago, because of no family attachments to run to if something goes wrong. The fact they diagnosed me as a borderline sociopath also gave me an advantage. Post-traumatic stress disorder has low likelihood of affecting my performance. I am no savior to the enhanced soldiers. If my life is in danger I often react with terminal actions as described by my boss. About 1 in 3 of the enhanced soldiers I tried to recover has been cremated because of me. The only problem with killing a target is none of the payment that I would receive if I brought them in alive.

Top dollar for bringing a target in alive is set at $400,000 and can be easy to claim. If you think I should be extremely rich with all the money for the recovered, you would be dead wrong. Along with the job comes the cost of the recovery team, the cleanup crew, and the get your ass out of jail team. They all charge excessive amounts and if you suck at this job you are sent to the recycling bin. Plus if you want any mechanical or additional physical enhancements you are going to pay for them. Hell this worn out looking t-shirt cost me $50,000. Now you know I am a Bounty hunter for some supped up Military deserters, do you have any questions?"

"Listening to your story sounds kind of ridiculous and outlandish. With that said, I do have a few questions." Reba said.

James poked around at the gray mush then finally ate it all in an instant and downed the coffee. He wiped his face on his right shoulder smearing coffee and oatmeal on his shirt. Reba leaned over with a napkin as James stared back up at her. He slouched back in the chair taking a deep exhausted breath in.

"Alright let me just let you know everything I answer will disappear due to my groups involvement. They will destroy all the recordings you possess and possibly give you a lobotomy. Not trying to threaten you, just wanted to make sure you are aware of what is going to happen."

"Well, a lobotomy would be nice since I would always be happy and forget about this piece of heaven. The first question I have is kind of a two part question, where did you acquire this supposed advanced prosthetic left arm and what is it made of? My second question is where did you find an eight round .44 magnum revolver? Eight rounds seems unusual for a revolver, that is a hefty cannon of a handgun as it is." Reba said.

"Oh, my arm and revolver come from around the beginning of the time I fell into my crew of asset recovery agents. I can start from when I lived in a trailer park over ten years ago. If you would like me too?"

"Go on, I ain't got nothin' better to do. Start from the damned trailer park." Reba said, as she rolled her eyes.

CHAPTER 4
TRAILER PARK

It all began about ten years ago when I worked as a computer help desk technician. At the time, I lived in a trailer park in Kentucky. Perfectly normal with no military involvement beyond getting a Monday off for Veterans Day. Being 27 years old living as far away from my past emotional pains as possible. I had a bad breakup with a long term relationship and found a place where I could distance myself from her.

Up front the trailer park gleamed in the sunlight and in the rear all decrepitly worn out. A tornado a few years before I arrived there had completely wiped off the front half of the park. Lucky for me I got to live in the back half of the park. The supervisor was a balding 40 something year old black guy named Tom. Good guy that knew how to fix everything in the park with mostly duct tape and a hammer. I would help him with computer issues a few times in exchange for a 12 pack of cheap beer and he would fix my leaking roof for the same price.

After helping Tom with his computer several times he had asked if I could help some others in the park with computer issues. Like a fool I said "why not," I could always use some extra free beer. Tom was also the one to get me hooked on the "good stuff" as he called it.

"Can't live if you don't got something to get you buzzed during the day." Tom would say.

Then with a tap, tap, tap, on the round can he went and handed me a wad of tobacco from his can. I went to say no, then decided against my better judgment and took the wad, shoving it into my lower lip. Deep burning wintergreen flavor filled my mouth.

"Careful, you spit it all out if you are dizzy." Tom Said.

The rush hit hard and I had an instant buzz. Of course, I felt dizzy, so I spit it all out as he stared at me and laughed.

"This ain't no kiddie bubble gum. This is the best shit a man can buy, Yak wintergreen long cut." Tom Said.

My head spun then I felt sweaty with my stomach trembling.

"Tom, I think I am going to throw up!"

"You throw up and I throw you out of the park!"

"Seriously?"

"No, just thought you were a man. Here ya go kid, you can have the rest of this can and decide if you are a kid or a man."

From that day on I made sure to always carry a can of Yak wintergreen in my pocket.

Heading back inside to the dingy trailer with old rancid carpet along with water rot on the rear bedroom wall next to the bed. Turning the water to hot in the shower only got the water lukewarm no matter how long it flowed out. The shower looked like something had died in it and the drain had a bad sewage stench. Not a single door remained on any of the cupboards . The windows had a nice layer of crusted white along with rust colors from the rusty old roof. The floor would creak and crunch under every footstep, almost begging to break open to the ground below. Paper thin walls made sure someone could hear all of your conversations and actions going on inside the trailer. All the trailers in the old section were like this and getting into a newer trailer seemed impossible due to the park owners using them to rent out to tourists.

After two years of being there the trailer park became home, away from everyone I had known. 'Knock, knock. Tom stood outside my trailer and he appeared a little spooked.

"Hey James, there is a new tenant in 308 and he wanted to know if you could help him with his computer?" Tom asked.

"Does he know the price?"

"Yeah, I told him but you might consider doing this one for free if he doesn't have the payment."

"Come on Tom, a 12 pack of cheap beer is not that hard for someone to come up with."

Tom gave a worried glance.

"Alright Tom, but if he doesn't have it you will owe me one."

Walking down the bumpy pothole filled road number 308 was four houses down, James was in number 304. Just as he went to knock on the door it opened right up. Standing in front of James a behemoth half a foot taller than him with blue gray skin and short strawberry blonde curly hair. This is why Tom trembled like he saw his life flash before is eyes. Looking him over it looked like he was some football linebacker with a weird skin condition. The guy was a behemoth monster of a man with giant bulging muscles and no fat at all on this one.

We shook hands briefly at the door and introduced ourselves.

"Hi, I'm Za." He said.

"James."

Za led me to his couch with the computer sitting on the coffee table.

"You look like ya want to ask me something." Za said.

"Just how big are you?"

"6'7" about three hundred."

"Just curious how you have not fallen through the floor yet."

"Ha, ha, ha, I did. Tore up the floor the first day after I fell through and had to reinforce it. Tom said he would take a month's rent off if I replaced the floor myself."

James observed the new plywood flooring with no carpet.

"I know I must look a little strange with my skin being this tone of gray. I got an infection and the medication has had a weird side effect on my skin." Za said.

"No, not concerned with that, just worried about falling through the floor of the trailer. It looks like you have taken care of that quite nicely. Now let me know what is up with your computer, and before we begin did Tom inform you of payment?" James asked.

"Payment?"

"Dammit Tom! Yes, payment as in beer for services of your PC. A man has to have standards for doing work after all."

"Hmm, alright let me see what I got. Got four left out of this pack here, hopefully it is enough for you."

"Ugh, I guess so. Just don't break anything on your computer next time without a 12 pack of the cheapest beer you can buy. If you try to buy anything that cost more than ten dollars for a 12 pack I will poor it on your new floor."

"Ha, man I like you and I don't like many people." Za said.

"Um, sorry I like women."

"You're a funny one, here's the computer."

"Okay let me see, it looks like your screen is just flipped over. Press and hold down the CTRL key and any arrow on your keyboard to rotate it. See, you try."

Za clicked as the computer screen rotated around constantly.

"How long have you been here in the park Za?"

"About two weeks. If you are wondering why you haven't seen me around the park it's because I work nights. Most people would notice me during the day especially with this allergic reaction to this medication changing me from a cool black guy from Los Angeles into a cool gray guy from Los Angeles."

"So, I am not the only one with jokes. Za, I will let the 12 pack slide for the night, but I will be back tomorrow for payment, since Tom paid me a 12 pack about an hour ago. Well, good night I have to go to work tomorrow. See you around Za."

The next day after work and a frozen dinner, James made his way back to Za's trailer to collect his payment of beer.

'Knock, knock. "Come in James, I saw you strollin' over from the window." Za said.

"Well, do you have my payment?"

Za slid a thirty pack of beer over to James.

"Whoa this is a little more than I expected." James said.

"I just need to confirm some information for my boss with you."

"What type of information?" James asked perplexed.

"Just some personal stuff we show listed for you. James I am going to be blunt, I work for the Government and need to make sure everything on file is correct. Are you going to be okay if I ask you some questions?" Za asked, sitting on his couch with a clipboard.

"I guess so, am I in some sort of trouble?"

"No trouble, just a few questions about your family."

"Okay, as long as I can ask you some questions back." James said, cracking a beer open.

"Sure thing, I wouldn't see it any other way. Now to confirm you are 27 years old and your parents perished at the World Trade Center in 2001?"

James nodded.

"Yes, I was going to meet them in New York with my older brother. They got there first and went to go site seeing before we all met up and my flight got cancelled due to the planes flying into the buildings. I didn't know they died until three days after everything happened."

James stared off distantly a little shaken when telling Za what happened to his parents.

"Okay good, sorry for your loss, it must have been hard. So, it also says your brother was on leave from the military and going to visit as well. Is this correct?" Za asked, leaning forward.

"Yeah, my brother Phil was leaving Fort Bragg and driving up when everything went down. He ended up getting sent with his Army regiment the next month to Afghanistan and got blown up a week later by an IED. So, I lost everyone in two months of time and went on wondering what I would be doing."

"So, that answers my question about your brother. What is your current job exactly?"

"I work at a call center for computer support for banking employees. If something doesn't work they call in and I can remote into their computer or walk them through the steps to fix whatever problems they may be having. A lot of the time it is fairly simple and having them reset their computer fixes the issue."

"Okay, those were the only things I need to send back to my boss. What questions do you have for me?"

"Well, is Za your real name or what?"

Za began pacing in a small circle in the trailer shaking his head up and down slowly.

"Let me lay it out for you with the brief history of Za. My parents were teenagers when I was born and both died in a drive by shooting when I was four years old. My full name is Waldo Harrison. My uncle Rudy took care of me as a kid since my dad was his younger brother and he had no other kids. Rudy would always bring home pizza from working at the local pizza shop and I would scarf it down. He would always say, "we shoulda named you Za for all the pizza you eat." When I turned fifteen my uncle got murdered in a drug deal gone bad and left me all alone.

From there I went on to a foster home and would escape to the gym to be alone and workout. I started playing football my junior year of high school as another way to escape my emotions. I would spend time in the library, field, or gym to avoid people. Another opportunity to escape popped up with an offer to go to West Point. All of a sudden it was 2003 and I had been playing football for the Army and on my way to go pro after my military service. Unfortunately I broke my ankle during a training exercise and received another redirect from life and here I am with this blue skin and red hair." Za finished, looking misty eyed and gloomy.

"Well, I will drink to a hard life if you will." James said handing Za a beer.

"Cheers, let the dead rest in our minds."

"So, now what should we do?"

"We can play checkers." Za said, with a hopeful look in his eye.

"Sure, why not. All I have going on tonight is this thirty pack. Or I should say twenty-eight pack. Remind me how to play again, I have not played since middle school." James said, cracking into another beer.

"Dude it's checkers. Just setup and I will school you."

They played checkers for about three hours when James left Za's place on his way back to his trailer. Outside the refreshingly cool night felt good, and feeling like a gaining Za as a new friend made the day better. 'Tap,'tap,'tap, taking a pinch of Yak and sticking between the lower lip and gum made it one of the best days in a long time.

Making his way back a bright glow coming from down the road towards where his trailer sat. Intensity of the glow increased with every step towards trailer 304. Making it back to the trailer the glow lit up the sky less than 5 trailers away. Running towards the glow to find out where it came from the odor of burning chemicals and smoke clogged James' nostrils.

"Help, Help!!" Someone screamed from down the way.

Brenda, James' neighbor stood there screaming.

"Tom is inside, he tried to pull Aaron out of there!!" Brenda screamed frantically.

Aaron the parks known troublemaker slash drug peddler. Good riddance if the scum bag dies, but Tom is another story. Frantically he glanced around for something to put the fire out with. Thick black smoke and searing hot flames meant the fire would probably take out most of the park. James, drunk and not thinking clearly rushed up to the trailer hearing a faint voice as he got close.

"Heellpp." a low voice whimpered out.

"Run out of here and find some hoses!!" James screamed back at Brenda.

"Someone call 911!! This fire is going to burn down the park!!" James screamed.

Walls of the trailer buckled out as the roof toppled down on top of everyone inside. Flames were licking up from the rear windows. Black smoke came up from the collapsed roof. Grabbing a baseball bat from out of Aaron's yard and taking a swing at the door a concussive force knocked James backwards into darkness.

Waking up to a white ceiling and beeping machines with a deep odor of smoke stained skin, the day had turned shitty. James found himself in the burn unit of the hospital when he glanced around to see his left arm bandaged up with a splitting headache. Reaching over pressing the call button attached to the bed a voice answered.

"Nurses' station." The voice said.

"What happened to me!" James yelled into the little microphone.

Then the door to his room opened and a nurse stepped through.

"Hi Sir, you were in an accident at the trailer park. You were lucky to survive." The Nurse said.

"I can't move my left hand."

"You are scheduled for an amputation tomorrow morning with Doctor Meyer." The Nurse stated, looking at a clipboard.

"Amputation!?"

"Yes, you received some second degree burns on your face and other arm, but your left arm below the elbow was much worse. It looks like the amputation will be removing your arm from your elbow down. Your hand is completely burned to the bone and halfway up your forearm. I can give you some medication to help you sleep if you want."

"What about the park? What about the other guys in the trailer?" James asked.

"I will find one of the officers and they can talk to you about what happened. That is only if you are up for it. Would you like me to get one of them?"

"Yeah, please."

"Hi James, I am officer Patterson. You are very lucky to be

alive after the meth lab your neighbor had blew up. Did you know there was a meth lab in the trailer?" Patterson asked.

"No, I ran over because I heard screaming. I thought the trailer park supervisor was in the trailer and went to help. Is he okay? Did the park survive?" James asked.

"Unfortunately we found two bodies in the trailer and suspect they are a Tom Harrison and an Aaron Welt. They were so badly burned that we will have to wait until we receive dental records. The park is okay since someone got into a big rig and pushed the trailer out of the park. Someone there is a real hero and saved the whole place."

"Officer, was there a truck in the park or near the trailer?"

"No, must have pushed it then drove off."

"Za" James whispered to himself.

"What's that?" Patterson asked.

"Nothing, thank you officer. I think I will get some sleep now, could you send in the nurse?"

"Sure thing, we can talk some more when you recover from your injuries."

Soon the door opened with the nurse with her dark hair and bright teal scrubs. She appeared to be from some pacific island with dark tan skin and a tribal whale tattoo on her right arm. About 5'7" and appeared to be not overweight but the right weight for her size.

"Did you go to the bathroom yet?" She asked.

"Not since I got here."

Then she grabbed what looked like a very long dull needle with a long tube attached to a bag from one of the drawers next to the bed.

"You need to go pee in the bathroom, or I will use this catheter for your bladder. So take the stand here next to you with the monitor and walk yourself to the bathroom and go pee. Don't flush the toilet and when you are done hit the call light, or this is going to be how your bladder empties." She said.

"Yes nurse, I will try to make an effort. That does not look fun for anyone at all."

"Good, and after you go to the restroom or decide on the catheter I will give you something to help you sleep."

The door closed once again and in a hurry James grabbed the pole next to him with the heart rate monitor. Trying to rush to avoid getting a giant needle stuck up his pee hole and whispering to himself "fuck, fuck, fuck, gotta go try." Lifting up the white dotted hospital gown became a little more difficult for someone used to using two hands. As soon as the gown got high enough to avoid getting pee on it, the gown would drop down. Finally, after many attempts James got the gown out of the way and started to go in the toilet only getting the gown a little wet. Turning around to go back to bed the hospital phone in the room rang all of a sudden. Could it be the nurse? James wondered.

"How would she know I went pee? There are no cameras in hospital bathrooms, or even in this room for that matter." James whispered to himself.

On the wall next to the bed a beige phone with a long curly cord rang incisively. James answered, "Hello?"

"James, it's Za. Come to the roof and I can explain everything. Give you 15 minutes to scramble up here or go back to bed and try to live a normal life."

'Click, the phone call ended.

"What the hell is he talking about? My normal life is already going to be over after tomorrow with my arm being sawed off. Well, maybe he can at least tell me what happened after being knocked out. Definitely not going to be able to go back to typing on a computer for work after this career ending injury." James whispered to himself.

CHAPTER 5
RE-ARMED

A brisk 'knock, knock' on the pale white interrogation room door. Opening the door Hector a tall, stout, Hispanic guy, with a goatee, brown eyes, black hair, and an eagle holding a snake tattoo above his right collar. Wearing a clean light blue short sleeve uniform fitting him perfectly except the pants issued to him were about three inches too short, but his boots helped make sure he wasn't showing any skin. A look of innocence on his face, like he would not hurt a fly but could kill a moose if he had too.

"Hi Reba, I don't mean to interrupt you. I am gonna grab some food from the taco truck and wanted to know if I could get you something?" Hector asked.

"Yeah, just two chicken tacos and a giant burrito for James here. He has a lot more to explain after his most recent story." Reba said with a smirk.

"How would you know I would want a burrito? After all I could be lactose intolerant or allergic to beans." James said.

"Well, I guess you will either die from your allergies or starvation, you asshole." Reba said.

"I meant to say thank you for getting me something

other than oatmeal." James recanted.

"We will take a half hour break for lunch where you can sit and eat in your cell."

Reba hauled James back to his cell in the basement of the police department directly below the interrogation room. Built in the last thirty years with bars painted light blue with rust spots and chips all over. Containing a metal bed with a thin mattress, metal sink, metal toilet. Sitting on the bed James could touch either the sink or toilet when he stretched out his right arm. Definitely just a holding cell since no one monitored him, which also made it into a private space. As soon as he sat down on the bed Hector came by with the burrito from the taco truck. Hector didn't say anything and tossed it through the open bars, running upstairs as fast as he came down.

Not wasting anytime with the burrito James ate as quick as he possibly could. It wasn't so much being hungry for food, but the craving for the half can of Yak long cut wintergreen. With a pinch of chew in his mouth the time came to think of an escape plan if things went bad. The tobacco cleared his head settling his nerves allowing him to focus. Looking for structural weakness in the cell there were none. Cement bricks and iron bars are not something James would be able to break. Looking around he pointed the end of his left arm, with what appeared like the bottom of a beer can on the end towards the ceiling. Waving it back and forth like someone looking for treasure on a beach.

"There you are, not as far away as I thought." James said to himself.

Reba burst down the steps all of a sudden wiping her face with a napkin.

"There who is James?" She asked.

"You heard that? Umm, it's just my left arm. Up over there in the corner. Is that your evidence room?" James asked as he waved the remaining portion of his left arm in a circular motion.

"No, the area over there is Sam's desk. The evidence room is down a set of stairs on the opposite side of the building from your cell. It is the second holding cell, but we use it for an evidence locker. Here take this let's run back upstairs so you can at least skip to the part where you put some magic arm on that nub you're waving around."

Reba handed him an empty styrofoam cup as she led him out of the cell. Back upstairs they went and click on went the digital recorder she had been using. Using the cup as a way to keep James from spitting on the floor in the interrogation room. She smelt like she ate her chicken tacos as well as a pack of cigarettes.

"Where did I leave off? Oh yeah the hospital and getting up to the roof. I hope those were some good tacos." James said, as he continued his story.

PEEKING OUTSIDE of the hospital room door and not seeing the nurse at the station down the hall made for a promising escape to the roof unseen.

"Hmm, she must be in another room." James whispered to himself.

Then he saw someone move forward at the nurses' station, reading a book not paying attention.

"This might be a little harder than I thought." James whispered to himself.

He crouched down into a crawling position looking for any signs for how to make his way to the roof. Then he saw a sign indicating the fifth floor next to a map of the seven floor hospital. The elevators were directly behind the nurses' station, to the left of the elevators displayed a sign for stairs.

Slipping back into the room with the attached heart monitor machine, he hit the nurse call button. Lucky for him his nurse is busy and the slim older nurse at the station would need to respond to the call light. The anorexic senior citizen of a nurse in the same teal nurse uniform leisurely strolled over.

"Did you use the potty like a big boy?" She asked.

"Yes, I did." James said.

She didn't even look in the bathroom for proof and handed him a paper cup with two pills and a small paper cup of water.

"Here, take these and go to sleep." She said very shortly.

"Can I turn these things down?"

James pointed to the attached beeping monitor. She unplugged it completely to his surprise and said "Go to sleep, so I can finish my stories."

Not even watching to see if James had taken the pills. As she stepped out the door James slipped out right behind her. A quick left around the corner and when she glanced back from the station it appeared as his door had closed.

Once she began reading her book, he started to slowly crawl under the waist high nurses' desk. Then 'brrrnng another call light went off and James seized his moment with the brief distraction and dashed through the door for the stairs. Running up the stairs as quietly and quickly as possible reaching the door for the roof. The door read 'Roof Access' with 'Door to Remain Locked at All Times'. James tried to open the door but it is in fact very much locked.

Knocking on the door James said "Za, are you there?"

Suddenly crunching whining metal sounds as the door crumpled apart with pure brute strength of Za.

"Hey James, glad you made it. Sorry, I was looking at the helicopter doors on the other side of the roof. I did not think they had another door." Za said.

Za wore a burnt black sweatshirt with Army in red letters across his massive chest and some track pants with flip-flop sandals. Grey skin with short curly red hair, and now showing red body hair through the burnt portions of his outfit.

"You probably have a million questions and everything will make more sense when Fred gets here. We should be good to talk up here since it is awfully close to 4am and the security guards never come up here." Za said.

Suddenly something crept out of the shadows in almost a slow motion. A figure no taller than 4'5" tall with a wiry build and a head the shape of a light bulb lurched towards them. Light gray skin appeared in the light with bulbous steam punk goggled eyes wearing a red polo t-shirt, brown pants, and tennis shoes.

"Hii Imm Fed." It said, speaking like someone with their tongue glued to the top of their mouth.

James felt apprehensive of this alien looking being since it appeared as described as an alien on all of those TV shows he would watch, of course without the clothing.

"I..I am James." He said, trembling.

"Ames I ave a popittion fa you to oin are eam." Fred said.

"Huh?" James said.

Fred waved over Za and asked him to explain.

"James, Fred wants to give you one last chance to go back downstairs and forget this ever happened or you can be part of something a little more interesting." Za said.

"Okay, I think I will stay and see what this is about."

"Well, this first part he says is going to take care of the issue with your left arm, but he needs you to unwrap it and stick it straight out."

Pulling away the white gauze dressing it became more blood and black stained as he began to unwrap his arm. After unwrapping his arm he could see he had lost his pinky and index finger. His hand now completely black like charcoal all the way to the wrist, with muscle and bone exposed up to his elbow. Fred came over to take a look at it and poked at James' hand with his finger.

"Is it urt?" Fred asked.

"No, not there but going up to the middle of my forearm feels like it is still on fire."

"Okay James, we are going to begin and Walter is going to hold you still." Za said.

The roof top shook as a wall appeared to be moving towards them from the shadows. A ten-foot tall monster with pale white skin, no hair, and a black suit appeared in front of him.

"Hi, you must be Walter." James said.

Za and Fred glanced at each other and chuckled.

"He can't talk, or even do much on his own without Fred. He is here to help hold you down for the next part of this little thing we have to do." Za said.

"What do you have to.." Before James could finish his sentence Walter grabbed around his waist with one hand and held his burnt left hand out like a tooth pick.

Fred held what appeared like one of those spring two handed weight devices from the 1980s. It had a circular center that would spin as Fred would pull it apart making a slight whirring sound. Fred pressed it against James fingers and black smoke would come out of the sides around the whirring center part. It wasn't until it ground past his wrist when it started to feel painful and Fred did not slow down. Grinding away, spitting out red mist, crunching on bone, blood spattered everywhere. James squirmed uncontrollably while writhing in pain with tears and screaming for them to stop, hoping to pass out so he might stop feeling.

Suddenly it stopped right at the elbow bone exactly. Fred pushed it back from a pulled out position into an inward position, it made a clicking sound and steam came off of it. Fred pulled the amputation device away and attached to James' elbow was what appeared like a bottom of a beer can but slightly bigger to fit his arm. A metal band an inch around now sat at the bottom of his arm with an upside down beer can on the end. Walter released James from his crushing grip and James fell to the ground wiping away tears. Taking a deep breath in to recover from the sudden trauma, Fred stuck James in the left upper arm with a needle.

"The shot was for infection." Za said.

"Oopps." Fred said.

Za and Fred had another little huddle.

"Just so you don't get mad he forgot he had some pain killer that would have made this a little less stressful for you." Za said.

"What the hell!? Are you the dumbest alien Doctor around or what!?" James screamed.

"Actually he is not a Doctor, and the alien thing is a bit complicated."

Fred pressed a button on what seemed like a garage door opener. A massive military helicopter came down on the helicopter pad.

"Let's go, we have to get you up to speed." Za said.

Fred pushed a blue bottled drink into James' right hand.

"Rink tis." Fred said.

It tasted like a blue sports drink in a tall bottle, because that's all it was. Fred wiped the red blood off of his face and cleaning up Walter's enormous hands. After an hour ride in the helicopter it finally landed at an old abandoned military base.

"James, come with me and you can get some sleep before you see the Doctor about your arm. Man you have had one hell of a night so try to get a few hours rest." Za said.

Za had James follow him down the short helicopter pad to an old dormitory 50 yards from the landing pad. It smelt like stale water, rust, and mold with old faded paint lined with 50 cots all covered in 10 years of dust. Sleep is all James could think about and passed out on the first cot in the room. Five hours had passed by in what felt like five minutes. 'Clang, Clang on the door.

"Wake Up! Time to see Dr. Death, I mean Dr. Garcia. She will fit you with something to go on the end of that stub. I can't wait to start with the real fun of getting you trained up!" Za had exclaimed.

"Huh, where am, oh yeah. Man I felt wiped out after last night. Guess it is all real then. Can I ask you some questions Za?"

Za shook his head no and pointed out the door across from the helicopter pad. The building had a faded red cross on it in the same half cylinder shape as the building he sat in. This was an odd looking base since all the buildings seemed to circle the helicopter pad in the middle making a star formation.

Za stood in the doorway watching James saunter over to the medical building pointing until James went inside. The door made a loud creaking sound as he pulled it open. A Hispanic female wearing a white lab coat sat at a metal table in the empty building with a large brown paper bag.

"Hi Mr. Hawthorne, I am Dr. Garcia and I will be over seeing your medical care. It appears everything with the removal of your arm went well?" She asked.

"Well, Fred forg.." Before James could finish she furrowed her brow and said. "He forgot the pain medication? Well, let me take a look at your arm."

He put his left arm with the metal cap on the end out and up to her face.

"Well, at least he gave you the antibiotic and it looks

good. Here you are." Dr. Garcia said, sliding the paper bag across the floor to him.

It clanged and rattled as it slid across the cold cement floor. Bending over to pick up the bag it began to make an electric humming sound. 'Clang, clang, snap. A silver skeletal arm came together at the end of James' left elbow.

"Don't worry we had your X-rays and whatever is missing we mirrored and copied from your right arm. It is hyper allergenic and won't tarnish easily." She said.

"So, a silver arm, is this for hunting vampires?"

"Actually James, it is pure platinum and the thing attached to your elbow is a gravity magnet set to attract the platinum pieces in your new arm. In the cap on your elbow your existing tendons from your arm are bound down so you will still feel pressure as if you still had your original arm. Of course, you won't feel any heat, cold, or pain sensations. It is actually a failed test design made by the...well never mind, it should work fine for you."

This new thing added to a compiling list of questions in James' head about what he is needed for. Fred came in the door by himself about to say something when Dr. Garcia stopped him.

"Hang on Fred put on your necklace and here James here's one for you."

Handing them both a thin wire necklace with a small blue ball pendant.

"Press and hold the ball on the pendant." Dr. Garcia said.

"Okay, I pressed the ball now what." James said without opening his mouth.

"Good they work. They are telepathic communication necklaces. Fred keeps losing his and I can barely understand what the hell he is saying without it. Make sure you press and hold the button when you want to talk with it. It only works if the other person is wearing one and will take you a little practice. Don't worry though Fred can understand you without it, but it does come in handy when you are working with a team and need to talk without talking." Dr. Garcia said.

"Thank you, Doctor. Now James, I will let you know what we need you for exactly in the building with the red door next door to this one. It is the only one with fresh paint." Fred said just by looking at James.

Fred walked out of the medical building and turned left.

"James, since this arm is new to you here is a glove to put over your hand. Stretch your left-hand straight out." Dr. Garcia said.

She had a can of what looked like paint under her chair. She opened up the can and it had a caustic flammable paint scent to it. Grabbing James' new left arm, she led his hand into the paint can dipping it all the way up to his new wrist.

"Some liquid rubber will stop you from puncturing your anus when you wipe yourself. I know a more skin tone would look better, but this is what we have." Dr. Garcia said.

The strange sensation of suddenly not having a lower arm and then having it again is the only thing on James' mind. Feeling her grab and pull down felt almost normal, all except the non-feeling of the liquid rubber. James flexed the fingers on his left hand now coated in black liquid rubber. Lucky for him it dried almost immediately leaving only a few small drops on the cement floor.

"Now go ahead over to the other hangar and talk to Fred about what is going on. I will be seeing you in the near future with some more upgrades."

James lumbered out and peered around for the red door to the left. Nothing there, no door to the left direction Fred had gone. Looking right, a freshly painted red door with a small window, peeking in he could see Za and Fred waiting for him.

CHAPTER 6
TROUBLE AT THE STATION

"You expect me to believe you have an arm made out of pure platinum and it sticks together with a magnet. Looking at my phone it says platinum is a non-magnetic metal like all other rare metals." Reba said.

"Yes, I know it isn't magnetic at all, but they called it a gravity magnet. Ten years before this started I would have called it out as bullshit. Reba let me walk past Sam's desk before I go back to my cell."

"Well, it is getting late in the day, we should continue this tomorrow."

Standing up from her chair she un-cuffed his right arm from the table and led James out of the room. Turning to go down the stairs to his cell Reba suddenly grabbed his left shoulder.

"I swear if this is some trick James I will tase the shit out of you."

They turned around and began to walk toward Sam's desk diagonally across the station past several other empty desks. Once they got to Sam's desk nothing happened at all and Reba became physically frustrated. She slapped the desk with her hand and gazed up to James.

"James where is your magic arm?" She asked.

Just then Hector came in the door with Sam closely following.

"Hector, we will be five hundred thousand dollars richer after we sell that platinum for cash. Go check on Reba and Special Ed downsta.." Sam said, realizing at that moment Reba is next to his desk with James.

"Where are the metal pieces we had for evidence Sam?" Reba asked.

"Well, they are back downstairs in the evidence locker." Sam replied, shakily pointing towards the stairs to the evidence room.

"Hector?" Reba said, asking the same question with her eyes.

"Why is the suspect not in interrogation or a cell Reba?" Sam asked.

Thinking fast Reba told Sam "His, call came in for transport to county by the Feds. Could you take him to county for me Sam?"

"I guess I could. Are you going to go home for the night?" Sam asked.

"Just after I put a new shackle on this guy for transport." Reba said.

"Come on Reba it's the middle of the night. Could we just take him in the morning?" Hector asked.

Reba gave Hector a deathly glare as he hung his head down knowing he said something stupid. Heading towards the back of the station with James she tugged him close to her.

"If your arm is anywhere it is in his car. I figure if your people are as big as you say they are you will have to come back here and wait to be picked up. If not then making Sam drive to county lockup and back with you is worth making me smile." Reba whispered.

Walking James over to Sam and handing him over like an animal on a short leash, Reba smiled and walked back to the interrogation room.

"Come on, walk close behind me. Hector will follow us out in case you try anything funny." Sam said, pushing through the double front doors.

Hector kept in close proximity behind them to make sure nothing happened. Sam opened the door to the backseat of his black police cruiser. The detective vehicle did not have a plexiglass window or a cage separating the suspects like a standard police cruiser would. A slight 'BZZT sound followed by ripping sounds of the backseat opening up with the platinum pieces cutting through like melted butter.

"Oh Sam, I wanted to do this ever since I met you." James said.

Positioning himself towards the passenger side door of the car for better leverage with his left arm now re-attached. James swung a full left cross with a closed metal fist into Sam's giant head. 'Crack, Sam's teeth crushed out of his mouth onto his driver side window. Sam went out cold in the instant of getting hit. Hector came running around to try and pull James out of the car from the rear driver side.

James only had a shackle around his waist and right arm which made kicking a lot easier than it would've been if his legs were shackled. Curling into a ball backing into the far corner of the passenger side James gave a forceful straight kick to Hectors face crushing his nose. Hector staggered backwards as James leaps out of the car crushing Hectors stomach inward with a hard knee.

Hector went over gasping for air on the ground like a fish out of water. Reba came strolling out holding a shotgun with a direct bead on James. He placed his left hand up, side stepping Hector.

"Okay, you had your fun. Come back inside before I spread you all over the asphalt!" Reba shouted.

"Reba, since you gave me a fighting chance I will come inside and keep telling you my story. You should find Sam to a dentist though." James said, pointing to the bloody tooth mess on Sam's window.

"Oh shit, oh shit. What did you do? Why not just run away? I didn't want him killed." Reba racked the shotgun keeping her aim directly on James.

"Don't do this Reba, I don't want to hurt anyone else. He isn't dead just unconscious with some of his teeth missing."

Suddenly James started pulling the bottom of his shirt with his left hand flat as he could. Trying to do the same with his right hand shackled to his waist, like trying to point out a stain on his rock n' roll t-shirt. He made a step forward and 'Boom, Reba fired the shotgun directly into James' chest. Still standing when the shotgun went 'crack, crack re-racked for a second shot.

Spinning to his right James closed the seven-foot gap and uppercut the shotgun with his free left hand. 'Boom, it shot into the air not hitting anything. Grabbing the gun with his left hand and pulling the shotgun forward and away lifting his right knee at the same time hitting Reba in the stomach knocking her to the ground.

"I thought I told you I have a very expensive wardrobe."

Reba didn't get hit nearly as hard as Hector but she still did act that way, coughing and grabbing her chest.

"Why, did you do that?" Reba asked, gasping for air.

"What? Defend myself from being pavement ground meat? Come on Reba, I will let these guys get moving to the hospital after I ask Hector one question."

"You ain't gonna run away?" Reba asked.

"Truth is, it would be much worse for me if I ran and

could result in more people getting hurt. I am really only here in town for my target then I disappear."

"Will you let them at least head to the hospital to be checked over?" Reba asked.

"Yeah, yeah I will let them go to the hospital after I ask Hector my question." James said, while racking the shotgun over and over ejecting the remaining shells.

Sitting on the ground Reba began to wonder how this almost average appearing guy with a prosthetic arm could cause so much havoc. James reached down with his left hand and helped Reba to her feet.

"Go ahead and ask your question then let them get going to the hospital." Reba said.

James just gave her an "OK" nod and walked over to where Hector began to gasp for his breath back on the ground. Dropping the shotgun next to Hector then helping him back to his feet. Hector stared at him like a wounded dog, full of fear and curiosity.

"The last time I had the wind knocked out of me like that was when I was 10 and my older sister caught me going through her diary." Hector said, with a smirk.

"Where is my backpack?" James asked.

Hector moved his head pointing with his nose to the car.

"There in the trunk, the pawn shop only was interested in your arm. Me and Sam talked about it, and we're just going to go drop it off for some quick cash. Sam said you were going to be leaving soon and wouldn't need it."

"Open it." James said sternly.

Hector opened the trunk and could see the blue cheap backpack had two things inside of it a metal cigar tube and a set of motorcycle keys.

"Something is missing." James said bluntly, looking up to Hector who stood seven inches taller than him.

Hector lifted the spare tire cover and there were two rolls

of cash with a piece of electrical tape around both of them. One roll clearly had the tape broken and bills missing.

"Okay, how much did you spend?" James asked.

"We only took enough for some food today and a bottle of expensive whiskey each to celebrate after we sold the platinum off."

"Okay, give me the bottle of whiskey from your car and take Sam to the Hospital."

Hector slowly walked to his car taking a napkin out of his pocket holding it under his nose. The napkin became blood soaked by the time he turned around and got back to James. He handed James the bottle and tried to pull Sam out of his car when Reba walked over to him.

"Here Hector, put these up your nose until you're to the hospital with Sam." Reba said, handing him two tampons.

"Are we going to be in trouble?" Hector asked.

"Well, I could remove your face with this." James said, flexing his fingers on his left hand.

"No Hector, head to the hospital then call me to let me know how Sam is doing." Reba said.

"Before I go, can I ask how much cash that was?" Hector asked.

"Ten-thousand, never know when I might need to buy a vehicle on a mission and I can't exactly have cash wired to me so when I go back to base between bounties I try to carry enough to complete the job."

Hector gave a confused look and walked off to the car with Sam and took off with lights blazing towards the hospital 10 miles away. The confusion for Hector came from only knowing James as a suspect. James walked back towards Reba with his cash under his arm holding the bottle of whiskey.

"Alright now they are on their way to the hospital can we take this cuff off my waist?" James asked.

"On one condition, you take your weird arm off when we are inside. It looks like something out of a horror movie and freaks me out looking at it." Reba said, lighting up a cigarette.

"Okay deal. Hey, look at this Sam bought us dinner plus a full bottle of 50 year aged whiskey from Hector."

James waved the bottle of whiskey in his hand using his head to point at the greasy bag in Sam's front seat.

"How could you eat after all of that?"

"More for me then, must be Sam's motto." James said, smirking. Grabbing the bag of food and whiskey they both walked back into the station as the next shift of officers arrived.

"Stay here for a few minutes and I will take a look at the items in evidence to make sure none of your other stuff is missing."

Reba un-cuffed James' right hand from his waist leaving him in the interrogation room. The greasy bag had three massive burgers and two large fries. James ate a burger and some fries in the time it took for Reba to look through the evidence stored across the station. The door opened and Reba looked a little irritated.

"Everything on the list is there, Sam never listed your backpack or cash. He must not have seen the cigar holder and just went for the cash. I also see he tried poorly to whiteout the listing for your arm and hand parts." Reba said.

"So, something I was wondering since I got here is where is the police chief for this station at?"

"He is on vacation for the next three weeks, and I am the officer in charge for now."

"Okay, here is what the little cigar looking container actually is."

James dumped out five small rubber pieces onto the

table. He placed one on the tip of each of his needle like fingers on his left hand and pulled on the lip of the container. The lip pulled out slightly and then the container opened up into a flat rectangle. The upper section had a small pager looking message screen and blue light up numbers on the rest of it.

"This is my phone I used to try to call my friend on earlier in the evening. He didn't answer, which could be good or really bad." James said.

"Wow that is a neat little gizmo, now what else can you tell me about the group you work for? Please try to continue where you left off."

Reba slid James another can of his precious Yak chewing tobacco and a bottle of water. James quickly drank the bottle of water Reba gave him and tapped the can packing another log of chew into his mouth.

"Sure thing, I will tell you since you have actually been nice to me. Except for one thing, you did shoot me point-blank with a shotgun while I was unarmed. In case you are wondering my shirt is made of a bullet and stab resistant material with the same look and feel as cotton." James said, lifting his shirt and showing a slight bruise on his right chest from the gun shot.

"Sorry for that, but you were like a man possessed in and out of the car. If you are such an elite fighter then why do you not have a muscular six-pack?"

"Beer, and I am supposed to blend in not be a fitness model. Jeez the only time I ever got close was the time during training, being forced to eat MREs for three months."

"If I shot you in the head you would die then?" Reba asked.

James spit into the bottle and smirked.

"Duh, wouldn't anybody. Getting shot in the head is one of those things that can kill me. I am not a vampire after all.

Oh, and shooting me in the foot would certainly take me down as well since these shoes are basic tennis shoes. I guess since I am still alive and able to speak I will continue to tell you what I remember. Besides, it helps pass the time while I am here."

"Let's send you back off to bed, so we can continue in the morning. It's late and I am exhausted." Reba said.

CHAPTER 7
JOB DUTIES

Awoken by a tapping sound of a pen on the cell door James glanced up. Reba leaned on the cell door with a pen and a cup of coffee staring into the cell. James got up and being escorted back into the interrogation room with Reba behind him. She pushed the record button on the digital audio recorder. It made a terrible shrieking sound until she turned it off again.

"Sorry about that. It's my arm, it makes digital electronics go haywire when it is attached." James said.

Sitting at the table this time Reba did not bother to cuff him as he leaned forward placing his left arm on top of the table. Releasing the entire arm from his elbow it maintained a complete shape until James relaxed. Pieces spread out with some smaller pieces rolling onto the floor. Reba bent over to pick up one of the pieces as it went rolling under the table.

"Don't worry about it, I can recall it back before I leave the room. Now let's get back to business of me spilling the beans while I am still here." James said.

Reba left the small piece of platinum and started the recorder once again. It worked without making any strange sounds this time. James sat back in the chair as Reba sat down across from him nodding for him to speak.

~

GOING through the red doors a gaping open space revealed itself dwarfing the internals of the other two buildings. Dug down about twenty more feet and fifty feet wider than the other buildings with a flight of zig zag stairs leading down to where Za and Fred were. They sat behind a rectangular metal table with an empty chair in front of them. Za waved his arms at James from down below. Fred appeared like a ventriloquist puppet compared to Za. Concrete flooring with concrete walls on all sides, the only way down are the stairs at the entrance. Completely empty except for the table and chairs for the moment.

"What is this place? Are the other buildings I haven't been in like this one?" James asked.

"This is the only Quonset hut like this out of the five buildings. All the rest are 20 feet wide by 40 feet long with 16 foot tall ceilings. This is going to be the lab and development building for our second level enhanced. Now to inform you of what we are going to be having you do." Fred said, pushing the button on his necklace.

"Ok, you need me for some sort of computer work?"

Both Za and Fred glanced at each other and started laughing.

"Man you made me cry, I'm laughing so hard." Za said.

"Ha, no James we decided to recruit you to help us hunt down AWOL soldiers with enhanced abilities. You are going to train and be weapons proficient after three months of training here. If you fail you will be sent back to your life minus your arm and memories of this place." Fred said, pushing on his necklace button once more.

In the light Fred had obvious skin tone from light gray to almost white palms. Each of Fred's hands had four fingers with two longer middle fingers and slightly shorter outer fingers. The fingers on his hands were almost twice the length of James' and had slightly round flattened ends. Fred had green egg shaped eyes, enhanced behind his egg shaped steam punk goggles. Fred wore a bomber style jacket, a child's dinosaur t-shirt, with jeans, and some silver slip-on boots.

Skin tone difference between Za and Fred differed since Za did not retain any skin coloration under his palms. He appeared bluer next to Fred and more unnatural. Za's red hair glistened in the dim room under the bright focused light over the table. His short hair cut retained the appearance of curls. Za wore a green Army t-shirt with black letters and black sweatpants. Wearing black and red shoes instead of flip-flops.

"Za will be in charge of getting your training started for the first month then you will be training with the other recruits while Za is gone. This is not going to be the same as military boot camp where the concentration is on team building, since I need you to remain an individual. In a sense this is going to be much harder as you will have to fight your way out of multiple impossible situations. Since you had your injury we had to bring you here a little earlier than everyone else. I expect you and Za to inspect the institution and if there is anything you require tell me now. During your time here there will be no alcohol during training."

Fred pulled a flask from his jacket pocket taking a long sip.

"So, is that some sort of weird alien drink you have there?" James asked.

Fred took a swig and said, "Whizzkey."

Fred tucked the flask back into the inner pocket of his child sized jacket.

"I have been chewing tobacco for the past two weeks is there any restriction on that?" James asked.

"No, here is a can I grabbed from your clothes before you got hauled off to the hospital." Za said, handing him a half melted half empty can of Yak wintergreen.

"Yak wintergreen, and what else would you be needing? Ahh, yes and clothes will be provided along with necessary bathroom type items." Fred said, pressing the button on his necklace.

"Nothing else for now." James said.

"This facility is a former military outpost used to test radio frequency effects on materials. It did not pan out well and subsequently got shutdown about 10 years ago. So, they did leave a lot of stuff here which we will be inventorying before everyone else shows up." Za said.

"So, when should we start?" James asked.

"After you take this, then you can start."

Fred handed James a giant egg, sausage, cheese, sour cream, salsa, and potato stuffed breakfast burrito.

"Oh and here's a drink."

Fred also handed James a large lemon lime soda.

"Man wish I could still eat those. Savor that since all you're going to be eating for three months is MREs." Za said.

"Yes, eat up you will need your energy. Now if you will excuse me I have a facility to organize."

Fred stood up and walked back upstairs through the doors.

"Man Za, what did you drag me into?"

"Well, we are going to have our work cut out for us since it looks like you have not worked out for about 2 years." Za said.

"Hey, I park in the middle of the parking lot when I go to work and walk all the way into the office!"

James laughed, spitting out some of his burrito as Za stared at him.

"So, back at the trailer park, was there anything actually wrong with your computer?" James asked.

"Nah, I had to check you out and see if you would be a good fit. Anyone could figure out the screen flip thing by looking it up online. Besides, I went to college and paid attention in computer class."

"Why would you want to use someone like me for this type of thing? I mean look at me I am not the most physically fit or smartest person for this."

"They need people to use with no family or other attachments that can blend in with regular people. The way they filter people and narrow them down is like this, one no family, two no relationship attachment, three no prison time, and four the most important a stupid face."

Now Za was the one laughing while James stared at him.

"Guess my code name will be Mr. Stupid Face." James said, laughing.

"Ha, ha yep you're perfect for this with that face."

"Okay, so I need to ask is any of the stuff you told me at the trailer true? Are you some sort of alien also?"

"Nah, man I am from South Central LA. I grew up around Crenshaw. The part I told you about in the trailer park is true. I just didn't mention how I came to be this way."

Za stood up as James finished his breakfast burrito and drank his lemon lime soda. James slurped the remains of his soda when Za nudged his right shoulder.

"Alright let's go upstairs and start with inventory and find you some clothes to wear. I mean you could wear a hospital gown and go barefoot the whole time if you were a true bad ass." Za said.

"I think everyone will believe I am some ass walking around in a hospital gown. Besides, I need to take a leak and I don't think Fred wants me peeing on the walls down here. "

* * *

Reba's phone buzzed away on her hip. She stopped the recorder answering the phone pausing James for the moment.

"Hello, hi Hector, how is Sam....Oh. Okay. Go ahead home, will you be okay for your shift tomorrow..alright see you tomorrow." Reba said, speaking into her phone.

"Well, how bad is it? Is Sam going to live?" James asked.

"Hector got him checked in last night, and they won't tell him anything since he isn't family. Lucky for you it seems he will live. Hector is going to be taking his patrol shift off this evening due to his broken nose. Ain't no reason to stop you, but I am partially responsible for Hector's injury, so I will cover the rest of his shift for him."

"Alright let's continue tomorrow. Do you mind if I keep my arm?" James asked.

"Keep your arm and yer tore up backpack, but put them under the bed in the cell so no one sees them. When I peeked in this morning I could see your arm shining off the sunlight. Just a minute I'll be right back."

Reba stepped out of the interrogation room for a brief moment coming back in with James' dark blue backpack. It looked like someone had attempted to fix his torn up back-pack with some fishing line and some duct tape. Standing up from the table James recalled his arm to attach itself again. The small piece under the table got hooked and caused the table to lift up then slam down.

"Oops. Sorry, I didn't mean for it to do that." James said.

"Just one quick question, where is the cash you had?"

"I placed the bills flattened out into my pockets. I figured they were safer in my pants than with the police. Now I have my bag back I will stuff it in there."

Reba opened the door to the interrogation room and looked back and forth. She heard a few officers talking but no one close enough to see her take James back down to his cell. She didn't want to run into anyone else with an un-cuffed suspect and a backpack full of evidence.

"Ok, come on. Let's go, back down to your cell for the night." Reba said, waving James to follow.

"Tonight and tomorrow night and I will be gone from your life forever." James said.

She opened the door and led him into the cramped cell and ran back upstairs. James took his left arm off at the elbow holding it over the backpack and it fell in pieces into the bag making a slight clanging. James didn't bother calling anyone since he had no reason to.

Stay silent and only make calls when absolutely necessary is what he needed to do. Besides after they ran his prints Fred would know his location and would only have him released or tell him to stay put if absolutely necessary. Considering the message of three days until the Feds come for him meant to stay put until then.

CHAPTER 8
PRE-TRAINING

The door for the cell clanged opened with Reba's familiar face. She wore a button up light blue shirt and navy blue pants with black police style boots. Reba looked professional and ready to get some work done. Even though her and James both knew they would be in the interrogation room for the next 16 hours with few breaks. James looked like his head fought the pillow with messy hair and the same clothes he came in with. He tried to push his hair into a semi presentable position but it did not work.

"Mornin' James ready to continue?" She asked, like he had a choice.

"What if I said lawyer and go back to bed?"

"Here take a few minutes and straighten up yourself."

Reba handed him a comb and a toothbrush. James soaked his head with water from the sink and combed his hair back.

"Alright let's do this."

They walked back up to the interrogation room, where two cups of coffee and some bagels were waiting for them.

"Ok, no lawyer since you got bagels." James said, smugly.

"So, what's up with your gun we have in evidence?"

"Well, it was acquired during my training. I know it seems odd just as everything else I possess is. Let me assure you it will make sense when I tell you about all of the fun me and Za had."

He sipped at his coffee and ate a bagel while Reba grabbed the recorder from her pocket. Reba placed the recorder on the metal table-top and pressed record.

"Let's start where you left off with your selection to this supposed secret group." Reba said.

"Alright, here we go!"

ZA HELD the door open at the top of the stairs and followed James to the barracks building. The door creaked open slowly and with a flick of a switch the lights all came on. There were only dusty bare foot prints from the bed and out the door from where James had slept the night before. With the lights on it looked mostly normal except for all the dust. Za began moving to the rear of the barracks with James following him. There were several full size lockers in the back with clothes left by the previous group of tenants.

"Here put this on." Za said.

Za handed James an outfit of a gray t-shirt, gray sweat pants, and running shoes. James began to undress.

"Wait, I almost forgot."

Za opened a drawer inside the locker with plastic bagged underwear and socks. Za handed them to James to change into.

"Around the corner is the bathroom and showers." Za said, pointing to the doorway on the left.

The rear of the building had two door openings on both sides of the lockers leading into the bathroom with showers. James looked around the corner and made a dash to go pee in one of the toilets. Basic with one wall lined with toilets and the other lined with shower heads and drains.

"Guess this is one of the few days I have privacy here?" James said.

"Huh, sorry was just watching you piss."

"Alright, now where should we begin?"

"Start counting clothes and writing down the sizes of each piece. Then we will move on to the beds by counting how many and everything on each bed. We also need to add what is missing." Za said, handing James a clipboard.

"Ok, let's get to it."

They counted every item of clothing and linen in the room and had a list of items they would need for Fred.

"Weird." Za said.

"What is weird?"

"There is a washer and dryer in here, over there in the middle, on the right wall where there should be bunks. Must be because this used to be a place for already trained soldiers and not newbies."

Za turned the washer on and then off, then did the same with the dryer.

"It looks like it is all still working." James said.

"Ten years of water sitting in a washer is a long time. Let's run the washer empty for a cycle before we wash all this crap."

Za turned on the washing machine letting it run a full cycle.

"That is going to take a while to run, should we do something else while we wait?" James asked.

Za had a smile growing bigger and bigger going ear to ear looking at James.

"Pushups, five hundred while we wait."

"Are you.." Before James could finish Za pushed him to the ground.

"Joking around is fine for the most part, but you need to do everything I command you to do while we are here."

James had not done push-ups for over two years and knew this was going to be painful. It took James an hour to do one hundred proper push-ups with long-winded breaks. By the time he got to one hundred ten the buzzer dinged on the washer. James soaked with sweat and extremely exhausted fell over.

He began to get up when the buzzer went off when Za said: "What do you think you are doing? Four hundred more to go!"

James kept at it and by the time he finished Za had washed and dried three loads of bedding.

"Okay, okay, I won't ask you anymore questions." James said, almost ready to pass out from exhaustion.

"Good, while this next load is getting cleaned we should go get some grub from the mess hall. It should be about 1600 hours."

James went to open the door but could not lift either of his arms. The sweat soaked shirt felt like a hundred pounds of dead weight. Za pushed the door open from behind James and pointed to the building that is going to be the mess hall.

"Man sorry about earlier, you can ask questions I just got a lot of extra stress with what is comin' up in the next few weeks." Za said.

"It is a lot for me to take in and I know it must get a little annoying having to train someone with no military background. Dude, I have never even been in a real fight."

Za pushed down on the handle to find the door locked. Za then pushed the door with his right hand, it creaked and crunched as he bent the deadbolt in the door. It opened to an empty dusty room with three enormous boxes and a huge metal sink.

"Great they took the stove and the tables out of here. Guess we will have to do with the water and those MRE rations for now." Za said, pointing to the enormous six-foot tall by four by four foot boxes.

James shrugged, since all he could think about is getting something to drink.

"Come on, go get a drink from the sink." Za said.

James walked to the huge stainless steel sink and turned it on. Brown water poured out at first then turned clear.

"Is this safe to drink?" James asked.

"I guess you will find out."

James bent over slightly to take a sip. The water had a metallic garden hose flavor to it. He drank his fill of water from the sink and then looked back at Za.

"You're still standing. Must be safe enough. The other two buildings are empty I checked them while you were sleeping this morning. Gonna need to add canteens to the list for Fred. Let's open up those MREs and eat some food."

Each box had been marked with '500 MRE' making them easy to count them minus the one James had and the three Za grabbed. They mixed water into the bags and ate with their hands.

"Za, what does MRE stand for?" James asked.

"Meal, Ready-to-Eat. We got lucky these are the freeze-dried packs since the standard packages would've already spoiled, and all we got to do is poor in a little water."

Za poured the last of his three pouches back into his mouth.

"Well, can we count on Fred getting a stove for the mess hall?"

"We can ask him, but he seemed confident the facility had all the necessary food processing equipment. If Fred thinks a sink with water is going to be all we need then this is going to be even harder on everyone coming here." Za said.

They headed out of the mess hall to go find Fred and give him their report with current stock and requested items.

"Over here!" Fred said, walking out of the medical Quonset hut.

"Here is the list Fred." James said, handing him a clipboard with the list of current items and requested items.

"Well, we will be getting more food here tomorrow and canteens will be coming in with the drop as well. Yes, some wash soap will also be necessary. Okay, looks good to me. James, why is your shirt soaked? Did you get wet playing with the shower?" Fred asked, pushing the button on his necklace.

"Za had me do five hundred push-ups, sir."

"Ha, ha, none of that sir crap here. I am here to make you a bounty hunter not a cordial soldier. Now I do believe Za has good intentions and you could use the exercise."

"Is there anything else you want us to do?" Za asked.

"Go check out the outer track of the facility surrounding the vast satellite dishes. Let me know if the track is suitable for running on. It is an exact one-mile circle." Fred said, pressing on his necklace and walking away.

James and Za walked behind the building with the red door, 300 yards away were two enormous white satellites circled by an asphalt road with a white line running down the middle. They walked around the circle with the giant satellites in the middle, clearing tree branches off as they walked. Every quarter mile a four foot high water spigot sprouted out of the ground.

"This one's good too." James said, twisting on the final faucet.

"Well, there is one way to find out if it is good to run on."

"Run on it?" James asked, knowing the answer.

Za tapped his giant grayish blue nose with his index finger.

"You do five and I will do twenty, once we get back around to the first faucet." Za said.

James looked at him and regrettably said: "Okay."

James started off with a light pace and Za stopped to drink water from the spigot where they were supposed to start. Once he passed the second spigot he heard a whooshing sound, as Za blasted past him like a semi-truck. By the time he got to the next quarter mile spigot Za whooshed past again. James made it to the fourth spigot already running out of steam, ready to fall over. Za kept whooshing by over and over again. James got his second wind even with his lungs and legs on fire he kept on. By the time he closed in on the finish it felt like he could walk faster than he could run. Za waited at the spigot where they started, not out of breath and definitely not sweating.

"Come on sweaty let's go talk to Fred and get you showered up." Za said.

"Ohh okay." James barely squeezed out, panting heavily.

They headed back over to the facility running into Fred as he walked to the helicopter pad.

"Good for Running on Fred." Za said.

"Good, just make sure he is better at it." Fred said, pressing his necklace with one hand and pointing to James with the other.

"I-I will-will get better." James said, still panting.

"Go take a shower and you guys should get some rest first drop is early tomorrow, and we will be setting up equipment along with physical training in-between." Fred said, pressing his necklace then taking a swig from his flask.

Za had a mattress on the floor since the cot's max weight is 280 pounds and the fact Za is slightly too tall for the frame on the cot. 'Shh, shhh, click the shower turned off from down the hall. Za showered up trying to put on one of the triple X gray workout outfits they had found in the facility. The fabric strained to stay together under his massive muscular physique.

Glancing over at Za it appeared he already began to transform drastically since the morning. His eyes were losing their brown color turning to an opaque white, the same as cataracts. Za started losing his sense of taste and smell at the same time.

James showered for a longer time than Za trying to clean himself up. He stumbled around trying to get a new outfit on, falling over several times due to fatigue. His cot looked better and better the closer he got to it. James passed out from exhaustion as soon as his head hit the pillow on the cot.

A loud smack sound on the concrete floor startled James awake. Za slapped his hands on the floor next to James' cot.

"Morning Za, what time is it?" James asked.

"0430, the doc needs to see you this morning after you take another shower. Man you still stink."

"Are you okay, your eyes are looking bad?"

"My eyes are still okay just look a little worse, but man I can barely smell anything or taste anything. I put some mint toothpaste on my tongue and it was like liquid rubber. By the way that says a lot for how bad you need to take a shower."

"All right, all right, here I go. Man, my whole body is on fire."

James turned himself to get out of the cot and get up and almost fell over. His legs were burning from the intense physical activity he experienced the day before. Every step became agony and undressing to get into the shower felt like fighting an invisible fire on the inside of his body. The shower felt good and cold. Za tossed some clothes around the corner. James put on the fresh outfit, a lot tighter than the outfit he wore the day before. Some sort of trick since the shirt was two sizes smaller and the shorts were the same.

"What type of joke is this?" James asked, stepping around the corner from the shower.

"No joke, man this is the size we need to get you to be by the time we leave. You wear an XL I just decided to move you down to a medium. It shows I got a lot of work to get done."

"Man, you can see my mid drift."

James kept trying to pull the shirt over his belly with no luck. Za headed out and over to the red door where Fred was getting things ready. James made his way back over to the medical center by himself. Dr. Garcia was sitting at a metal desk near the entrance, filling the rest of the building were eight bathtubs filled with what appeared to be BB's.

"Hi James, we need to get a preliminary physical and some physical information. I will be doing this with all the recruits and since you are here early we can test the tanks." She said, pointing to the bathtubs.

Each of the tubs was eight feet long by four feet wide and had a stand with a laptop computer attached. The tubs were as deep as they were wide.

"Go ahead James go get into tank number 1."

Dr. Garcia pointed to the tank closest to her. He began to walk over to the tank and was about to get in.

"What are you doing? Take off your clothes first. What physicals have you done where you wore your clothes?"

James shrugged and painfully undressed again and sat in the tank.

"Now let the beads go all the way over your face. Fully submerge yourself in them." Dr. Garcia said.

He did as she told him, finding it odd he could breathe as the copper appearing beads went up his nose.

"Yes, now breathe through your mouth for a moment. Nod if you can hear me. Good. You may feel a slight burning sensation."

She had a screen showing a green outline of the entire patient's body. Dr. Garcia clicked on a picture button which said initial scan then popped off with an: "Are you sure? Yes., No." Button. She clicked yes.

It felt good and warming for the first ten seconds then it went to a burning hot back down to freezing cold within a matter of seconds. Paralyzed in the tank with pain and tingling all over, abruptly stopping. He sat up breathing heavily in a panic.

"Okay James, not so bad right?" Dr. Garcia said.

"Itt...it felt like I was dying all at once."

"That is just the initial scan now time to see if everything is working properly. The readout is showing increased lactic acid in your muscles as well as tearing on your muscles related to increased physical activity. Lay back down please."

James reluctantly laid back down into the bead bath. This time it warmed up becoming searing hot followed by soothing cooling.

"Okay, sit up now." Dr. Garcia said.

He sat back up with an appearance of relief this time.

"What did you do? I feel great." James asked, puzzled.

"Each one of these beads contains a thousand nano-bots that appear like tiny spider viruses. They can repair minor injuries within seconds and can repair life ending injuries in minutes. Just make sure if you lose anymore limbs they are thrown into the tank with you to make the repairs complete. They react with an electric charge and are controlled with the computer that is attached. In cases where blood loss is greater than 25 percent this fluid bag will need to be introduced."

Dr. Garcia pointed to an upturned milk jug with what looked like water and a rubber hose attached.

"Now looking over the data you are 246 pounds, putting you 66 pounds overweight for your body type. The nanobots cannot do anything for your weight, but I am sure Za will get you on track for that. Now this tank appears to be working correctly I will need your help this morning setting up the other seven tanks." She said, pointing to the other tanks.

"What happens if it doesn't work correctly?"

"You would be pulled apart cell by cell and be a red goo in the tank."

"How sure were you this would work on the first tank I was in?"

"Not to sure, since this is the first time I have used the tank on a human. I have plenty of practice on primates if that makes you feel any better."

"That is just great, I am the guinea pig for this place."

Dr. Garcia pointed to the second tank with a smirk on her face. James put his clothes back on and walked over to the computer on the second tank. He got everything connected the same as the first tank. Cables were to some extent easy to figure out since each one had its own place. She handed him a thumb drive and said he would have to load the software and test each one by running the self-diagnostic. It took about three hours to get the tanks setup and running. Dr. Garcia undressed and hopped into the second tank.

"We must be sure they all work correctly." She said.

He ran the software and found it simplistic. James ran the same scan she ran on him and after she shot up and said, "Okay, you don't need to run the scan on me anymore just run the Health diagnostic in the upper left corner."

Dr. Garcia hopped out of the tank and ran over and laid back into the third tank. She was fit and attractive with a lean body and slightly tan skin. James was a little ashamed to see her running around naked hopping into each tank while he sat there clicking on the screen. They continued to each tank until they were done. Za popped his head through the door as Dr. Garcia was getting ready to put her clothes on.

"Sorry, am I interrupting something?" Za asked.

"Nope, just finishing getting the nano-bot tanks running." She said, putting her clothes back on like it was normal to run around naked.

"I would not expect my patients to do anything I would not do myself." She said, looking at both Za and James.

"Come on, it's time for some grub." Za said.

James followed Za with Dr. Garcia tagging along as they headed over to the mess hall and ate the ancient dried MRE rations.

"Fred is supposed to be getting the food supply this afternoon, so hopefully this is the last time we have to eat this garbage." Dr. Garcia said.

"What type of food is he going to be getting for us?" James asked.

"Well, for everyone that is not the same level as Za it will be a meal that is similar to a microwave dinner with better nutritional value. For you James the first month you will only get two meals a day, morning and night." Dr. Garcia said.

"It's because he's fat!" Za said, laughing and spitting food out at the same time.

"Thanks Za, I will remember that!"

After they ate an endless stream of helicopter freight

drops came and went for about two hours. Each drop similar to the size of a semi-truck freight container. Just as soon as it would drop Fred would be directing Walter, the giant robot, to push the container out of the way for the next container.

Za had James back on the outer track running again for another five miles. Exhausted and drenched in sweat again James and Za went back to talk to Fred.

"Walter kinda gives me the chills." James said.

"Me too. That thing is the freakiest thing I've seen."

They started laughing when they ran into Fred finishing up with Walter.

"James, Za, Help me set up the re-invigoration chambers. Then get some rest. Tomorrow is the big day when the rest of our team arrives." Fred said, pressing the blue button on his necklace.

"Where would you like us to start?" James asked, in a helpful tone.

"Let me show you how they go. It is considerably simple, but will need both of you to work as a team." Fred said, pressing the button on his necklace.

Fred walked through the red door with James and Za right behind him.

"Connect the lines like this and pressurize each container to the number 8 on the dial. One of you will need to turn the dial while the other one press's the pressure plate below in."

The Chambers were fourteen feet tall and eight feet wide with clear glass. They looked like giant fish tanks. There were twenty of them lined up in rows of ten on both sides of the room. Each had a staircase to the top with controls above and a pressure plate switch at the bottom.

Fred made it appear easy using Walter to push the pressure plate at the base of the first chamber while he turned the dial back and forth at the control panel on the top. Za pressed the pressure plate on the second tank he setup with James, while James tried to set the pressure to 8.

The difficulty came in the screen having two wave lengths, which had to match. With the green screen there were numbers in little square boxes number 1 to 10. The bottom wave and the top wave on both wave lengths had to touch the number 8 on each one. Too much pressure and the wave lengths would go to askew beyond the number 10 and go off the screen. Not enough pressure and they would stay too small in the middle of the screen.

"Put a little more pressure on it!" James yelled down to Za.

James twisted and twirled the dials and after thirty minutes of having Za put pressure on and off it finally got as close as he could get it to the number 8.

"Fred, how is this!?" James yelled out.

Fred scurried up the stairs.

"Not quite there. Here try doing it like this." Fred said.

Twisting the dial all the way around clockwise twice then the other dial counter clockwise half a turn. It stopped perfectly on the number eight.

"How the hell?"

"Well, me and Walter finished with the other tanks. I guess the rest of the afternoon is left to you and Za." Fred said with the necklace, going back to some other task.

"Walter was built by Fred some time ago. He gave it a mannequin Head with two cameras for eyes. The thing also has a center camera in between its two pectoral plates in the top center below its chin. Damn thing weighs close to five thousand pounds. Walter was the name of the first human Fred met, so he designed the robot after the impression he got from meeting a human. Just remember the goggles he wears control the monster." Za said, talking in a low voice to James as they left Fred and Walter.

They went back to the barracks and didn't say anything until James looked at Za.

"Push-ups?" James asked knowing the answer.

"Push-ups, let's go 500."

James went down and up 500 more times and went to the showers afterwards. They ate another set of rations and went back to the barracks. James sat on his cot opening his can Yak Wintergreen putting a plug in his lower lip. Not ready to go to sleep yet they both sat up looking at each other alone for the last time in the barracks.

"So, how about the Doc?" Za asked smiling.

"She is more or less good at getting things running, I guess."

"No fool, her running around naked like that, man I wish I could have switched jobs with you this mornin'."

"Why? What did you get stuck doing instead?"

"Man, I had to setup the weight room in one of the huts and the other one with the shower I had to setup a bunch of these shitty beds."

Za shook the cot James was sitting on shaking his head.

"Why would we have separate housing?" James asked.

"Well, I am hoping it is for some more females."

"Ohh, aww a big red haired monster, how I must have such a beast for my own."

James laughed as he saw Za getting slightly upset.

"Shut up! Man, I just want to get this over with so you can see what is going on." Za sneered.

CHAPTER 9
THE FIRST MONTH

James and Za awoke the next morning to the sound of a helicopter coming to the landing pad. They rushed out the door to see the troop transport helicopter unload their counterparts in this bounty hunter gig. A mix of 19 men and women exited from the first helicopter then another helicopter landed unloading 19 colossal gray blue skinned men.

The last group similar to Za had different variations of blue and gray as well as different shades of red in their hair. They were all muscular but in different forms, some were lanky and muscular and some were broad and muscular. Za still looked to be just an edge bigger in physique than all the rest even if some were taller he had the bigger biceps and chest.

"Alright everyone, get to the following barracks, for men go right and women go left! Fifteen minutes get into your physical training gear! Meet in front of the satellites on the road directly behind us!" Dr. Garcia said, yelling and pointing in all different directions.

Za and James were already dressed, so they headed over to the meeting point.

"Hey you two, give these out and make sure everyone has one." Dr. Garcia said, handing over a bunch of wire necklaces with the blue button bead on them.

They took them and went on their way to the meeting spot. James and Za walked around handing out the necklaces to everyone as they arrived at the meeting point on the roadway. The only issue they encountered was with a guy named Mitch Burton.

"Why the Fuck do I need this!?" Mitch shouted.

"So, we won't have to wash my friend Za's shirt again. The old washing machine doesn't wash blood out too well." James said, smartly thumbing his finger over to Za.

Mitch put the necklace on and walked off pounding his feet.

"What did you tell him?" Za asked, walking over to James.

"You're a lonely man looking for some good nighttime cuddles."

"Get over yourself and get ready for a double workout."

"Dude, I'm on a roll. Sorry, I get carried away sometimes."

The ground shook and the trees swayed back and forth from the trail leading to the road where all the new recruits were standing. Walter lumbered out with Fred standing on his hands, like a prize found by a child. Fred wore his bomber jacket with a kids cartoon character on his shirt this time. Same goggled egg eyes and elongated four fingers on each hand.

Walter lumbered until he stood with the satellite towers behind him holding Fred up above everyone. Some recruits looked terrified and ready to flee. It might have been the giant figure or the fact an alien from another planet stood in its hands.

Fred pressed the button down on the bead of his necklace and said, "Welcome everyone. Please raise your hands if you can't hear me."

He giggled a little and trying to break the ice for anyone that has not seen a being like him.

"My name is Fred, and I am in charge of the enhanced asset recovery program. I may appear to some of you as a scary out of this world being. To re-assure you my species has been here for a lot longer than you could imagine. My family is a refugee group from a planet beset on a war we hope to prevent on your planet. Our operations often run beyond what your Government would consider black operations."

"What the hell does this have to do with us! Most of us here have been in black ops. Your life story doesn't matter! So, get to the point light bulb head!" Mitch's final words.

Walter grabbed Mitch right as he stopped talking and threw him like a toy army man. Mitch flew up and into the outer perimeter fence three miles away from where they were standing. The force and speed had turned him into small pieces of bloody grated chunks. Most of the pieces went through the fence except for some clothing.

"Please hold any questions until I am done. As you can see I do not take insults well and neither does Walter. No one here should need to worry since I knew Mr. Burton was already marked as self-destructive, what happened here was going to be inevitable."

Fred clasped his hands together turning to face the crowd.

"So, back to my introduction, it takes my people roughly two hundred of your years to get here from what you have marked as the Zeta Reticuli planet cluster. Besides some physical and minor intellectual differences we are basically the same as humans. We live the same life span as humans, which means two to three generations sacrificed themselves to get my family out to this planet. I do not have telepathy or mind control as some would believe.

The reason for our larger heads is processing of a harsher atmosphere and slightly higher than average IQ compared to human counterparts. Slightly in the sense of ten points higher at our genius level and the same at our bottom glue-sniffing level. My IQ is 161 which is in the mid-range for my race's IQ. I am dumb at some things where others may be smarter which is why I will rely on each one of you to make very dedicated decisions. Now let's see if anyone has any questions and I promise Walter will refrain from removing anyone else." Fred stated.

No one moved or said anything for thirty seconds, then a hand raised from the crowd.

"I have a question. What is genius IQ?" James asked, honestly pushing the button on his own necklace not moving his lips.

"It would be anything over 160 for extraordinary was what was told to me. Yours is probably in the 120 range James." Fred answered depressing the button on his own necklace.

It was the only question anyone had asked since most of the people there wanted to begin training, and the rest were still in shock at what they saw happen to Mitch.

"Okay, now let me get all the future second level enhanced to stand to the side here." Fred said, pointing to his left.

"Everyone take a look over here these are going to be your trainers for the first month here. They will be responsible for making you stronger and better than you already are."

Fred pointed out to the group of giant blueish gray men.

"As you can see they have an obvious pigment change going on as part of the enhancement process. In the next three weeks they will be peaking out and getting less human daily. By this time at the end of the first four weeks of training they will be losing taste, smell, and some vision. This is normal, and we received nutrition supplies for them specifically, so they will survive getting into the re-invigoration tanks." Fred stated, looking over the nineteen remaining recruits on the right.

"Everyone has been assigned their own personal future level 2 enhanced person for training. With the exception of one of course. At this time I would like to ask anyone that feels this is not for them to leave. No harm will come to you and you can return to your regular life. Of course, we will need to sedate you and give you a medication that makes your last three months of memory go away. So, does anyone want to leave?" Fred asked, looking over the crowd and scanning for a hand.

A man and a woman raised their hands and were led out by Dr. Garcia.

"Okay, now we will be training and judging you at all levels of performance as well as improvement. Since we now have three extra level 2 enhanced without trainees they will work directly with me and help supervise overall training. At any point during the training you can simply leave. Just remember after the training is complete you belong to the Government for a period of time determined by past service. Anyone without any military service will be required to give twenty years to the Asset Retrieval Core. Okay, everyone pair up as I call your names out." Fred said, pressing his necklace and looking over everyone.

James panicked a little since he only knew Za and anyone else would not do for him. Lucky for him his pairing with Za was determined early.

"Well, looks like we are stuck together for the long haul." James said.

"Man, you were always going to be stuck with me. Verified you early on through a preliminary personality evaluation. Some of the others also know their level 2's." Za said.

"If you're a level 2 then what does a level one look like?" James asked.

"Look at those four guys over there they could be level ones. We will know as soon as we see what numbers they put up in the weight room." Za said, pointing.

The four guys he pointed out looked like roided out body builders from some sort of freak show.

"Your stronger than they are?" James asked.

"Maybe, or at least about equal. After the procedure is complete I will be much stronger, taller, and attractive."

"So what would unusual numbers be in the weight room for those guys?"

"Anything over a thousand pounds for bench is usually a dead giveaway. The gravity bar weights here make sure we don't need to worry about breaking bars or equipment. I guess the weight machines use something similar to your left arm. Plus most guys like to brag about how much they bench."

"Za, I feel stupid. Look at me, my belly is hanging out and my shorts look ridiculously small. I feel like the fat kid at a bodybuilding competition."

"You have to use what you got. I wanted you to know you will be fighting an uphill battle no matter what you do. Besides, if everyone is staring at your belly it distracts them from staring at me. Come on, let's go get to the weight room and see where you're at."

They made their way back to the newly setup weight room while everyone else was still getting acquainted with the facility. Entering the weight room they encountered all types of weight machines and benches reinforced for added weight of the enhanced level 1 guys to use. At least that is what James assumed. There were no racks or rows of iron weights like a normal weight room. There were three of each type of weight bench and squat racks.

"So, these are gravity weights, and they basically use a magnet to pull them down to the ground by setting the number on each of these you can increase the weight up to 3000 for bench and squat and 400 per free weight. The free weights have a little rubber pad in the middle of a circle to stand on so you can get a good burn with those. All the weights balance like real weights and you have to lift off as you would with a squat rack or bench press. Just like the real thing you can hurt yourself awfully badly if you push off more than you can lift." Za stated, like lecturing for a college class.

The bars all appeared normal except they had a four-inch by four inch square on each end. Each side of a workout station contained an individual keypad to input a total weight. Miniature three-inch screens squeezed into the bar ends would illuminate with numbers to show weight in red.

James pressed the buttons on the control pad for the weight on the bench press and put in the number fifty to test it out. The number blinked and stopped on both sides with the number fifty. Za stuck his hand out and pressed the clear key and put in 1200. It did the same thing this time James made an uneasy face.

"Ahhh!!, My arm." James said, collapsing his left side onto the metal plate on the floor.

Za panicked and went to get James off the floor, but before he could James stood up.

"Just messin' with you. Platinum is as magnetic as a piece of wood see." James said, knocking his rubber coated metal hand on the metal plate on the floor.

"Move"

Za pushed him over and laid down on the weight bench. He breathed in and out, pulled up and down a few times on the bar. Then he growled out, "one, two, three, four, five, six, seven, eight, nine, ten."

Za was breathing a little heavier but not much.

"Just make sure you warm up with a lower weight before you start." Za said.

Za typed in 135 and had James go for it to warm up. James had worked out fairly good in the past, but two years of eating the wrong things and drinking beer made him soft. He was still able to do a set of ten to Za's slight surprise.

"So, I will set up a workout schedule for you to follow and make sure you follow it very closely. Chest and back today, legs and arms the next day, then whatever we missed the third day and repeat for six days in a row. Day seven will be max out day for everything you have worked out. Each day you will be running, doing push-ups, and starting today pull ups. Understood?" Za said, stating not to engage with a question.

"Yes I understand, but what about sit-ups or other stomach workouts?"

"Sit-ups and crunches are for sissies trying to show off. Believe me with these workouts you will have stronger abs than someone doing a thousand sit-ups."

They continued on with lifting weights for another hour then went back to the mess hall as others were entering the weight room. There were long tables to sit at now with long metal seats to match the tables. Now the food menu was two choices for James which were beef and chicken in what looked like a microwave dinner tray. Each tray was a self-heating MRE with foods separated into each section. One corner was the meat section then a green vegetable mush and something that was moderately close to mashed potatoes.

James swore after trying both of them they were the exact same thing with different colors for beef and chicken. The fact was they were, and they were also a failed test MREs due to the size of the boxes. Ultimately the military went the route of self-heating bagged meals. Food for the up and coming future level 2 enhanced soldiers was two large cans of something with a label clearly torn off for three meals a day.

"Za! What the hell are you eating!? It smells like wet cat food."

"Nah, man its dog food, look at this they were in the dumpster around the corner."

Za slid a dog food label to James.

"Beef and lamb flavored dog food. How can you eat that like its ice-cream?"

"Man, everything tastes like flavorless tofu right now and if I want to keep up with the program I have to take in these calories. Believe me if I could smell or taste it I wouldn't eat it. I would rather go cook up some Zeta whatever alien and chew on those tasty fingers."

Za started laughing as he swallowed another plastic spoonful of dog food. There were only a few people eating in the mess hall. Everyone was trying to keep to themselves for the most part.

"James, besides doing the workout schedule you will have a fight training schedule as well. Have you ever hit a punching bag or done any type of fight training?"

"I have done some basic boxing moves someone showed me on a heavy bag but nothing beyond that."

"Okay, this is good and bad at the same time. No matter what you do during a fight just remember there is no such thing as fair in fighting. You fight for your life every time you have to fight someone. Since you have no formal martial arts training doing this will be more natural. Most people you meet who have studied some form of martial arts, they waste a lot of time going through some sort of posing motion trying to intimidate opponents. You are not intimidating and will have to be the one to throw the first kick to the nuts."

"Where did you learn how to fight?" James asked.

"The first place was outside my apartment when I was ten and a crackhead tried to rob me, luckily my uncle saw before I was getting ready to stab the guy with his own broken crack pipe. Then I was in many more after that one. I got the full fight training in the Army when I went to West Point for school. They trained me to be more than a fighter and turned me into a dangerous killing machine. I will show you what was shown to me, and we will begin each time with me showing you some moves and then full on you attacking me. Since we have those recovery tanks for you, I won't have to go easy."

The schedule for James for the month was coming together as far as workouts and training. James would find himself running his five miles first thing in the morning followed by breakfast. Then off to the weight room for a few hours of weight lifting for whichever muscles were to be worked out during that day. Right after weight training fight training was a casual showing of the moves Za learned while at West Point along with some street fighting moves.

James would try to do the moves Za showed him in an actual fight with Za. After the fighting James would go to the medical building and hop into a recovery tank with broken ribs, arm, shoulder, leg, legs, back, fractured skull, crushed throat, and broken noses with many other gruesome injuries inflicted by Za. After the recovery tank it was dinner then off to do pull-ups and push-ups for 2 hours instead of a set number. Za said it would give better results.

After a month straight of grueling workouts and hand-to-hand combat, it was time for Za to go onto the next phase. Za had lost all of his teeth by the last night of the month and looked emaciated. James' appearance was opposite of Za's. James was starting to appear fit and as a side effect of being beaten daily and going into the recovery tank daily he was in the best shape of his life so far.

Za's skin was a pale blue and his once bright red hair looked dull and aged. He looked like he was in his 90s and not in the prime of his life. Even though he looked weak he still brought James another beating of his life and after going to the recovery tank James went back to the barracks to get some rest with Za waiting on him.

"Hey Za, what's up?" James asked.

"I saw something back in the medical office I was going to grab for you. Just give me a minute."

Za got up rushing out of the barracks. James took out his wintergreen Yak and began to tap the can. Suddenly it was not in his hand but in the hands of Jim Berthlow. Jim was a level 1 enhanced and looked like a gym rat from a bad 80s science fiction movie. He was pale as snow with a jet black flat top and clean-shaven 6' 5".

"What's this? Someone gave you this crap?" Jim said.

"I don't want any trouble, so just give me my chew back."

"Ha, without your helper monkey you won't be much trouble at all."

Jim moved his head and neck in a pointing motion towards the door.

"Last warning." James said, getting ready for a fight with someone far physically superior to him.

"You should have left on your first day here while you could still breath. Now I will kill you and dump your chew on your dead body."

Then all of a sudden. 'Bonk, it was Za giving Jim a dropped fist on top of the head.

"Man, you leave him alone if you don't want him to kill ya. I trained him to kill and not be a little girl like you." Za said, staring at Jim as he looked up from the ground.

"Sssorry." Jim said, handing the chewing tobacco back to James.

"I leave you alone for a minute and this is what happens? Damn you better be ready after tomorrow when I am gone for the month or longer. Here is what I got for you from the med room."

Za stuck his hand out with a thick book in it.

"Wow, I wish I had this when I first got here."

It was a manual for the Platinum Gravity device. It detailed the uses of James' arm and how to make use of all of its functions.

"It looked like some sort of technical instructions that I couldn't follow but maybe you will be able to." Za said.

"That is one of my super powers of being an instruction manual nerd. Za, this says I can use my hand as some sort of yo-yo to throw and retrieve as a weapon. Man if I knew all of this earlier I would have definitely kicked your ass once."

"One out of 30 times would have been interesting. Now get your happy ass to sleep. Tomorrow is the beginning of something bigger for both of us."

CHAPTER 10
TRAINING MONTH 2

The morning came with Dr. Garcia at the door of the Quonset hut all the men were staying in.

"Twenty minutes and head out to the field by the satellite dishes." She said, firmly and left.

Everyone began to scramble in a big commotion running for showers and getting changed. James realized Dr. Garcia had left a box of rain slickers at the door. The rain was hard beating on the hut and the slickers would be nicer than getting soaked as James had been out in the rain many times with Za. Everyone had their gray training outfits on, rain slickers, and necklaces with blue beads, so they could hear Fred's voice in their heads.

Fred was standing in Walter's hands again like a little puppet in the rain with an umbrella covering himself while Walter got soaked with rain. The rain was pelting down hard making the grass in the infield squishy as everyone stood in front of Fred.

"Welcome back my remaining Recovery Agents. I would like to ask all level 2 enhanced to stand behind me while I speak to everyone." Fred said, pressing down on the button on his necklace.

The group of faded blue men walked around and stood in a row directly behind Fred. They all looked like they had just been sick with the flu for a week with glazed over eyes. Bitter toothless faces peered out with an occasional clapping of the lips. All the 20 level 2 enhanced were dying by choice at a chance to become complete with the re-invigoration chambers. Looking at the group without the level 2 enhanced was a lot more sparse than when they had started.

"As I look out at everyone here currently it concerns me how strong your will to continue truly is. We started with 10 women, 6 non-enhanced men, and 4 level 1 enhanced men. Now we are down to 7 women, 3 non-enhanced men, and 4 level 1 enhanced men. All 20 of the level 2 enhanced behind me have no choice since if they do not continue with entering the re-invigoration chambers they will die. The remaining 14 will be assigned to two groups designated by what the level 2 enhanced have reported to me while observing your training. If for any reason at this time you wish to leave you can and return to your lives before. Right now the only remaining non-military person is Mr. James Hawthorne.

This concerns me since the level 2 enhanced observing your training placed Mr. Hawthorne well below the level of what is expected out of a Recovery Agent. Some things to note are the loss of every hand-to-hand combat training match with your level 2 as well as constant use of the recovery tanks. James you can either stay and try to make it, or you can simply leave now. This work is not for everyone and your background without prior military training may inhibit your further progress. Will you stay or will you leave Mr. Hawthorne?" Fred concluded, looking right at James.

"I will stay! Recently I have been given something to help me stay to the end!" James shouted, trembling nervously.

"Very well then, no more recovery tank usage unless you

are actually dying, from now on. As for everyone else training will begin tonight at 1800 hours lasting until 0600. Your squad postings will be on the doors of your buildings as well as on the medical building door. All of you in front of me are dismissed until then and all the level 2's behind me will follow me into the building with the red door next to the medical building."

James just about sprinted back to the men's barracks splashing through the puddles in the rain. He blazed through the door and back to his cot where the manual for Platinum Gravity device was underneath. The only hope for remaining and keeping his new left arm was inside the manual. As he opened the first page of the manual a piece of paper dropped to the ground. It was a note from Za explaining what he needs to do to keep from being forced out.

The note read:

Hey man,

Sorry for putting the beating on you every time, but it was the only way I could make you strong in such a short period. The recovery tank kinda made you heal your muscles faster as if you were taking steroids. Looking at you now from when you started you look like a piece of steal compared to the doughnut I met. Hell, I wanted them to think you were weak but just found out they might force you out for not winning a few fights. If you are reading this you stayed and should be tougher than any creature they grow in a lab. One reason you lost every time was your tight clothing made it easier for me to pick up on your movement. There were a few times I thought you had a chance but just caught you a second faster than you could react. Sorry if this makes me a cheater, but I told you to be tough to win.

P.S.

Also I kept the manual hidden from you until the day I left to give you an advantage while I am gone. Look in my pillow case there are three sets of large shirts and pants to make you less predictable.

-Za

"Asshole!" James shouted, while going over to Za's pillow.

James found the larger more size appropriate outfit and put it on. Then ran back to his cot and began looking through the manual. There were chapters on budget and overall project cost being over 100 million to develop with a 15 million per developed unit cost. The three chapters he had focused on were hand launch and retrieval, detachment of the entire unit for storage, as well as heat and electricity warnings. The cap on the end of James' left arm seemed to be the most complex component giving the user the feeling of pressure similar to what they would feel if they had their actual arm. It also regulated the release and retrieval of the hand with a maximum distance of ten feet.

As everyone else began to come back to the barracks they took a minute to look at the squad assignments which James had ignored. He was dropping his hand to the ground and retrieving it like a kid with a new yo-yo. It was sloppy at first with his hand going beyond his wrist and snapping suddenly back into position. Jim saw him playing with his hand and attempted to kick it away before James made the retrieval motion. James' hand snapped up and pulled Jim off balance making him fall over on the ground hard.

"Sorry about that." James said.

"Do yourself a favor and just quit loser. Everyone knows you're not going to last."

Jim got up and walked back to his bed to grab a canteen. James shrugged and kept at it and eventually made his way outside. He stood in the open field next to the asphalt road and began throwing and retrieving his hand at max distance. The first full throw was hard with an open hand, it snapped back and landed James on his back. He wiped mud off himself and threw it again this time he pulled his arm away to absorb the impact. Still, it toppled him backwards and off balance to the ground again.

"This is going to take a lot of practice." James said to himself.

While everyone else was getting rested up with the day off, James kept on practicing throwing his hand opened and closed. The way his hand was set once it was thrown was how it remained until it was reconnected to his wrist. A metal hand encased in rubber was a great advantage as a throwing device. It would be deadly to anyone if the rubber was taken from the metal hand with the needled finger tips. It was getting darker and James figured it would be time to join up with his squad soon enough.

As he made his way back to the barracks to check which squad he was assigned to he glanced at his reflection in the rain puddles. James remained caked in mud from falling over so often, and would need a shower since the rain stopped a few hours ago. Just before entering the barracks he looked over the squad list. They separated the men from the women into two squads except James was on the bottom of the women's list. There was a squad of six men and seven women plus James on the women's squad.

As 1800 hour neared the barracks began to empty into a damp misty night. Everyone went back out to the circle track to meet with their squad. It was almost pitch black outside due to the cloud cover. The first assignment for both squads was to gather wood and pile it in piles at different locations on the inside of the track.

It was a simple task made harder by the rain earlier in the day, gather wood and start a fire. The wood was soaked from the rain during the day and with no dry wood it seemed almost impossible to light. With some help from some gasoline the wood ignited all around the field with a bright blaze. For the next four hours everyone was tasked with gathering and placing wood in the sonic testing building attached to the satellites.

It was a pale white building the size of a double-wide trailer and was perfect for storing the wet wood. The rest of the evening was spent going over what the training outline for the month would be for each squad. Night training from 1800 to 0600 for the rest of the month was set to begin. James' squad was set for all twelve hours to be spent doing the following:

Hour 1: Yoga

Hour 2: Weight room

Hour 3-4: Firearms

Meal break 15 minutes

Hour 5: Field Medical

Hour 6-7: Running

Hour 8-9: Combat training

Hour 10-11: Survival Training

Meal break 15 minutes

Hour 12: Cleanup/Resupply wood

Return to barracks

"Firearms, when do we pick our guns?" James asked.

A lean Asian women standing next to him heard his question.

"Tomorrow, during our firearms training time, plus once a week we will be doing physical combat against the other squad during our last hour instead of cleanup. Rules are set to be tap out, knockout, or give up. Everyone will compete with an uneven number we will be attempting two on one fight training against one of the level 1 guys." Barbara the squad leader replied.

Yoga took place in the womens' barracks with the cots all moved to the back and blankets placed over the cold concrete floors. James stumbled and fell over attempting to do the most basic moves. It made him feel foolish each time as some women giggled and laughed each time he fell to the ground. After bearing his way through yoga it was on to the weight room, he was much more comfortable with weights. The most exciting part was coming up for him, a chance to pick a gun. James never owned a firearm, and had never even fired a gun.

Meals were brought into the barracks by the squad leaders of each group. The commissary was temporarily off limits while the firearms were laid out. James ate his meal before some of his other squad mates even opened theirs. The excitement he had was mounting. James could hear the other squad outside cheering as they went into the commissary first.

Finally, they headed over to the commissary to pick out their guns. Each table was lined up with different handguns, semi auto and revolvers. All the guns were slightly different from each other in length of barrel and weight. Some guns were as light as two pounds while the heaviest was seven pounds and looked worn out. All the guns were a .44 magnum load with nothing higher or lower.

Almost every color was available on the table green, black, chrome, blued steel, and the rusty looking thing in the middle. Each revolver was modified to carry eight shots over the standard of six shots. The other squad already got the pick of the litter and now it was their turn to go. James saw one he wanted on the table, but was stopped suddenly by Barbara.

"Alright, ladies we go first while our black sheep goes last." Barbara said.

The gun James was reaching for was a green semi auto with a three magazines next to it. It was the first one picked up off the table by one of the other women. After everyone was done picking their guns three were left on the table. A black short barreled semi-auto, a chrome six-inch barrel revolver, and the giant eight and a half inch barrel rusted revolver. James looked at each one carefully and picked up the six-inch barrel revolver. As he was walking away with it he turned and ran back and grabbed the rusty revolver instead.

It was a massive handgun weighing close to seven pounds with a brown rubber hand grip. The rusty look was caused from the coating of iron on the outside of the gun. Although it appeared to be rusting away, internally it was clean and had no rust inside. James learned pretty quickly the outer rust could be used for quick camouflage by simply wiping the gun across body parts or clothing.

One important missing component was a sight on top of the gun. It appeared there was no way to attach a sight to the gun as the top was smoothed out. The last inch of the barrel end had three horizontal holes on each side with three dotted holes on the top for porting. On the front of the gun facing the barrel was a tiny hole above the barrel. James was hoping to find some sort of laser sight but there was none.

"Okay, now everyone has their guns let's go get some target practice in for the night!" Barbara yelled over everyone tinkering with their guns.

It was beginning to rain lightly as they headed over to the target shooting spot at the rear of the field. The mud and what was left of the grass was sloshing under their feet as they all walked on. There were mannequin parts piled up to the right of where they were to be shooting. There was debris from the other squad from earlier all over the road.

"Setup your target, and we will line up and begin firing after everyone has a target built!" Barbara yelled.

It was difficult to see with the darkness from the clouds and the rain killing out the fires they had started earlier. Some were lucky and grabbed full mannequins while everyone else had to add a few parts. The rain slickers' hood also made it difficult to see as the rain was beginning to pour down heavier. Boxes of ammo were setup by Barbara in a line thirty yards from the mannequins.

"Everyone load your guns, and stand behind the ammo cans! Now you will only fire what your gun can hold then we will check the targets!" Barbara was almost screaming over the heavy rain.

James fumbled to load his massive revolver while everyone else had their guns loaded within a few seconds it took James over a minute. He got glares from his squad members for what felt was the millionth time that day.

"Fire!!" Barbara screamed, not even a second after James was done loading his gun.

Booming sound from high-powered revolvers drowned out the rain and bright flashes of light would light up the mannequins. As James took his time he realized everyone had at least an iron sight to aim with, and he would be firing with no assistance.

Trying to look down the barrel and aim he carefully pulled the trigger and a crashing boom sound came from his own cannon of a gun. It was lifted up out of anticipation of a shot and went somewhere into the woods completely missing the target. He took a deep breath and fired again, missing again. Then tried to fire off the next six shots in quick succession and grazed the target taking a chunk out of its right elbow. His rusty revolver had almost no kick due to its hefty weight, but James was still all over the place due to his nervousness of firing a gun.

"James!! What the hell took you so long to shoot at your target!! You completely missed the target!!" Barbara was screaming at him.

"I hit the arm, I don't have any sights like everyone else. Give me a break."

"You hit the arm!? Give me your gun!" Barbara yelled at him as she stuck her hand out for his gun.

She loaded it in a matter of seconds and without taking a glance at James' mannequin fired off eight shots. The mannequin exploded into white cloudy pieces everywhere. Barbara slammed the gun back into James' chest.

"You should just leave." She snarled at him

Lucky for James they only had time to shoot three more times before it was time to begin medical training. Every part of the night felt like another way to try to shame him away from the program. This was one of the most emotionally challenging days for James. For a time he considered leaving and going back to the regular world as an amputee with a questionable future.

After getting through medical training without being scorned they headed to the track and started to run. Running was a good way for James to clear his head and focus on how to stay and surpass expectations.

Combat training was taught by Alyson Whitmoore a six-foot tall black girl from New York. She was an up and coming MMA star before she joined the Army. Short black hair with a body carved from solid oak. For the past five years she was one of the lead hand-to-hand combat trainers for the Army. She would train both men and women how to take down an opponent and survive. She paired everyone up and would demonstrate on James how to perform a move. Most of the combat training was demonstrate and recreate what move was shown.

James was glad since it meant not getting beat to a pulp by Za and sent to the recovery tanks. During survival training everyone was taught how to filter rain water and make fire out of just about anything available. They also began learning which plants were edible and toxic. The last hour of the night as dawn was approaching was spent cleaning up the mess from shooting guns earlier in the night and resupplying what wood they could gather.

"James! Before you head into your barracks head over to the medical building for a physical re-evaluation." Barbara called as everyone was heading back to their barracks.

James opened the door to the medical building where Dr. Garcia was sitting next to a long metal table.

"Barbara said you wanted to see me?"

"Yes, James strip down and lay here on the table. Then drink this." She said, handing him a small cup with pink colored medicine.

"Yum, bubble gum, what was that?"

"Just something to stop you from moving while I implant you with your optical sight for your gun. You picked the only firearm to require an ocular implant. I will be drilling straight up under your chin through the base of your skull to your optical nerve. Once I have made the hole this little guy the size of a flea will attach itself to your optical nerve center and will allow you to use your gun's sighting system. Of course, I have you scheduled for physical evaluation, and this gun was technically not meant for you, but since I like you I will do this under the table. Think of it as our little secret. Do not tell Fred I did this or it will be big trouble for both of us."

James was paralyzed but could still feel the cold table under him. As he laid frozen Dr. Garcia moved his chin up and tilted his head back. The drill whirred and went quiet as it was slowly pushed under his chin. Burning pain and coppery flavored blood filled his mouth and a greeting of great pain was followed. The feeling of the drill being removed as a colossal syringe with the implant followed.

James went blind and could not see as the implant locked itself on with tiny metal legs.

The table wheels squeaked as it was rolled next to a recovery tank and stopped. Tilting sideways over the tank James plopped in as the nano machines repaired the injury. James popped up and screamed out.

"That was horrible! You could have blinded me!"

"Well, good news is you are down to 200 pounds. Now let's see if your gun and the implant work together. Just lift your gun and point it at something."

James lifted his gun up and a light appeared to shine similar to a laser beam. The colors changed with an offset to make the beam appear on different colors. As he shined it on something green the color changed from green to dark blue. It had seemed to default to green and would contrast to a more visible color on a hard to see background.

"Okay, it is pretty cool. So what if I lose the gun?" James asked.

"Don't lose the gun and remember this only works while the gun is held in your hands. Go ahead and run off to sleep. I didn't set the recovery tank to full recover, it was set to repair your head trauma. You should still feel tired." Dr. Garcia said.

James lumbered back to the barracks where everyone else was already sleeping and passed out until the night had come.

Night came with a clarity and briskness leaving James extremely excited to try out his gun after getting his ocular implant. When it became time for firearms training everyone met in the mess hall again to choose their holsters for their new firearms along with scopes. While everyone busied themselves picking out scopes James grabbed speed loaders and put-on his holster. The speed loaders were also modified to hold 8 rounds and drop in when pressed against the gun's cylinder.

The holster made for his gun came as a dark brown leather the same as the belt. His belt had three open spots on the left side to hold the speed loaders with the holster and gun on his right. Only a simple snap held the gun in the holster sliding over the hammer of the gun. It struck James as weird that his gun belt contained nothing more than a few pieces of leather with nothing else to offer other than a holding place for his hand cannon. The others had either leather or nylon belts to fit their guns and extra speed loaders or magazines.

"What you aren't going to grab a scope?" Barbara asked.

"Don't need one, I will show you in a few minutes how I do."

They set up the mannequins again this time standing forty yards out and all ready to fire. One thing James didn't anticipate was his simple snap holding up the time it took him to draw and fire his gun. After a brief struggle un-holstering his gun he hit the target. Everyone finished shooting while James struggled to fire his last three shots off.

"Alright everyone stop for a moment. James will be standing out the rest of the evening to practice drawing his firearm and if he decides to stay, he will be allowed to shoot tomorrow." Barbara snarled.

James practiced drawing, holstering, unloading, and loading his gun for the rest of the night. As the week went on he showed an amazing improvement. Now almost as quick as some women with the semi auto handguns. James still made some beginner mistakes like firing early or slightly off due to anticipation of his shot. Barbara and the rest of the women took notice on how hard he tried and how much of an improvement he made.

"Looks like you are getting a lot better than I ever thought you would. Keep it up and you can stay with us. Tonight is the first night we fight the other squad so be ready." Barbara said.

Time came to test their fight skills against the men's squad. Out of the women's squad Barbara chose to referee the fights due to the uneven numbers. Each fight was set with simple rules of give up, knock out, tap out, or quit. James went up first fighting one of the few non-enhanced guys on the men's side. Fighting a former Recon Marine made for one rough appearing first fight.

Miles was the name of the guy he ended up fighting. Red hair with a flat top, standing two inches taller at 6 foot 2 inches, with a barrel chest and long muscular arms. In some form of intimidation he raised his arms in the air before the fight began. Cheers from the men's side were loud with yells of "beat the loser Miles!" James stood in the middle of the circle made by the squads and got ready. Barbara stood between them and stepped back in a quick motion.

"Fight!" Barbara yelled

James got into a fighting stance and got a swift kick to his shins knocking him over. He caught himself with his right hand and twisted to try to sweep his left leg at Miles. Miles jumped back and James was left open on the ground with his back turned. A crunching kick from Miles connected with James' right shoulder.

James hurried back to his feet as Miles raised his arms once again showboating for the crowd. Both teams were now cheering for Miles. James unlatched his left hand in a fist and dropped it to the ground. Miles turned around to face James again and was met with a solid crunch under his chin from James' upward yo-yo swing of his left hand. Everyone went quiet as Miles collapsed to the ground.

"Winner." Barbara said, after a five-second pause pulling James' right arm into the air.

"Cheater! He Cheated!! Let me fight him and I will destroy the cheater!!" Jim howled.

"We can fight next time Jim. That is if you're ready to lose." James said, rubbing his right shoulder.

The rest of the women's squad didn't fare as well as James with everyone else either tapping out or quitting. Last two to fight were Jim Berthlow and Alyson Whitmoore. When it came time for Jim to fight Alyson, he stood and waited for her to attack. She threw a quick punch to the throat and Jim laughed it off. As she moved back to try and kick at Him he caught it and snapped his elbow down on her thigh breaking her femur. Alyson did not cry and went down as Jim stepped back going for her head with a downward stomp.

"Stop!!" Barbara screamed.

James stood almost five feet away and threw his left hand in a fist backwards out five feet and twisted upward bringing it forward in a bowling motion. Jim moved forward fast and before he could connect with his stomping foot, James connected with the wild upward throw of his fist with Jim's jaw. Jim went crashing down motionless. No one moved for a brief moment, then everyone realizing James had saved Alyson's life cheered. Jim was hauled up by one of his teammates and taken back to the barracks.

Fights for the early morning were over and with Alyson's broken leg it became obvious they would need to change their tactics. A few of the women helped carry Alyson to the medical building while everyone else headed back to the barracks. Suddenly the adrenaline vanished and the pain of a badly bruised almost broken shoulder began to make itself known to James. As he started to head back rubbing his shoulder he could feel someone watching him.

"Hey, James is it!? That was some crazy shit back there! Hey, wait up!" Miles yelled.

"I guess so, I don't want to see someone die when we are all training for the same goal."

"The only person saying you cheated in our fight was the big dumb ass Jim. I get it you used what you had and won. Hell, I would have done the same thing." Miles said.

"Really, I saw an opening and took it. Not much more than that."

"No way, you got some skill. Use your left hand as much as possible. Win at all cost."

"So, you don't think it was cheating?"

"Just be careful from now on, everyone will be expecting you to use it. The others side with me on your hand being a necessary tool, and we will keep Jim away from you. He is a bit of a dick anyway."

"Good to know, my shoulder hurts like hell now after I calmed down from all the excitement."

"I screwed up there too. I was going for a clean break, but hell guess you walk away with a bruise and I have a few loose teeth. Let's get some rest and let your squad know they were very close with a couple of those choke out moves." Miles said, opening the door to their barracks.

Jim was in the corner brooding as the other guys calmed him down and reminded him fighting would be reserved for the end of the week. James crawled into his bed laying on his left side due to his sore shoulder. It was a brutal reminder of what was in store for them when they began to work as Recovery Agents. Having both squads once hating him now seeing a glimmer of what Za saw in him made James sleep easier.

As the week went on Alyson was in a new mindset with teaching more choke out moves to the squad along with more aggressive tactics. Eye gouging, crotch punching, nose ripping, and more unfriendly techniques reserved to stay alive were taught and practiced. James was finding more questions about what Za taught him come up constantly during training. By the end of the week it was time to fight squad vs squad again.

This time James was asked to referee the fights due to the uneven numbers. The women's squad performed much better and took half of the wins for the week. Jim was still extremely aggressive, but when he realized James wasn't fighting claimed something was in his eye and could not fight.

With more confidence in the adapted fighting style the squad went over what went right and wrong during the week. So far the first week turned out the most brutal compared to the second week. Moving into the third week Jim insisted he would be fighting only James. Brisk clear weather lead them to the end of the week.

Fire behind the fighting circle blazed blindingly in the clear night sky. Everyone circled up and got ready as names were randomly chosen for fighters. James was asked again to referee which was no big deal since it was better than getting beat up. Peeling open a fresh can of Yak and putting a wad in was the best way for James to prepare himself. As the first two fighters were getting ready to fight James got a weird feeling something was off.

James would count down the fight in a unique way by throwing his left hand over the fire making a 3, 2 ,1 count-down alternating his fingers as his hand returned. As he began 3, 2, ... James got straight kicked in the back causing his hand to drop into the fire. Followed by another hard kick sending him stumbling forward towards the fire.

"Cheater! You won't even face me, I'll show you how a fight is won!" Jim Screamed.

"Wha.."

Just as James went to retract his hand he was kicked behind the knees falling towards the ground. The same time hitting the ground a fist went hard into his ribs cracking them followed by a hand on top of his right forearm and a hand behind his elbow. A snapping crunch followed as his right arm cracked in the wrong direction. Jim hauled James up off the ground and slammed him down hard on the ground. Blood began oozing out of his mouth from somewhere inside. Leaving the ground again as the brute picked James up by the shoulders to toss him into the fire.

"No recovery tank for you! You're going to be dead! You cheating piece of shit!!" Jim Screamed, getting ready to throw James into the massive 10-foot round fire.

Dulling vision went from dark to light as James drifted in and out of consciousness. Jim lifted James up fully extending his arms ready to throw James in the fire. When Jim began to move his arms downwards 'Snap, the sound of James' left hand re-attaching suddenly. James swung his palm open on his left hand and pressed down hard on Jim's face.

The burning black rubber hand with skeletal metal pieces showing through pushed hard on Jim's face. James pressed down as hard as he could with his palm fully opened. Jim's nose felt like a marshmallow being squished under his palm. Jim staggered backwards screaming.

Jim fell onto his back from the heat of the melting rubber and metal on his face. The unexpected scent of melted rubber and burnt flesh wafted in the evening air. The squads rushed in to pry James off of Jim's lifeless body and took them both to the medical building.

Everyone crowded into the medical building as James was stripped down and placed into a recovery tank. It looked like there might be two less in the running to become Recovery Agents. James laid in the recovery tank for over an hour while Jim laid out on a metal table with all types of tubes and hoses connected to him.

No one said anything as James sat up from the recovery tank and looked over to Jim. No effort was made to try and place him in one of the recovery tanks and the sound of a helicopter above grew louder. Jim's nose melted flat with a piece of gooey rubber in the shape of a hand covering most of his face.

"Why, isn't he in a recovery tank?" James asked.

"Level 1 enhanced DNA has been altered making the recovery tanks instant death for them. He is being taken to a specialized hospital facility to try to stabilize him." Dr. Garcia said.

Suddenly a helicopter had landed at the pad in the middle of the facility and three medics came with a stretcher to take Jim away. The helicopter still running took off into the early morning sky as quickly as it had landed. Everyone except James went back to their barracks to rest after all the excitement was over. James was putting his blood stained clothes back on and getting ready to head back to his barracks when Dr. Garcia waved him over to her desk.

"Remove your hand and place it in here." Dr. Garcia said, pointing to what looked like a paint can.

"What is this for?"

"It is some chemicals to melt the rubber and whatever else was left on your hand off. I have a little something here for you. Or should I say five little somethings."

James looked at his left hand and saw it was a miss-contorted form of rubber with metal pieces showing. The palm of his left hand still had some flesh melted onto it with some other white material. His hand was stuck open due to the rubber material cooling and hardening.

James released his hand and dropped it into the silver

paint can container. It looked like water before his hand was dropped in then as his hand made contact with the liquid it sizzled and the clear liquid turned black. Dr. Garcia picked up the container and dumped it into a deep sink. Then she sprayed it down with water from high pressure faucet with a nozzle attachment.

"Now retract it." She said.

James retracted his hand and noticed how much easier the movement was without the rubber coating. It was the first time since first receiving his new arm he saw the needle pointed finger tips. He touched the tip of his left hand to the index finger of his right hand to see how sharp it was. Blood and shooting pain from his index finger followed. Dr. Garcia handed him a band aid, immediately, since she expected he would test it like someone testing a knife blade.

"So, as you can see the reason I put your hand in the liquid rubber first thing. You are more likely to hurt yourself than someone else. Since the platinum arm you have was a discontinued project they never tried to come up for a solution for the finger tips. I got a little creative while you were here and made these." Dr. Garcia said, handing James five silicone finger tips.

"Why are they still black?"

"It gives the illusion you have a typical prosthetic arm. First glance someone sees your hand and doesn't think much of it. I spent a month making those by copying and mirroring the skin on your right hand. Hopefully they work well."

"What if I lose one?" James asked.

"Don't. Now scram out of here, I will have something for the squads this evening. Let everyone know to come here before starting training. I have to tell Fred what happened today and find out what we are going to do next."

James went back to his barracks to rest for the day while

Dr. Garcia went to the building Fred was currently working on the level 2's. Early in the evening as everyone was getting ready for training James made the announcement for everyone to meet in front of the medical building.

Both the squads were in front of the medical building awaiting their new instructions. Dr. Garcia came out of the medical building to give everyone some news on what was going to happen after the fight between James and Jim.

"As you can see Jim Berthlow is no longer here. He was sent to a medical facility last night and is in a stable condition. Jim will not be returning. As you may or may not know anyone with genetic alterations cannot use the recovery tanks. After explaining to Fred what had happened, weekly fights will not be occurring anymore. If, you take a look you will also notice we have a few others not here this evening. Three women and one of the enhanced guys have left. The squads will now be combined into one group and be led by Barbara Nyguen. This is all I have for you at this time if anything changes I will let everyone know." Dr. Garcia stated.

It was only a week until the level 2 enhanced group was going to be ready to come out of whatever was being done to them. The last week Barbara had the new squad follow what her squad was doing originally. James found out he was a lot better at Yoga than some level one guys. After the week had ended it was time for the Level 2's to be let out. James was excited to see Za again after his adventurous month and almost being kicked out of the program.

CHAPTER 11
TRAINING MONTH 3

During the last night of the second month of training Dr. Garcia greeted everyone as they came in for the midnight meal. Everyone was quiet as Dr. Garcia climbed onto the metal table where some had their MRE meals already opened. She carefully stepped around the food and went to make an announcement to the remaining Ten. After the event with Jim Berthlow they were down to 4 women, 3 non-enhanced men, and 3 level 1 enhanced men.

"Now we are coming into our final month of training, the training will now shift once again from night to day. As a little bit of a relief the next evening there will be no training. The Level 2 enhanced group will be coming out during the day time and we will be getting another announcement from Fred at 16:00 hours." Dr. Garcia stated, then climbed off the table and left the mess hall.

With training for the night completed everyone went back to the barracks to rest for the afternoon announcement. James slept for about four hours then woke due to anticipation of seeing Za again. It was the same feeling a child would have during Christmas. He tried to leave the barracks as quietly as possible with the only sound being the door hinge making a slight screech.

Once outside the blinding sun made it hard to see what was happening at first. Then as his eyes adjusted he saw Walter's giant frame coming out of the building Fred and the level 2's were currently in. Walter was carrying two enormous black bags, adding them to a pile next to the helicopter pad. It took a moment to click in James' brain the bags were people. Failed level 2 enhanced being removed before the big reveal Fred had planned.

James ran for the door Walter had walked out of to find out if his friend had made it or had died in the process. Monstrous creatures peered up at him as he crashed through the door. Fred was standing in the middle of them all pointing to wooden boxes stacked at the back wall. Walter was behind James before he could try to run away.

"Welcome James. It is good to see you and your improvement has impressed me very much." Fred said, pressing the button on his necklace.

All the creatures turned away and went back to going to the wooden crates, all except for one. It made its way up the stairs to where James was standing. The creature towered over James and made a fist. James readied for a fight slipped the finger coverings off his left hand onto the ground and stuck his arm back ready to throw with his palm flat. When the creature stopped with its fist directly in front of James he began to recognize it as Za. He bumped its fist with his and could see a familiar smirk appear.

"We did it bro, you kept in and I made it!" Za bellowed.

"It took me a minute to recognize you. Did you grow taller?"

"Just a lil' bit. Man, we got some catching up to do. Let me grab some clothes out of one of the crates and I'll meet you in 15 outside."

James turned to go outside as Walter stepped to the back out of the way. It was a strange feeling with everything working out for once in a long time. Walter went back inside the building and did not come out again. Questions were swirling in James' head as he waited for Za to come out of the building. Za came out of the door wearing pants and custom-made high top shoes.

Za was now 8 feet tall and 857 pounds with dark reddish brown fur covering his body. His face, hands, chest, and abdominal section were the only parts without fur. Za appeared to look like a picture of a bigfoot James had saw in a magazine. His teeth had been regrown larger than before, with long fangs on his upper and lower portions of his mouth.

"Come on let's go to the track so we can walk and talk. The sun feels good." Za said.

"So they turned you into a bigfoot?" James asked.

"Man, I guess you got it right. Just so you know my sense of smell and hearing have gotten a lot better."

"What do you eat? People?"

"Nah, we eat plants. Well, plant material. In a sense we have these big teeth to better eat tree bark."

"Can you see farther? Or in the dark?"

"Eyesight is just about the same as yours. Guess they could only make two senses enhanced." Za said.

"How much better is your hearing and sense of smell?"

"I know you stink and need a shower and have a can of chew in your right pocket. There are three squirrels in the tree we just walked by and one dropped to the ground to look for food."

"Can you pick up a car and throw it?" James asked.

"Pretty sure I could pick up a car and maybe drop it on the ground. Fred also told us our skin is much more dense making 9mm rounds feel like being shot with a bb gun."

"How did you acquire a pair of shoes?"

"Fred asked what we would want for clothes before we went in with shirts not being an option. I asked for a set of sweet kicks. He had all this stuff made while we were in the tanks. Fred was able to calculate our growth and these things fit perfectly. You know I needed a little of my own style."

"What about the bags Walter was carrying out?"

"They didn't make it. Guess it means there will be extra clothes for the rest of us. Man, nine guys didn't make it."

"Well, thanks for the manual after making me the bottom bitch of the group."

"Just trying to keep things interesting for you." Za said, smirking.

James went on explaining to Za everything that had happened in the past month. They had circled the track for almost two hours. Za was interested in seeing the gun James had chosen after hearing about his optical sighting. It was something Za needed to see to believe just as seeing Za as a giant creature was for James.

Making their way back to the mess hall where the guns were stored James showed Za his choice. The giant cannon of a gun looked like a small toy in Za's hand. Za couldn't fit his finger into the trigger guard without the trigger being pulled back. They grabbed some rounds of ammo and went back out to the back end of the track where the squads had been practicing target shooting.

Za would throw mannequin pieces in the air and James would explode them with his gun. The time would fly by as James caught Za up on what was going on while he was out. James holstered his gun and looked over to Za as he took his fingers out of his ears.

"Well, we better head back Fred is going to give another one of his speeches." James said.

"Guess, ya right. Gotta find me a gun and we can have a little competition later."

The remaining recruits gathered in on the track with the two satellites in the background just as they had the month before. Fred walked by himself this time with no assistance from Walter this time. Walter was still busy cleaning up the level 2 enhanced that did not make it. The little grey alien was wearing khaki pants and a red baseball jersey with the number 21 printed in white on it. He stood as tall as he could and pressed down on the blue button on his necklace to give his latest update for everyone.

"Hello, everyone. Congratulations on making it this far. We are coming to the end of the training and will be getting everyone ready for what to expect when working in the field. Level 2 enhanced will be moving out of the barracks and living in the woods. It will better suit their new physical needs. No one is to engage level 2 enhanced in combat of any type. Everyone else will continue training the same as before with some small changes. Handcuffing and asset recovery will be covered beginning next week when Amir Nasser arrives.

He is the leader of the Termination squad and is eager to meet you all. We lost 9 in the process of completion of transformation to level 2. Now if there are still 21 of you left at the end we will have a special test to move the number down to 18. Training will resume tomorrow morning at 0800. Level 2 enhanced will still be separated from the other 10 unless Amir request otherwise. This is all I have for you for now."

Fred marched past everyone back to where Walter was loading enormous black bags into a Helicopter. The level 2 enhanced group headed out to the woods and the rest of the group went back to the barracks. The week went by quickly and the only difference in training was seeing an occasional level 2 knock down a tree in the distance.

A single black helicopter landed at 8am during the end of the week with 30 guys in full black military gear with masks covering their faces. They all held massive caliber automatic rifles with no difference in them except for the leader.

Amir Nasser was the only one not wearing a mask, only a bullet proof vest with no shirt underneath. His arms were multiple black cables tied together from his shoulders down to his hands. Amir stood 5'9" tall with a thin muscular build. He hopped down from the helicopter and his men fanned out behind him. Amir held up a set of handcuffs ample enough to cover half of an average person's forearm. Everyone gathered around as he began to speak.

"I am Amir Nasser, the Commander of the Termination squad! These are what you will be using to bring in your bounties alive! My squad unfortunately has no use for them, but I will show you how they work so you can avoid having one of your bounties taken out by my crew! Everyone in the termination squad is here to eliminate targets! We are not enemies of yours, rather we are the ends to a mean!"

Everyone looked at each other as the Termination squad circled behind the remaining 21 with handcuffs. They moved in silence and only the level 2 enhanced could hear them coming. They took out 4 inch needles from under their right sleeves all in unison. They held the needles up next to everyone to see what they were doing.

"The pins my crew is holding contain a drug to disorient and receive compliance from enhanced units. They act the same as a pen, there are 3 microscopic bearings in the pins that release the drug into the targets system. It will take a regular person a week to recover from them so try to only use them on enhanced units. Now lock them in!" Amir shouted.

The Termination squad locked restraints on everyone

before they had a chance to respond. One of the level 2 enhanced tried to resist and got a pin in his arm. He dropped both arms to his side immediately and was cuffed without any other incident. Everyone was now handcuffed with the bulky restraints.

"Those cuffs have a cable extending out to a max of 4 feet and retract with the press of a button on the rear down to 4 inches. They will not extend out until they are unlocked with a 4 digit code. Now if anyone would care to try and get out of them you may go ahead now." Amir said, with a smirk.

Everyone that was not a level 2 was wearing a black zip up sweater including James. There was grunting and even a few growls as everyone struggled to try and take the cuffs off. The cuffs also had a limit on how tight they could close leaving James a little wiggle room with his left arm. Just as Amir was getting ready to speak again one of the Termination guys standing behind James began to wave his arm in the air and point at James.

James had released his left arm and slipped it out of the cuff with ease. Then he reattached it with the gravity matrix pulling it back together. James slipped his left hand into his pocket and grabbed the can of Yak he put in there before leaving the barracks. He peeled the can open and put a wad of chewing tobacco in his lip while the guy from the termination squad was waving his hand in the air.

"What did I do?" James asked, spitting on the ground.

"Interesting, ok everyone meet up in the mess hall and we will un-cuff all of you. Everyone except you." Amir said, pointing at James.

Everyone headed to the mess hall to have their handcuffs removed as James waited to see what Amir wanted. Amir simply pointed back to the helicopter waving James to come with him. James followed Amir back to the Helicopter and sat across from Amir. It was quiet since the turbine engines had stopped running halfway through Amir's speech earlier. They both stared silently for a brief moment before Amir began to speak.

"What is your name?"

"James Hawthorne."

"So, how did you end up with the piece of hardware you have there?"

"It was what they had at the time, not really my choice."

"Let's take the cuff off your right arm." Amir said, typing in a code on the right cuff.

"My left arm is some sort of failed project, and I guess I got it since it was a leftover unit."

"Can you take it off and let me see it?"

"Sure, but after ten seconds all the pieces will fall everywhere until I recall it. Let me put it on the seat next to you so you can check it out."

James released his left arm from his elbow and placed it on the seat next to Amir. It was a solid unit for ten seconds before the effects of the gravity matrix wore off and the pieces fell apart on the seat. One of the ends of his pinky finger rolled off the seat onto the ground and Amir picked it up. He rolled it between his own mechanical fingers looking at it in the light. Carefully pulling the black silicon protector off of the end of the pinky and examining the pointed tip of the finger. Amir put the piece of pinky down handing James the protective silicon cover and grasped one of the long forearm pieces.

"What type of metal is this, silver?" Amir asked.

"Platinum."

"Interesting, how does it work?"

"Do you see this thing that looks like the bottom of a beer can on my elbow?" James said, pointing to his left elbow end with his right hand.

"Yeah."

"It is a gravity matrix configured to attract the pieces of the arm together and configures them in the correct order when the user wills it back together. The thing I had the most trouble with was being able to release it since no one ever thinks about removing their arm."

"How does someone will their arm back together?" Amir asked.

"The manual says to make a fist with your hand and the pieces will retract. Which is pretty weird since my arm is not attached to my body. I guess it is a combination of the tendons and nerve endings inside of the matrix." James said.

"So, why is it made out of a metal that can be easily bent and dinged up?"

"From what the manual says, the matrix acts almost as a sort of magnetic gravity field keeping the pieces stronger than what the metal was ever supposed to be used for. It copies the bones in my right arm by being flexible and rigid at the same time."

Before James could say anything else Amir grasped the forearm metal bone with both of his hands and bent it into a "U" shape. James looked sternly at Amir for a brief second as Amir picked up the other forearm piece and made another "U" shape. Now both of James' left forearm platinum bones were in opposing "U" shapes. James stared at them for a brief moment before Amir grabbed what was left of the hand pieces and threw them out of the helicopter.

"Now show me how you are going to fix that!" Amir shouted at James.

James concentrated on making a fist with his left hand and the forearm pieces returned in two outward "U" shapes and began to unroll and straighten. Then the rest of the hand returned almost instantly back to James' left wrist. James put the silicon rubber cap back on his pinky finger and put out all five fingers in front of Amir's face. James rolled his hand around his wrist a couple of times while wiggling his fingers.

"Amazing, it straightened out and went back to how it was before." Amir said.

"Oh, and it also allows me to release my hand at the wrist to be used as a kind of yo-yo weapon."

"So, how does it generate energy to do this type of thing?"

"The matrix uses the blood that would be routed into where my arm was, like a mini turbine to generate energy. Guess if I die or lose the rest of my arm it would shut down."

"Well, I do not extend this offer very often, but considering this and your ability to think on your feet. I want to formally offer you a position in the Termination squad. Of course you will have to complete your training here." Amir said.

"Really?"

"Yes, really. You won't make the same amount as a Recovery agent, but the job is more stable and safer. Here is my personal number so you can call me if you ever want to join my crew."

"Cool, thank you Amir."

"Now let us go and see what is going on in the mess hall with everyone else."

They stepped out of the helicopter and made their way to the mess hall. The sound of hollering and laughter could be heard as they approached the door. As they peered inside they could see the level 2 guy that was poked with the pin in a crawling position. He was mooing like a cow and crawling in a small circle. Amir stepped up on the table at the back of the room by the door.

"What the fuck is going on here!" Amir shouted.

The Termination guys immediately stepped back from the crowd and stood against the walls. Everyone else stepped back and watched as Amir made his way to the level 2 guy mooing like a cow. Za was sitting in the back next to the door. Every once in a while the guy mooing would lick the concrete floor look up moo and crawl in a small circle.

"Stand up, and shut the fuck up!" Amir shouted as he stood, behind the level 2 guy.

He stood up and got quite immediately. Standing still like a statue as Amir shoved him towards the rest of the group. Amir looked tiny compared to the level 2 enhanced guy, but the effects of the pin had made him docile. Everyone was watching as Amir appeared ready to say something, but instead walked out of the mess hall waving everyone back outside shaking his head trying not to laugh.

"Your next two weeks will be spent the same as the last, except for 3 of those days will be spent attempting to capture and bring in an enhanced unit. Level 1 and Level 2 will be trying to evade recovery during this time. You will have the whole day to recover your target. Since the numbers are a little off some of you will be teamed up during this training." Amir stated.

When it was time to work with the Termination squad only Amir was present to show everyone how a target was ranked. A targets rank depended on time a target was AWOL and the threat level to the general public. Some level 1's were more dangerous than level 2's due to their ability to blend into a city and cause more casualties. Amir also mentioned a level 2 could be apprehended by another level 2 or a group with one or more enhanced working with a non-enhanced.

Everyone was given a Roll-Device for receiving a targets rating as well as a picture with the targets last known location. The device looked like a cigar tube with two caps on the end. It was 6 inches long and unrolled to 4 inches with a full colored screen. Both the ends were the batteries attached with a small wire and an onscreen keypad with numbers on the lower right. It was also to be used for a phone to call in a completed recovery or phone other Recovery agents. Amir mentioned a better version of the device was being placed into the hands of agents in the last month and these were the old models.

The cuff units were 6 inches long with an adjustable diameter of 18 inches at maximum down to a minimum 3 inches. To adjust the cuff from maximum to minimum size was done with a slide on each one when closed they would only close down until they were opened. When they were opened the cuffs could be fully opened up to an 18 inch maximum diameter. On the cuff cable holding both cuffs together was a button which pulled the cuffs together from a maximum of 4 feet down to 4 inches. As the cable would tighten it would wind around the inside of the cuffs until the button was released.

Devices were complex yet simple at the same time to make them user friendly. On each cuff was what looked like an old pay phone keypad, with numbers one through nine and zero on the bottom with no special characters. Each side required the first two digits of an unlock code to be entered on the left cuff first followed by the second two on the right cuff within 20 seconds to unlock the cuffs. If someone failed to unlock the cuffs in four attempts they would lock up for a half an hour then allow code entry once again. Amir told everyone to make sure the cuffs were reduced to their smallest size before carrying them out into the field.

Two weeks of training with cuffing and recovery techniques mixed in had passed and now it was time for the final test. Everyone was a little on edge considering anyone could be eliminated after all the hard work that was put into training. Even the level 2 enhanced guys seemed nervous for what was going to happen. The night before the final test Dr. Garcia informed the group to meet in front of the building where the level 2 enhanced were created at 0800.

It was a warm morning with a slight breeze in the air with a stench of fresh paint wafting in the air. Everyone was nervous for the final test and some even puked up breakfast. James took a pinch of Yak and put it in his mouth to calm his nerves. Fred was standing in front of the the building which the level 2 enhanced had either died or survived to become beasts. The door had a fresh coat of yellow paint on it for some odd reason. Fred was wearing blue child's size shirt with a green airplane and neon blue pants.

"Welcome everyone, let's get some rules out of the way first. Three minutes is all the time you have. All of you will be graded on time. If you make it the full three minutes you have completed the test with a full score. There are some more rules, but I will only disclose those to you once you enter the building. Last the longest and you will become a recovery agent." Fred stated, holding the button down on his necklace.

On the front of the building was a newly installed digital timer set to 3 minutes. There was also a digital timer above the rear doors of the building with 3 minutes set. As everyone wondered who would go first a name scrolled across the timer. It was Alyson Whitmoore's name scrolling across where the digital timer once read 3 minutes. She was the first one to enter for the final test.

The delay was about 2 minutes before the digital timer began to count down. It got down to 2:26 then stopped. Then a sudden clang of the rear doors opening and closing with the timer resetting to 3:00. A new name began to scroll across the board and it was Waldo Harrison, Za's real name. Za went through the doors with a bit of confidence in his walk. Due to Za being 8 feet tall and stronger than a freight train.

Another roughly 2 minute delay and the timer began to count down from 3:00. This time the timer got down to 2:15 and stopped. A familiar sound of the rear doors clanging open and close with another name scrolling across. Barbara Nyguen, a five foot five 120 pound South Korean orphan and leader of the women's squad. She was tougher and meaner than anyone James had met and this would be where she could prove it.

This time the timer delay was only a minute and the countdown timer seemingly went down forever. Barbara got the timer down to 1:15 before the clang of the doors opening and closing. One difference was there was a lot of shouting going on at the back of the building after Barbara went. Something happened and it sounded bad but was being muffled by a sudden white noise coming from a helicopter landing behind everyone waiting to complete the test.

James was beginning getting a little anxious and grabbed for his Yak Green in his right pocket. He tapped the can, empty.

"Damn."

Lucky for James the next name was Miles McCallester on the scroll board. James sprinted back to the barracks and grabbed his can of Yak and ran back. By the time he got back Miles was already out and the next name began to scroll. He opened the can with his thumbnail and placed a wad of chewing tobacco in his lower lip. The name scrolling was James Hawthorne followed by 3:00.

"Shit." Spitting and taking his fresh wad of tobacco out of his mouth and throwing it on the ground.

James walked through the double doors down the stairs to an empty building the size of a football field. Fred was standing by a white line at the end that looked like the 20 yard line of a football field goal. Walter was on the other side of the white line near the rear doors. Fred began his speech by pressing the button on his necklace and looking at James.

"Congratulations on making it this far, for the final test of your training you will be given three minutes. If you can last the full three minutes you will be awarded an automatic win. If you can stop Walter at any time during the three minutes you win. If you turn around and run back across the white line to the front doors trying to avoid Walter the timer stops. Let me put it simply to win you must beat Walter. The timer starts once you cross the white line." Fred Stated, as he stated to everyone before.

James stared out and up towards the towering machine in front of him. It had a white mannequin head with what appeared to be wavy surfers' hair and two golf ball sized black lenses for eyes. The suit it was wearing appeared to be new even though several others had already went up against the abomination. Something new James noticed was a humongous softball sized lens at the base of its neck directly under the machines chin. Walter's giant translucent yellow ballistic gel covered robotic hands with a visible metal skeleton inside terrified him. Bulging oval feet poorly painted with black paint shook the ground as the behemoth took a step.

Walking towards the line James noticed Fred walking in towards the right corner and picking up a set of gloves. Fred slid the gloves over his six inch long middle fingers and then over his four inch long outer fingers. Just looking at Fred gave James more chills than looking at the mechanical monstrosity currently in front of him. Fred finished slipping the gloves on standing near the far right corner over the line and made a go on motion to James.

"Should I go now?!" James yelled.

"Yes, go, go." Fred Replied, pushing the button on his necklace.

It was a good enough distraction to let James step over the line and start sprinting towards Fred. James was almost four feet from Fred when a sharp clamping pain shot down his right leg. Walter had James thigh in his hand and was crushing James' femur. Splintering sounds and a rush of sudden dimming vision hit James all at once due to his leg being popped like a zit.

"I knew it. You were controlling it the whole time!" James shouted.

"Now you will lose with the lowest time. Good byyeeah!"

Fred was too busy trying to control Walter and talking to James when James threw his left hand palm flat. It was a five finger ninja star that connected with Fred's own right thigh and stuck. Fred collapsed and Walter released his grip from James' leg. The timer stopped at 2:34 and Doctor Garcia came running in with a few of the others that already went through the test. Fred was placed in the recovery tank first due to his panic while James waited for his turn.

"Damn man, does that hurt?" Za asked.

"Fuck yeah it hurts. My knee cap is showing and most of my thigh looks like a squeezed tube of toothpaste. Hell it was worth seeing the look of fear in Fred's face when I got him in the leg with my hand. Look he's done can you put me in?"

Za dropped James into the recovery tank just after Fred had come out of the tank. Fred was pissed about being outsmarted by a guy he was going to flush out a few months earlier. It all happened fast enough for no one to really notice anything was going on from the front of the building.

Fred continued with the test without missing a beat. James waited in the back and helped others the best he could. Two of the level 2 and 1 of the level 1's got broken bones and had to wait to be taken to a medical facility while Dr. Garcia gave them some pain meds to keep them calm. After everyone was done Fred opened up the back doors leaving Walter in the building.

"Hello everyone, so far the person with the worst time is James Hawthorne. Before anyone says anything I have to say James was also the only person to win the final test. He realized what his surroundings were and seized the moment. Not one of you even came close to accomplishing what he has done. I was so angry and impressed at the same time. Here is the video for everyone to see."

Fred pointed to the open door behind him and Walter was projecting a video playback without any audio into the darkness of the open doors. James looked away when his leg was being squeezed and grabbed a quick pinch of Yak. A smirk went across James' face when he saw the look of terror he gave Fred. Everyone was silent for a brief while, processing what they had seen. Suddenly James felt someone rubbing his back in excitement.

"That's my boy!! You showed that little fucker who's boss!! Fuck yeah man!!!" Za screamed out in excitement.

"Za calm your ass down. He is still our boss." James said, speaking through his teeth.

"Yes, he in fact did show me something new. Now looking over how everyone performed I have an opportunity for all of you. If anyone would like to be a guard at one of the prisons we hold the people the recovery agents bring in let me know. If no one wants to be a guard the bottom two will automatically be assigned guard duty with the possibility of becoming a recovery agent after a year. I will be sending the injured enhanced in need of medical attention out of the area and they will be back in no less than four hours. This evening after they have returned I want everyone to be ready to meet up with Amir Nasser at the

Helicopter pad to receive your gear." Fred said, pressing down on the button on his necklace.

James did not realize this would be the last time he would see Fred in person, and the last time he has seen Walter. Fred was still in charge of the recovery agents and passing on assignments, always working in the shadows. The time waiting to grab their gear seemed to go by at a fast pace. Excitement was everywhere and the two with the lowest times were even happy to receive a chance to work at the prison.

"Yo, did you hear?" Za said.

"Dude, don't give me an open ended question. Yes, I did hear you're a little bitch."

"Whoa someone is cocky, I will give that one to you but that's it. They're given all the level 2's a combat weapon to go with our guns."

"Cool, does anyone else get anything?"

"Nope, just the level 2's." Za said, with a grin.

"What are you getting exactly?"

"Check it. I am getting a bat that when you twist the handle turns into a bladed club."

"Coool." James said, sarcastically.

Za made his way in first to see Amir at the helicopter pad and got his bat and a shotgun with a 100 round barrel magazine and modified trigger for his enormous physique. The bat weighed three hundred pounds and had a tension spring in the handle to twist. Once it was twisted the inner round form would spiral into four curved blades. It attached to his back with an electro-magnet. Pressing the center of his chest where the bat sheath was strapped together Za was able to release the bat. Za was annoyingly happy with his new toy.

As Za was skipping around with his new toys James made his way to the helicopter pad. There was a cheap folding table and wooden crates all behind it. Amir was sitting and handing out weapons and clothes for everyone. Amir handed James three black t-shirts and three pairs of jeans all in silence. Then Amir handed James his gun belt with 3 new speed loaders loaded with eight rounds each and his old cannon Rust.

"James my offer to work for me still stands. I saw the video of your test and I am extremely impressed. If during anytime you doubt being a recovery agent call me. I understand being an amputee and loss more than anyone. Look at me I am a quadruple amputee. I have this mess of metal hoses for arms and legs now, but after joining the Termination squad I feel like a complete person. I will get off your back for now." Amir said.

"Thank you, Amir. I will keep that in mind. For now I want to try my hand at bringing these people in alive for a little while."

"Okay James, as you wish. Just remember I will always have my door opened for you."

James walked away from Amir with his new gear and saw Za playing with his bat. Opening and closing the blades then taking a swing at a huge pine tree splitting it in half. James stripped off the worn out grey sweats and put on a pair of jeans and a black t-shirt. The shirt felt like any other cotton shirt and fit loosely and comfortably. As he went to put on the gun belt he ran his fingers over the top of five pins stuck into the inside along the right side, horizontally covered by the belts overlap. He slowly removed a pin and as Za was examining his new toy he stuck him in the side with it.

"What the..." Za began to say.

"Come on we have too run to the copter over there. It's time to leave." James said.

Za began to lumber towards the copter when James turned tapping him on the shoulder to grab his bat.

"Grab the bat and put it on your back. Then go to the copter and sit down on the seat next to me." James said.

Za grabbed the massive 300 pound bat and put it on his back and lumbered over to the helicopter without turning back. It seemed Za was in a sudden trance caused by the pin pricking him in his side. James grabbed the pin and placed it back in his gun belt. Za was completely compliant and silent for over two hours into the flight. After the two hours he was the same as someone waking up a little groggy. Then he seemed pissed off at James for sticking him with a pin when he wasn't paying attention.

"Tha fuck man! Not cool." Za sneered.

"You were playing with your toys, so I decided to try one of mine. Besides it was time to go and you were going to miss our flight out."

They landed four hours west of where they were at another military base. This time it was full of typical military planes and cargo with a lot more going on than the hidden training camp they were at before. The helicopter landed with James and Za being separated from the rest of the group sent in all different directions. Za and James were then put on a cargo plane with a bunch of gear and traveled further west for another 5 hours.

After the plane landed the pilot guided them to a transport truck with two enormous boxes loaded in the back and a map of where their next stop was. James was told to drive and Za was to sit in the back with the cargo boxes blocking any view of him from the road. It was a 17 hour drive to Northern California for the first mission. The truck was not supposed to stop for more than five minutes in a four hour period and not exceed any speed limit. When James attempted to go faster than a posted speed limit the truck would lurch and slow.

It was a grueling drive with no real breaks to rest for James during the drive. Luckily Za was able to talk to him through a sliding panel between the two front seats. Most of the drive Za would keep him awake with conversation until Za fell asleep. Once they got to the final destination at the end of a closed road in rural Humboldt county California they saw an armored truck sitting on the road. The armored truck had an extremely poor black spray paint job.

"Hey Za, wake up! We're here this must be our contact. I'll go talk to them you watch my back if you see anything funny."

"Huh, alright." Za snorted waking out of a dead sleep.

CHAPTER 12
BACK AT THE STATION

Reba was looking at James like he was telling an unbelievable tale, leaving her with more questions. Reba lit the last cigarette out of her pack and inhaled most of it in one inhale. She put the cigarette out in an old coffee cup. James looked up at her waiting for her next questions. Just as she was ready to begin again James stood up grabbing his stomach cringing.

"Hey Reba, could we take a quick bathroom break? That burger is begging to come out."

"Sure, I'll escort you down to your cell. You have 15 minutes. I have a few questions still about all of this crap your tryin' to feed me."

Reba took James back down the stairs outside of the interrogation room to the holding cell. The greasy cheeseburger from last night had worked its way out of his system. It was a little after 4:30pm and he had told Reba what he had known. This was only the third time he was arrested during the job and the one and only time he was locked up and ordered to wait. The other two times he escaped immediately with no one giving chase. This time seemed to be different and he had a bad feeling about what was going on while he was on the inside.

James finished up and gave the cell door a quick reverberating knock with his left hand. Reba came back down the stairs and brought James back into the interrogation room. Reba had a fresh pack of cigarettes and was lighting another one up. She slid James a cup of black coffee to help keep him awake for her next set of questions. He took a sip of coffee, getting a slight burn to his tongue from the recently microwaved coffee.

"So, does this answer your questions about my training?" James asked.

"Some, but I have a few questions about that and the way you were just let out to go and recover escaped targets."

"How much longer do you want to keep going? It is getting late in the day."

"I have nowhere to go and you have the largest murder investigation going against you in this small town. All I have is time. Tell me more about how a quadruple amputee can lead this so called Termination squad. It seems funny to me that someone with hoses for arms and legs is in charge of a group everyone is afraid of."

"Well, not really afraid of, but they do make my money disappear. Amir didn't have hoses for arms either. They looked to me like the protective metal an electrician would use to shield cable. He told me the black cables were powered by separate power packs sitting inside of the cables for each portion of his limbs."

"So, he had battery packs in his arms and legs?"

"I guess, that is an easy way of understanding it. These packs were buried where his bicep and forearm would have been the widest. The cables were different sizes, so it gave the appearance of him having natural arms and legs. His legs were the same way even though he never showed them to me. The only thing was they were made to make him look like some buff guy with black cables for arms."

"Why didn't he cover his arms up then and appear more normal?" Reba asked.

"Well, I can only guess he wanted people to know he was more than human, and it was more intimidating."

"Okay, fair enough. What about Fred being an alien in command of a squad of Earthlings? Where does he come from and why is he running the squad?"

"All I know is his species is a group of refugees from a waring planet that have been here for 7000 years. They have a vast settlement on one of Saturn's moons and return regularly to trade for supplies with our government. I think the reason he is in charge is because even though he is what most would consider an alien, he is just a guy doing a job. It is very similar to what most of us do anyway."

There was a loud knocking at the door all of a sudden. Reba opened the door slowly and saw it was Hector with a bag of food and a distraught look on his face. Reba led him into the cramped interrogation room where he stood next to James. Hector had a broad metal strip on his nose, tapped down with surgical tape. He was breathing heavily through his mouth and sweating profusely.

"What's wrong Hector?" Reba asked.

"Sam had a heart attack when he was hit the other night. I told the Hospital he was hit by a car. They have him in emergency surgery. It looks like they are going to do a quadruple bypass to his heart. The Doctor also said if it wasn't today he could have had a massive heart attack on the job and would be dead. I ggguess it was a good thing he was knocked unconscious because he was not overworking his heart."

Hector began to cry thinking of losing a mentor and friend all of a sudden. As he was sobbing and trying to breath he pushed the bag of food onto the table. Some more burritos for James and Reba to eat for dinner. James reached for the bag to pull his food out when Hector snatched the bag back and handed it to Reba. Reba took her burrito out and handed James the other one.

"Keep that son of a bitch away ffrom mme!" Hector sobbed.

"Hey, buddy look at it like this if I didn't send him to the hospital he would have probably died on the job. He might have even killed someone if he was driving when he had a massive heart attack. You should be thanking me for saving Sam's life!" James shot back at Hector.

"Now boys, what James did was a little extreme, but he did act in defense of his property. Which, here in Texas is the law. Hector you should take the rest of the night off and put your head on straight. I already asked some of the others to work over for you."

Hector glared at James then turned to the door, opening it and slamming it as he left. James was peeling the aluminum foil from the massive burrito filled with fried pork beans and cheese. As he ate Reba placed her burrito back into the bag and left it on the table. She finished off her cigarette as James made the burrito in his hands disappear in less than a minute. Reba glared at him and began to speak.

"Okay, I do have one burning question. If the level 2 guys are so enormous and obvious to people how would someone like say Za travel? I mean an eight foot sasquatch would stand out pretty easy in a crowd."

"I guess you're right he would stand out like a sore thumb in the city. They would set them up in the back of semi-truck trailers and ship them around. The trucks had special government permits so they would avoid weigh stations and inspections. Za showed me one of the trucks he was traveling in and it was setup just as a luxury RV. A lot better than taking the bus." James said.

"Taking the bus? Don't you just fly from place to place?"

"Well, not unless absolutely necessary. My position is to blend in and not be seen by a target. A helicopter is usually a dead giveaway someone is coming after you. I travel by car, bus, taxi, and sometimes motorcycle. Besides since I am a Recovery Agent I have to pay for everything out of my own pocket. Our motto is 'With big money comes, big expenses'. That is if we had a motto."

"If you are going to be whisked away by someone when this is done, tell me how many times you have been arrested in the last ten years then?"

"Actually, I have only been arrested two other times. Both times I went peacefully into the back of the police car and escaped at the first stop. The first time they put cuffs on both wrists without paying attention to my left arm. All I did was detach my left hand and used it to break out the window and run. The next time about three years ago I handcuffed the arresting officer to the front of his patrol car and left his pants on the driver seat. Luckily he didn't have a dash cam."

Reba stared in disbelief at James as he began to tear his fingernail across a new can of Yak wintergreen. James took an ample pinch and placed it between his lower lip and gums. She put her right hand on the back of her neck and stared at the floor shaking her head. The story this far was getting to be too much for her to follow.

"How is it so many enhanced soldiers are able to escape?" Reba asked.

"I asked the same question many times. The way it was explained to me is how many regular soldiers go AWOL? It is around five thousand a year. So, an average group can just walk away. How do you keep someone that is faster, stronger, and aware of their abilities from leaving? They are told of the Termination squad to try and scare them from desertion. It works on a few, but most think it is a boogey man story to keep them in line. The Military would rather they run off than risk harm to other soldiers or exposure to the fact soldiers are currently being enhanced." James said.

"What happens when you bring one of your targets in?"

"If they are alive they go to a kind of reform school slash prison to be ready again for battle. One problem with it is if they fail they are executed."

"What about dead ones?"

"Some military docs dissect them finding as much use out of them as possible. The organs are used for transplants in other enhanced injured in battle. I don't completely understand it, but for whatever reason an enhanced can have direct organ transplants from another enhanced of the same level without any fear of organ rejection. If I was to guess it would have something to do with their altered DNA."

Reba began rubbing her forehead with her left hand shaking her head. She pulled out another cigarette and lit it up. James yawned and stretched his arms out with his fingers extended. The stainless steel table had a lot of scratches on it from years of interviews in the small room. James began taping his fingers on the table, when his left hand fingers hit the table it sounded like a fork hitting metal. Reba had her left hand on her face covering her eyes partially when she began to gain interest in something.

"Your left hand there you said you could stab it through things, right? Show me and stick it through the table." She said.

"Umm, well it is like trying to stab through metal with a scalpel. Sure, you can stab through flesh easily, but a dense metal table. No way. The best I have ever done is stab my fingers into the trunk of a car and that took a lot of force. All it would do is put little dents in the top of this table. Even if I threw it up in the air all it would do is ricochet off and probably stab me in the face." James said.

"So, throw it at the door or somethin' so I can see it."

James stood up and knocked on the white painted solid brick walls. Then he knocked on the door gently with his right hand. It was a solid steel door painted white with a layer of aged tan muck on it. Finally James stood on the table and pulled a piece of the drop ceiling above them down. He took the chair and put it on top of the table and poked his head up above where the piece of drop ceiling was.

There was electrical wires running down to the light and some pipes running over head. He grabbed a bulky four inch water pipe with his left hand. James stepped down off the chair without his left hand. He pushed the table against the door with Reba scrambling to the corner on the other side of the small room. James' right thigh was pressed against the table as he raised his left arm into the air.

"Okay Reba, this is either going to be really cool or really stupid. Here I go."

James recalled his hand to his wrist with it gripping the water pipe above. He went up into the ceiling with little effort. It looked like he was sucked up by some invisible force halfway then he dropped back down when he let go of the pipe. James looked over at Reba who was in shock with what she saw. He put the table back and climbed up the chair with Reba handing him the drop ceiling back. The pipe had a slight bend now, but it was not James' problem.

"How'd, you do that?" Reba asked, still amazed.

"This doo dad on my elbow can retract all parts of my arm with a thousand pounds of force. Since I way a little less it looks like I can magically fly. Well, fly up to ten feet at least. It has gotten me out of some bad situations."

"Alright, now I am a believer. I do have one final question. You were released to be a Recovery Agent with only three months of training? Seems like a short training period for someone going after these so called Enhanced people."

"Not exactly, we had a year of field training we had to do. I guess it is pretty similar to being a new cop. They don't just let you go out straight from the academy, do they?" James asked.

"No, they don't. So tell me about your field training. That is if you can remember it."

"I can give you the brief rundown of what we did. It would take a week to tell you everything I learned."

James stretched his neck back and forth spitting into his empty coffee cup. He stood up and pulled the chair out for Reba to sit in now. She had been standing or leaning against the wall for hours and was beginning to look uncomfortable. Reba sat down and tapped her cigarette letting ash hit the ground.

"Let me stand for this since you have been standing the whole time. I am impressed you stood for so long. I thought you were going to have Hector grab another chair." James said.

"It is part of the interrogation technique taught to us to have the upper hand on a suspect. Now you showing me what you did makes me think you are telling the truth about only being here because your boss said so. Hell if just some of what you are telling me is true you could leave anytime you wanted. So, go on tell me about this field training you had."

"Alright, I can tell you about the first and last missions I did, since those are the only ones I remember from about ten years ago. Beside they were two of the most fun missions I ever did without being alone."

James glanced back and forth in the room leaning forward grabbing his can of Yak from the table and tapping it. He twisted it open and put a fresh wad of long cut chewing tobacco in his mouth in front of his teeth and lower lip. Reba put out her lit cigarette and grabbed another one lighting it up crossing her arms. Leaning back against the wall with the table between him and Reba he began his story of his first and last field training missions.

CHAPTER 13
FIRST FIELD TRAINING MISSION

Za was waiting in the back of the truck as James went to inspect the dilapidated armored truck. James knocked on the driver side window of the truck with no response. It appeared to be abandoned on the end of the road with no one in it. All the doors were locked and it had an ample cover of dust and some green mold growing up the windows.

"Hey Za, no one is here!! Maybe the guy lef.." James began to say.

"Ya boys lost!?" A voice from the trees behind the armored truck yelled.

The truck Za and James was in shifted upward as Za jumped out moving to where the voice came from. There was a commotion coming from the woods where Za went. James could only hear some grunting sounds and see the brush and smaller tree branches sway. James was confident whomever it was would be in for a big surprise once Za got a hold of them.

"Ahh, ya beast lemme go! Fine den!" The voice yelled from the woods followed by an electric buzzing sound.

After the buzzing sound was the distinct sound of a

gargantuan body dropping to the ground. James ran towards the commotion through the woods. He saw Za laying on the ground with an Asian guy pulling purple elbow length gloves up onto his arms. James thought the guy didn't see him, so he snuck around behind him to try and sneak up on him.

"Aye, see ya. Guess de ain't makin da new boys any betta dan da old ones. Liam Harper is my name over here. Ya must be James and da big fella must be Za." Liam said.

"Your Liam? I thought.."

"Now donna you go thinking migh be dangerous. Ya expectin some sorta army man?"

"Kinda, well I wasn't expecting someone with purple gloves and eyeliner." James said.

"Ha, I wasn' spectin someone to jump me when I takin a piss."

"Also what is up with the accent? I just want the awkward questions out of the way now."

"Well, I was told you were both southern boys and wanted to make things more comfortable for you two." Liam said.

"You have us mixed up with two of the other new recruits. We're California guys."

"Far out dudes, let's catch some gnarly waves over the horizon. Just messin' with you, I myself grew up in Michigan. The accent thing is just something I practice when bringing targets in. Sometimes they respond better if someone sounds like they grew up where they did."

"What did you do to Za?" James asked.

"He is fine and is listening to everything we are saying just give him a minute and he will be up."

"So, what did you do to Za?"

"Oh, sorry sidestepped the question. I put my hand on his arm as he reached for me and gave him a little jolt."

Liam was wearing a grey tank top muscle shirt with leopard print designer jeans and neon orange cowboy boots. James was not expecting anyone like this at all to be the person training him and Za to capture enhanced soldiers. Liam took his purple velvet gloves back off slowly revealing black translucent hands and forearms. His bones and blood vessels were all visible when in the sunlight with rectangular 2 inch by 4 inch separated lumps circling his arm before his elbow. The lumps also circled the mid-section of his biceps sticking up from under the skin similar to a the size of 5 stacked credit cards.

Liam rolled up and placed his gloves in his front left pocket of his leopard print jeans. Za was beginning to lurch back up to his feet again as the effects of whatever happened were wearing off. James stood by watching Liam, still a little confused at what was going to happen. Liam slowly reached for James' left hand and then in an instant his arms where glowing a neon blue. He shocked James left arm and it dropped off with a clanging of his hand and arm dropping to pieces.

"So, that is all you can do? Make your arms glow?" James questioned.

"No, I sent an electric shock through your arm. It looks like you have some built in type of safe guard for this type of thing."

"Ha, oh yeah it has an electrical safety built in when a high amount of electricity is detected. I also think it said something about the same thing happening with high wattage emitting things such as a microwave would do the same thing."

"Well, the move I made just then sent your friend to the ground. Lucky for you there are some safeties built into that arm of yours."

"What about your arms, what are those things under your skin? Battery packs or something?"

"So you've heard of the level 1 and 2 enhanced already, well I am a different type of experimentation. I got these rubbery implants in my arm so I don't shock myself." Liam said, poking one of his implants with his index finger.

Za was now standing to the right of James rubbing the back of his neck. James also remembered the manual saying the electrical disconnect would last for 30 minutes before allowing the parts to be reconnected. Za was shaking his head in disbelief there was a different type of enhanced out there. It seemed Liam was not quite a level one, but was very muscular with a different type of enhancement.

"Ya got enhanced? Like you're some sort of level 3 or somethin'?" Za asked.

"Nope, as far as I know I am a one of a kind. They had tested the same thing on six other guys before me and they all died from the shock. It wasn't until they finished with me they decided to put these electrical buffer implants in. They have been workin' for me for a good six years now with the only issue being a tingling feeling for about 20 minutes after I discharge electricity." Liam stated.

"Huh." James said, looking at Za.

"Huh, is right." Za nodded back.

"Now boys, time to follow me back to your truck to take your equipment out." Liam said, slipping his purple gloves back on.

"Do the gloves stop you from shocking pe.."

"Who are you callin' boy!" Za interrupted.

"No, I just don't like burning up a good pair of gloves. I meant boys because you two are fresh to this." Liam said.

"Well, just watch it with that boy shit!" Za snarled back.

"Come on Za let's go grab our stuff and get the show on the road. Liam, both me and Za are exhausted from the trip so we are a little more irritable than usual." James said, trying to calm the giant.

"Alrighty, pickup your junk then come over to my truck. I have a camp about 100 yards out from here." Liam said.

Za grabbed the two enormous 6 foot tall crates from the back of the truck and ripped them open. James grabbed his gun belt, 3 speed loaders, two sets of the bulky handcuffs, and his hand cannon Rust. Za grabbed his bat, shotgun, bandoleer, four 100 round shotgun ammo drums and two sets of handcuffs. They clang, clipped, unclipped, loaded guns, loaded drums, loaded speed loaders, and re-clipped gear on. Something which should take five minutes took over thirty minutes due to exhaustion and the fact James could only use one arm.

They made their way back over to Liam's truck, James made a wide loop to retrieve his arm from the ground. Pointing his left elbow towards the ground making all the pieces clang back together. James shivered from a cool breeze as the sunlight was dwindling away. Even though it was early summertime the weather was a cool 64 degrees during the day and 44 degrees in the evening.

Liam had changed into a black t-shirt, camo cargo pants, black combat boots, and dark green leather elbow length gloves. James and Za made their way over to Liam as he was buckling his own gun belt with no giant handcuffs attached. Liam's gun belt was identical to James' and the gun appeared to be the same size as Rust. Liam now appeared to look somewhat like what they expected to see when they drove up except his black shirt had a printed unicorn with a rainbow going from its horn to its tail.

"Hey, why aren't you wearing cuffs too?" James asked.

"We are only going after one guy. Besides they throw me off balance. How do you like the shirt? Got a screen t-shirt printer in the back of my truck, I can print anything if you want something different than black." Liam said.

"What's up with the unicorn? Seems kind.."

"Gay? Yes, in case you lovelies haven't figured it out I am gay. Play your cards right big guy and I can show you somethin' you never seen before." Liam said, interrupting Za.

"How many pairs of cuffs should we bring then?" James asked.

"Just one, unless you want to have some extra fun later." Liam quipped back.

"Sorry Liam, I appreciate your offers but me and Za are not gay. Well at least I am not, sometimes I do question Za's sexuali.."

Za slapped the back of James' head in a quick motion for him to knock off the jokes. James' vision went blurry and he almost blacked out.

"Knock it off let's get over to camp." Za said.

"Liam, do you happen to have an extra sweater in your truck?" James said, with a brief shiver.

"Here take this one." Liam said, handing him a black hoodie.

The hoodie was well worn with a jumbo white "O" printed on the back. James took off one of his cuff sets and just as he was going to take off the second set Za set his two sets in the back of Liam's truck.

"Lucky you get to carry the cuffs with that giant ass target on your back." Za said, smirking.

They followed Liam to his campsite where there was a small tent with a single sleeping bag and a burned out campfire. The campsite was in the middle of a grove of redwood trees over 200 feet tall. Za was ripping bark off one of the trees with his teeth and eating it. Chewing sound coming from Za reminded James of a large cow eating.

"Does that taste good to you?" James asked.

"Imagine you are eating the most perfect steak ever. This is so much better fresh."

"This is the first time I have ever seen a level 2 eat. Most of the time they are trying to kill me. Well, I was gonna explain how payment and all the bureaucratic bull shit works, but it is goin' on five past 8:30 and I am sure you are both tired. James there is a sleeping bag you can use or you can sleep on the cot." Liam said.

"I'll take the sleeping bag since I haven't acclimated to the weather yet. What about Za? Never mind."

Za was already sleeping on the ground with redwood bark and a log for a pillow. Liam made his way over to Za to try and wake him. Liam shook Za's shoulder first with no response, then tried lifting the giants eyelids with only a grunt for a response, and last he gave him a slight jolt. Za shot up like someone sticking a fork in an electrical socket.

"Mother fucker you're dead!" Za shouted.

"Honey, would you kindly move out a few hundred yards that way into the woods?" Liam said, politely.

"Fuckin' shit, fuckin' okay." Za said, getting tired again lumbering away into the woods.

"Sorry Hun, I am not a light sleeper, but I do not believe anyone can sleep with that freight train running." Liam said, looking over at James winking.

James wriggled into the army surplus green sleeping bag with its built in pillow. Liam climbed into the cot next to him off the ground. The sleeping bag smelt moldy from being wet at some point and not drying out. It was dry now and that was all that mattered to James, besides it smelt better than his trailer back in Kentucky. James closed his eyes for a blink and when he opened them it was morning.

A pleasant aroma of fresh meat being cooked was flooding the tent. James wiggled out of the sleeping bag to see Liam cooking two small skinned and feathered birds over the campfire. After three months of preserved low grade meat James was excited for something fresh. Za was eating a large piece of redwood bark the size of a skateboard like a giant candy bar.

"So, you brought some chicken to eat? Are those game hens they look a little small?" James asked.

"Za caught these and gave them to me to apologize for snapping at me last night. I already ate my two and these are gonna be for you. Now these are not chicken they are better, pheasants. If I hear one word of these taste like god damn chicken, lord help me, you will be shitten your teeth."

Liam handed James the stick with the two birds on it and he ate without saying anything. They did not contain an ounce of chicken flavor. Considering all the chicken he ate the last five years was in some sort of breaded nugget form or MRE. While James ate his pheasants Liam broke down the tent and rolled up the sleeping bag. Liam placed the tent and the sleeping bag back in his truck and brought down a bulky military style hiking backpack.

"So, did you get this stuff from when you left the Army?" James asked.

"Army? I was not in the Army, I was a Marine. Got all this crap from a surplus store two years ago haven't used it until today. After three months of basic, I got trained, turned from a turd into a man killin' machine, then to this." Liam said, waving his hands slowly over each arm.

It was cool brisk morning with a light layer of fog. The giant redwood trees turned into colossal ghosts gradually disappearing in the distance. Giant oversized shoe prints were the only thing James could see as he went to locate Za. The shoe prints went straight into a giant tree James almost walked into due to being focused on the shoe prints.

"Za, where are you!" James yelled.

"Next to you." He whispered.

"I just got chills, you creeped me out there."

"Yo, guys come on over! I have something for both of you!" Liam called out.

Liam handed them both roll devices which appeared to be slightly different than the ones they played with when they both were training. Still looked like a cigar tube with two caps attached at both ends. The main difference was they were solid black with no scratch marks on the outside and the caps were slightly smaller on the ends.

"So, these technically are not yours until you complete training with me for the next 12 months. Latest and greatest in cigar technology, your standard issue cigar holder has two satellite antennas, just pop them off like so, twist clockwise to take off each one, place them within four feet of the device for signal, roll up the screen, press the tiny switch in the middle up, then once within three feet they will magnetically re-attach like so. Usually I just open it up and place the little antenna end caps in my pocket. Any questions?" Liam stated.

"I'm gonna lose these little caps." Za said.

"Well hun, lucky for you I have a sewing kit in my truck and can sew up a pocket to put on your hammer strap going over your shoulder." Liam said.

"Hammer? You mean History?" Za said, taking his bat off his back.

"History? You named your bat History? Well, show Liam the blades while you have it out."

Za gripped the giant 6ft long 300 pound bat and pulled down on the pommel then released it. A loud clang followed by the bat twisting out four ninja star curved blades. Za gripped the pommel again pulling back then releasing it once more to make the blades turn back in. Liam looked in amazement and made a motion to try and hold the bat. Za stretched his right arm straight out to hand the bat too Liam.

"Wait Liam, it isn't..!" James tried to stop him.

Liam went to grab the bat and went toppling over to the ground from the sudden drop of the weight into his arms. He sat on the ground for a minute and dusted off dirt from his clothes and stood up. The massive bat was laying on the ground next to him. Liam went to try to pick it up and after a straining try he got it off the ground for a brief moment, squatting holding it with two hands by the pommel.

"I tried to tell you it is a lot heavier than it looks. Za likes to fuck with people and make things look lighter than they are." James said.

"Give me History. She is one and only made for me out of solid steel. No light weight alloys here. Pure solid forged steel." Za said, taking the bat away from Liam and placing it on his back.

"Ah, I see you playin games with me. Alright my sweets lets get a move on we can talk while we walk. It is a ten mile hike to where the last known whereabouts of the target is."

They began walking into the dense forest of giant redwood trees following Liam. Za picked up the backpack Liam had and hooked it onto History's handle. The fog was beginning to thin out as the morning sun got higher in the sky. Za was naturally camouflaged with his red fur and dark skin against the enormous redwoods. Without his gear on Za would simply disappear into the background of the forest.

"Yo Liam, I just thought of somethin', how do we charge up our dick phones?" Za said, shaking the roll device up and down.

"Dick phones? Hun, I hope for your sake if this was your dick they upgraded it with the rest of you. They charge up with the sunlight. A kind of extra charged solar power by the miracle of nanotube technology. The antennas are also the batteries, so don't lose either part of your dick, Za! Oh yeah, they last eleven hours fully charged and take three hours to charge. The one great thing is sunlight even on a cloudy day will allow for it to charge and it can be used while it charges." Liam responded.

They hiked up and down small hills through the dense forest walking at a quick pace until they were 3 miles out of where they needed to be. Stopping at a small stream 3 feet wide flowing away from the direction they were heading. James waved Za over to grab a canteen from the backpack and take a quick sip of water. Za took the bag off his back and opened it up to everyone's surprise it was not survival supplies.

"What the shit is this Liam!" James yelled, grabbing his gun from his gun belt.

"Paint me pink, I am so embarrassed. That is my makeup kit. I keep my survival stuff in the same type of bag." Liam said, apologizing.

"Damnit Liam, you couldn't keep your crap in different bags? Well, good thing we are almost there." James said, placing his gun back in the holster.

James was feeling a little thirsty after their seven mile hike and kneeled down by the stream of water. Liam was looking through his makeup kit and began to apply some more eyeliner. The water felt cool and looked pretty clear with a few small patches of algae on some of the rocks. James cupped his right hand and went to place a sip of water in his mouth.

"You drink that, your dumb ass will be shitten blood for a week." Za said.

"It's a stream with fresh flowing water. Survival training they taught us moving water is usually pretty safe." James replied, putting his hand up to his mouth.

Before he could take a sip Za picked him up by the back of his shirt like picking up a baby and put him face to face with him.

"Toxic." Za growled in a low voice.

"Okay, now put me down so we can talk to Liam about what's next."

"What's next? You do realize I am just putting on eyeliner not plugging my ears. Za is going to run ahead and stop about 300 yards outside of the farm with this radio. Play all songs on the track and turn it to full volume. We will be about a half an hour behind flanking the drying shed from the left and right. James will go left heading in first and I will go right." Liam responded.

"So, I just play this radio and stand there? Plus why is there a radio in your makeup bag?" Za asked.

"Well I planned the radio thing and lucky for you I brought my MP3 radio in my makeup kit. So it kinda worked out. No, don't stand around, hit play and disappear back into the trees. There are a few more things for the plan with James, but nothin' major. Have your weapons ready when you are close." Liam replied.

"When do we find out who we are going after? This whole time me and Za have been left in the dark about who exactly we are going after. Plus what is the payout for all of this? Amir said there was some sort of pay scale."

"Gosh darn me! I totally forgot all that stuff. Guess I had it planned for the first night but you both were so exhausted. Here I will forward the target info to each of your roll devices. Pay and all of that is written down in my truck. For this job if we bring the guy in alive it will be a little over 50k for each of you." Liam said, opening up his roll device.

James and Za both popped open their roll devices putting their antennas on a downed tree and sitting on the giant log. The screens flickered to life as they unrolled the devices for the first time by the both of them. A little message box popped up with "Liam Harper has sent you a Message." They both clicked on the message and a full color picture of a level 2 enhanced popped up with a mini arrow in the left corner pointing down.

A dark coal colored face with dark red hair was on the screen. As they scrolled down below the picture was information on the target. Name, age, weight, escape date, escape location, followed by a countdown timer spinning down to termination. The list on the roll devices showed:

Name: Gilbert Long

Age: 28 years old

Weight: 624 lbs.

AWOL Date: 6/23/09

AWOL Location: Sierra Army depot CA

Term. Timer: 160 hrs. 23 mins. 14 seconds.

"Wait a minute it says depot, like Army storage building. Seems kinda weird, I expected some sort of unusual secret place for all of these guys to escape from." James said.

"Perfect place to grow your enhanced soldiers without spyin' eyes. Everyone is watching Area 51 so the best cover is the most and least obvious places at the same time. Besides as you saw what they did with our lovely Za, it was done at an abandoned military facility. They just perform the transformations in different locations so no one will be able to figure out what is going on." Liam replied.

"Can I please get a bigger one of these!" Za said, shaking his roll device like a tiny cigarette in his enormous hands.

"Well, actually they do have different configurations, but you will have to purchase your own upgrades from now on. No more free rides my loves." Liam said.

"How much?" Za asked.

"The biggest one the size of a laptop when opened and a

paper towel tube when rolled up was around 165 the last time I checked." Liam replied.

"Well heck, Za for that price I will buy you two after this mission." James said.

"No, sweetie one hundred sixty five thousand. We get paid well but gear gets expensive fast, you will need new things such as the needles in your belt to subdue unruly enhanced, thirty thousand per needle. Now I wouldn't go without them, but try to use your gear in a smart fashion." Liam said.

"Damnit, I wasted a pin on Za earlier to get him loaded up to go. There goes thirty grand."

"Ha, fuckin' dumb ass." Za said, laughing.

"Alright, alright now you know a little more can we get this done? Za run ahead like planned and turn on the radio. Hide out in the outer region until we are there. I will send you a message on your roll device when we are there, it will vibrate when rolled up." Liam said sternly.

Za disappeared into the redwood forest in a brief instant leaving James and Liam. They made their way directly up the creek where it began to reek of dead fish. The dead fish scent grew stronger and stronger until they finally got to an enormous marijuana grow. Waste pipes from the grow were polluting the creek with fertilizer being used for the grow.

The grow site was two acres of leveled ground for plants with a few small modular buildings on a hill to the right from where James and Liam were standing. Directly to the left to the middle of the grow site was a gigantic barn with peeling brown paint. A low sound of techno music was being blasted out from the radio Liam gave Za, just next to the barn. There was no one around anywhere, it seemed surreal no one was watching such a considerable grow.

"James, I sent a message to Za telling him where we are. You go ahead to the barn and check it out I will go up to the right to the trimmer buildings." Liam said, pointing and motioning where to go with his hands.

"What about Za?"

"He is our backup if anything happens. Za can move faster than we can and if you see Gilbert yell. I will do the same. Got it?" Liam whispered.

"Got it."

James pulled his gun from his gun belt holding it up ready to fire moving closer and closer to the barn. The music was getting louder with each step. He carefully stood with his gun up leaning against the door of the barn. Making a quick left pivot movement and placing his gun to the inside of the building only to see it was completely empty. A distant yell came from up on the hill where Liam was.

"Heyy! I see him in the Field!!"

Several redwood trees began to sway as an enormous bigfoot like creature came bursting out towards the middle of the marijuana field. Clearing the plants in a fierce run towards where the target was. Ten foot tall plants toppled over, being plowed down by the shockingly quick beast. Then another yell back from the center of the marijuana field came out.

"Yo! He's passed out!" Za called out.

James and Liam both sprinting as fast as they could saw a naked level 2 enhanced passed out from eating marijuana plants. Za rolled Gilbert over as James put the cuffs on him, while Liam called out for a helicopter pickup. Gilbert was beginning to come around after Za carried him out of the middle of the field. Still disoriented he was more curious about who the guy with the skeleton hand was, more so than the other level 2 enhanced setting him down outside of the field.

"Skelly hand, you are scary. Oooh I am sooo.. sccared." Gilbert said, slurring out his words.

"I don't understand is he mocking me or what?" James asked.

"Well, babe level 2's can't exactly drink alcohol without some adverse effects, so when they eat enough pot they get drunk stoned. This is only the second time I have seen this. Good for you loves it mellows them out so no wasting any of those expensive needles." Liam said.

Within 15 minutes a container the size of semi-trailer was being lowered down by a storage helicopter. Inside the container was a smaller room on the far end with a cable attached by an open eye hook to the floor, and the door to the container was solid with no way of telling what was inside. Three people came out of the helicopter wearing full blackout gear and aircraft helmets. They took Gilbert into the container and clipped the handcuffs to the cable in the small room within the container. All three sat down in one of the four seats inside the container and waved as the door was closing, and the container raised back into the helicopter.

"Man that's cool!" Za yelled, over the sound of the helicopter leaving.

"Only downside to helicopter pickup is they take your cuffs with them, considering they will cost you twenty five for another pair. Lucky for you my sweets this pair is on me. Next one's are on ya'll." Liam said.

"Twenty five thousand I am assuming. Damn does anything come cheap?" James asked.

"Ammo boxes for magnum ammo cost us about sixty dollars for a box of 50. Armor piercing tipped and radioactive tracing to determine if one of ours shot the target, and about forty five dollars for a box of fifty armor piercing slugs for the shotguns. Let's make our way back to my truck I have some lunch items for you James, and Za you can just eat on the way."

They got back to Liam's armored truck before noon and found the truck they came in was gone. Liam walked up to the back of the truck and touched a one foot by one foot patinated copper square where the lock would have been. A popping sound of a lock releasing was followed by Liam pulling the rear door open with the handle to the right of the copper square. Inside the truck on the left side was clip in hangers with spots for ten handcuffs on the upper left going across to the cab. There was a two foot open cage cabinet running under the handcuffs full of .44 magnum ammo all the way to the back of the cab.

The cab was separated from the front of the truck by a solid wall with a small window over the driver's right shoulder. Just below the ammo was a grey cabinet filling the rest of the left side of the truck. The right side was a small metal desk next to the door with a fixed stool in the middle just big enough for a regular person to sit in. Behind the desk was a bed touching the left side of the truck storage bin with pillows and a bright neon green velvet sheet. All of the camping gear was thrown on top of the bed in a disorderly fashion. On the desk was a t-shirt screen printer taking up all the space of the desk.

"So, where is lunch?" James asked.

"One second." Liam replied.

Liam touched the floor next to the stool where a smaller six by six inch square was next to the door. The rear of the truck expanded out three feet wider than it was before and the cab remained in its same position. Liam climbed into the truck and opened up the lower 3 foot high cabinet by grabbing a handle in the middle and twisting it down. A cold breeze came from the cabinet and it lit up.

"Sorry, all I got for now is some bread and bologna in the

fridge. We will have to do some shopping on our way to the next target." Liam said.

"Damn, that's cool." Za said.

Liam handed James a bread and bologna sandwich along with a cold bottle of water. James and Liam ate while Za munched on another piece of redwood bark. Liam made his way to the front of the truck and pressed his hand against a six by six patinated square of copper where the door handle was. The front door popped open about four inches and he pulled the door all the way open.

"So, the panels are hand print panels?" James asked.

"Nope, electrical charge opens them up sugar. James you can ride up front and Za you can ride in the back." Liam replied.

"Liam how the fuck am I supposed to fit in here. It is wider but not any tall.."

Liam started the truck up and flipped a switch on the left of the radio. The rear of the truck went up from six feet tall to nine feet tall. Then he flipped another switch below the other switch and the entire roof behind the cab came down on the side of the truck. Now the truck appeared the same as a pickup truck with a sizeable camper trailer on the back. The roof panels which were now side panels showing "Zeke's Rare Animal Transport."

"Animal transport?" James asked.

"Just in case any one sees are large sugar bear in the back. It took me two weeks to figure out what to do if I have to transport a level 2 enhanced. I tried to bring them to the bases myself but it was more of a pain in the ass than callin' in a copter." Liam said.

"Wow, now can your bed hold me and History?" Za asked.

"Well hun, how much do you weigh again?"

"Eight hundred fifty seven pounds, and History is a perfectly balanced 300." Za replied proudly.

"Eleven fifty seven, nope you can stand. Your bat can rest on the bed. How in the blazes do you weigh over 200 pounds more than Gilbert?" Liam asked.

"The math was supposed to be somethin' like 3.15 multiplied by your original weight before transformation begins. Mine calculated out to 850.5 since I weighed in at 270 pounds before beginning the program."

"Wow, I'll be damned. Where to now Liam?" James asked.

"Well, how about you pick the next one and Za picks the next. As long as you two can take turns."

James opened his roll device and the screen lit up with a message 'New Active Cases Available'. Touching the box with the message a small one by one inch square appeared on the top left of the screen with a brief description of level 2 or level 1 with a countdown timer. Touching one of the pictures it expanded open to a full picture and information was available just as before with Gilbert. The only difference was at the very bottom of the screen there was a green accept button or red cancel.

"Just read through and pick one you think we should do. From now on I am basically an expensive taxi driver. Granted I will follow your plans and lend assistance. The bulk of the work has to be done by both of you. This is your final test to be either let out to go to work or be a prisoner with a job." Liam stated.

"Pick a good one James, ooh look at this one." Za said, pointing his massive finger at the screen and shoving it in front of James.

"Level 2 on the Oregon coast. Sounds nice but I want to try something a little different. Here look at this Level 2 in

Western Idaho, plus it says he is 848 pounds vs 730 in Oregon." James said.

"Up to you this time, but if we get done soon enough I pick the one on the coast."

They loaded up into Liam's armored truck with Za standing in the back and James sitting in the passenger seat. In-between James and Liam was Liam's makeup backpack. Liam had a bad habit of reaching into the bag and grabbing makeup out while driving to apply it to his face. Eventually he let James drive so he could focus on his personal beauty.

CHAPTER 14
LAST FIELD TRAINING MISSION

"Well, we shit the bed on the last mission. Just lucky for us no one else got killed. Za your turn to pick, where are we gonna go for the final mission?" James asked.

"We did not shit the bed Jamesy. Just pooed on the floor next to it. They had a gang of people tryin' to kill us and no one kills my honeys under my watch." Liam replied.

"Here we go, check it out. Brother and sister both level 1, last known location was near Portland Oregon." Za said.

They climbed into the armored truck and made their way from Bakersfield California to Portland Oregon. Liam and James both had agreed it was better to travel away from freeways and take more indirect routes to avoid Za being sighted. Before they had come to this agreement a trucker had seen Za pop out of the truck late at night and attempted to call the police. No cops came because the story of bigfoot at the truck stop sounded too ridiculous.

As soon as they were on the coast the truck shook with a loud banging sound. Za was knocking on the rear panel between the cab and the back of the truck. His face was a sad pleading grimace that would make a good ad for save the sasquatch. Liam pulled off the road as soon as he could and the rear door blew open in a flash. The suspension shuttered up and down for five minutes after Za leapt out.

"Ahhhh. Thank you, I had to pee so fuckin' bad." Za said, with relief.

Za loaded himself back into the back of the truck and they were on the road again. James and Liam thought early on they would be able to give Za some jumbo bottles to pee in to save on searching for a secretive place to stop. They soon found out his urine had a strong ammonia odor that would stain clothing the same as a skunk. The aroma was not as potent as a skunk's but was strong enough to last several days.

"Za did they mention your piss smelling this bad when you were signing paperwork to become a giant honey bear?" Liam asked.

"Well, if you two must know it is kind of a sweet aroma to me. I don't know why the fuck you two are complaining about stinking. I have enhanced smell and can smell the fart you had 3 hours ago." Za replied.

"Alright Za, where should we start with this one? A bar, a motel, used car dealership, or something else?" James asked, through the small square hole over his shoulder in the truck.

"You still using the used car dealership as the first place to go. C'mon that only worked one time. When we get there you and Liam go look up friends of theirs and I will go to the local parks and see if I can sniff anything out." Za said.

The brother and sister were Nevaeh and Tristan Leit, from Portland Oregon. This was all the information available to them on the roll devices. Also the last known location sighting was not based on an actual sighting but off of a phone recording from them talking to friends on burner phones. When a level 1 or level 2 escapes the phones of relatives, friends, and any other associates are flagged for recording and review. Once an estimated location is made it is up to the recovery agent to locate the target from then on.

"I think the only reason we are going after these two is Za thinks the chick is hot." James said.

"I agree completely. She is an attractive women, too bad the brother went the other way in the looks department. Why couldn't they be identical twins, so me and Za could go on a double date." Liam said.

"Yeah, you got me. She is so fine. Milk chocolate skin with a beautiful short dark chocolate curl on top." Za said.

"You got all of that from the 4 inch photo of her head on your roll device? I hope for your sake she is nice enough to just give up." James said.

After two days with stops for sleep and bathroom breaks they made it into Portland without any issues. Liam pulled into a wooded park on the north side of town and let Za out. Za got out and took another leak on what he thought was some trash on the ground. It turned out to be a guy in a sleeping bag at the entrance of the park. The bag wriggled around as Za finished his business then it popped open.

"Hey I'm sleeping here! I'll cut you up ass clown if you don't..." The guy said, stopping seeing the giant beast in front of him.

"Sorry man, didn't see you down there." Za said.

The guy looked up with his mouth open and eyes wide not knowing what to do. He stiffened up frozen in fright from Za's appearance. His jaw began to quiver up and down trying to speak, but would only make gasping sounds. Za kneeled down to help the guy out of the urine soaked sleeping bag. Peeling the guy out of the sleeping bag in an attempt to help him up was more of a challenge than it should have been. The guy curled up in the fetal position inside the bag trying to hide in disbelief of what was happening.

Za grabbed the bag still kneeling down tearing it in half slowly to pull the guy out. The bag opened up with the guy going flat to the ground. Several spoons, needles, and a few black bags poured out with the guy. Now the guy was scrambling to grab his drugs before they could be taken by the giant.

"Man, I don't want your shit. Why the hell are you doin' that fucked up stuff anyway?" Za asked.

"I...I..Ittta makes the days better." The guy said.

"Shit like you got it so rough. Go get your arm half burned off from a trailer explosion, then have a bat shit crazy alien grind the rest of it away with no pain meds." James called out.

"Whaa....?" The guy tried to ask.

Then the guy saw a man with a metal skeleton left arm with a hand gun larger than anything he had ever seen.

"Well, guess you heard me, Liam wait in the truck while I see what's going on. What are you doing Za?" James asked as he walked over.

"Pissed on dudes sleepin' bag on accident." Za replied.

"Hey bud, what's your name? I am James and this is Za. Don't worry we are not here for you." James said.

"Travis...Travis Williams." Travis said.

"Well Travis, what brings you down to sleeping outside of a park in a sleeping bag. Did something terrible happen to you to make you want to forget your life? You are a young guy and can have a better life if you choose to." James said.

"I...I failed. I was going through my residency and I failed. I can't go back to the world, I can't." Travis said, trembling.

"Alright here is what we are going to do, first here is a hundred bucks for a new sleeping bag. We are going to leave you alone to be you. I am not a therapist but you seem to think the world is over so just stay here and act like it is over and die slowly. Me, personally I would rather live and risk dying fast." James said, handing Travis a 100 dollar bill with his left hand.

"Whoa, whoa, whoa, you were gonna be a Doctor. You fuckin' idiot quit the shit and get back at it. Man I wish more of my African brothers would be Doctors. Your fucking shit ass is coming with me to see what is going on." Za said, seething.

"Za, come on he has made his choice calm down, we have work to do." James said.

"Nah, this fuckers gonna learn how good he's got it!" Za shouted.

Za took off his bat from his back and smashed it straight down on Travis' small drug supply. It was buried deep in the ground when Za grabbed a boulder used to block cars from driving into the park and placed it over the drugs. The rock was the same size as a small car. Travis began to cry and tried to throw a tantrum until Za picked him up off the ground with both hands under his armpits facing him up and away.

"Look at this world out here. This is where you live not in there. Now get your ass to the hospital." Za said.

"I don't understa..." Travis said being interrupted.

Za dropped Travis to the ground with a mild downward swing causing him to break a leg and arm on the fall.

"Well, let's go up the road a little ways and break off with the plan. This guy is either going to get help or just lay here crying. Guess we will never really know." James said.

"Yeah let's go. This bitch can just stay here and cry." Za said sternly.

James and Za loaded back into the truck with Liam heading up the road for 10 minutes before deciding on a plan. Za entered to the north west of the park they saw Travis sleeping in front of. He headed out in an attempt to locate any signs the twins were hiding out somewhere outdoors. James and Liam decided to ride the local public transportation system stopping at the past known hangouts of the twins. Liam picked a bus line going in the opposite direction of James. They were to meet up at 7pm back at the spot where they ran into Travis.

Liam climbed onto the bus going the opposite direction after James had already left. Too busy putting on eyeliner when he got onto the bus Liam had forgotten to leave his gun behind. Someone screamed on the bus, the driver stopped immediately and Liam got off running back to his truck.

James went to a grocery store in downtown Portland where Tristan had worked. It appeared to be his first job since no one at the store recognized the picture James showed them. He asked the manager why no one would be able to recognize a kid employed there less than five years ago. The managers only response "turnaround." It appeared the store did have pretty high turnaround since the manager had only been there a month.

Liam went to one of Nevaeh's high school friend's houses only to find out they had died in a car crash two years ago. After that he went to one of Tristan's high school buddies homes, only to find out the people that lived there had moved away. Down to one strike left, Liam went down to the bar closest to where the kids former friends once lived. Lucky for Liam he came accross one of them leaving the bar as the other one snuck out another door.

It was getting close to time to meet up with James and Za. Liam was a strong believer in reconnaissance before apprehension. One thing that has kept him from being seriously injured and alive. Liam watched the twins climb into an old decommissioned police car and drive off down the street and turn right. Liam went into the bar to talk to the bartender before going back to meet up with Za and James.

"Hey barkeep, you know those two that just left?" Liam asked.

A short heavy set girl with bright blue hair looked up from below the counter. In the middle of cleaning glasses before being interrupted by Liam.

"Tristan and Nevaeh, the two that just left?" She asked back.

"Yes."

"Tristans an old boyfriend from way back in middle school and Nevaeh is one of my best friends. Are they in some sort of trouble?"

"No, no dear, I work for a fitness magazine and would love to talk to them. Would you by chance know where they are staying? Or about when they come around the bar so I can talk with them?"

"They just stopped by for a cocktail after lunch and have been coming by almost every day, around one O'clock. Never did tell me where exactly they were staying just said they were camping outside of town."

"Thank you sweetheart, could you do me a favor and not tell them we spoke. If you don't tell them I will give you a two hundred dollar finder fee. Half now and half later after I speak to them, no matter if I use them in the magazine or not, deal?"

She rubbed her forehead with the back of her hand unsure what to do.

"Eight hundred."

"How about eight hundred and you give me a dry martini? I can see your boss has some cameras up. So, me handing you money and walking away could get you in trouble with your job. If I leave you a four hundred dollar tip for the martini it is less conspicuous. How does that sound?"

She looked back and forth like being watched constantly by the cameras.

"Deal."

She made Liam a martini with what looked like an expensive bottle of vodka. It tasted cheaper than it looked, because it was plastic bottle vodka poured into an expensive bottle. Liam downed the martini leaving the tip on the table walking towards the door. She called back to him before he could walk out.

"By the way the cameras are just for show. My boss bought some fake ten dollar things online and had us put them up to deter people. Our deal is still good, hope to see you soon."

Liam feeling slightly burned walked out through the door and back to his battered looking armored truck. James sat on a bus wearing Liam's old hoodie with the white "O" on the back zipped up to conceal his arm. His bulky gun and gun belt were around his shoulder under the hoodie. Za meandered back to the parking spot next to the park with nothing to report. James also did not come across anything, and all they had is Liam's lead.

James made it back late to the meeting spot due to the bus running late. He could not see Za, but knew he lurked close by hiding in one of the trees. James ran over to Liam's truck and knocked on the armored window. Liam opened the door stepping out with a grin going ear to ear. After the bus drove out of sight Za came down from 20 feet above them in the timber tree next to the parking lot.

"Well?" James asked.

"Ain't got shit, people just talkin' about babies and their stupid ass dogs!" Za said.

"Not you, him!" James said, pointing at Liam.

"Ha, you sweets ain't got nothin'? I know a place where they will be and likely are, plus where they are hiding out." Liam said, still grinning.

"Okay where?" James asked.

"Just a little ways up the road in Forest Grove." Liam replied.

"Sounds tasty." Za said.

"Well, what's the plan?" James asked.

"Za's mission, so it will have to be Za's plan." Liam replied.

Liam informed them of the bar they were going to daily in the afternoon, their vehicle, and possible camping locations around town. They drove up to Forest Grove and drove around the outside of town to set up their own camp. Liam noticed an old police car parked on the side of the road near a nature preserve. Liam pointed the car out to James and Za when they went by. He stopped the truck five more miles up a winding road stopping at a parking lot for a golf course. The lot was completely empty with only an occasional car passing by on the road.

"Okay Small Fry, what's the plan?" James asked.

"So, I think I will head down and try to scout what they are doing tonight. After I get some recon I will have a better idea for the plan." Za said.

Za ran off across the street back into the wooded area towards where the car was parked. James and Liam waited making a quick sandwich each for dinner in the back of the truck. Liam was finished with his sandwich before James took his first bite. Just as James took his last bite the truck tilted up on the driver side then slammed down hard on the suspension.

"God damnit!! Za that better be you!" James yelled.

"Heeyaa!!" Liam yelled at the same time spilling bottled water all over himself.

"Yo, come out." Za said.

Liam lifted the lever for the door and came out first followed by James. They were standing in a bright moon lit night sky on a gravel parking lot. Za looked a little excited to give news about something. Liam got back in the truck and began to throw a sleeping bag out for James to sleep in outside.

"Man she is so much finer in person." Za said.

"Oookaay, what did you find out about bringing these two in. Any idea if they are going to leave tomorrow, or if they have any, I don't know weapons to kill us?" James said, with serious sarcasm.

"No weapons, no plans to leave yet. The brother is planning on stayin' at the campsite tomorrow and she is going to get lunch and bring it back for him. Guess he is working on their next move and we arrived just in time before they split out of here."

"How do we know she is going to go to the bar after getting the food?"

"I heard her say she wants to say goodbye to Jenny before they leave. Her brother said bring him back a whiskey sour." Za said.

"Plan?"

"Okay, my yummies you have to go find some place to sleep and I will pick you up in the morning. Here, at let's say ten. I am going to get my groove on tonight." Liam said, climbing into the cab of the truck.

"Liam, your part of the plan is to watch James from outside. In case he fucks it up!" Za yelled, over the sound of Liam starting the truck.

Liam waved as he sped off down the road into the bright night sky. Za waved for James to follow him into the wooded area to find a place to sleep and go over the next day's plan. James tried to follow Za through the thick brush but found it to be almost impossible. Stopping constantly to find a different way around and look for a giant waving arm. Za made his way through the shrubs and wooded areas like a fish swimming downstream.

They stopped at a tree two miles closer to the twins and Za cleared a few downed trees for James to roll out his sleeping bag. Za tossed 50 foot logs like they were paper towels into the woods. Birds and other sleeping animals could be heard scurrying away as the trees came crashing back down. He was getting into a rhythm tossing downed trees just to toss them making a clearing more than a 100 square feet.

"Stop, you lug! I only have a sleeping bag, not a condo!" James yelled at Za.

"Sorry Bitch, just tryin' to give you some luxury."

"Alright, now what is the plan for tomorrow?"

"So, you wear the Army jacket Liam got from the surplus store. You will leave all your gear with Liam in the truck to be non-threatening. All gear, so no fuckin' nunchuck hand. Make sure you button up your sleeve on your left arm. Mention you were in the Army and lost your arm in Afghanistan to try and get a little sympathy from her. Then talk her into giving herself up peacefully." Za stated.

"The only time this went peacefully was our first case. She is going to kill me without my arm. You want me to get my ass kicked by a girl again?"

"Don't worry she won't hurt you, she is an angel sent from heaven." Za said, looking up into the sky.

Taking a deep breath and breathing out James said. "Alright, it is your mission. If I die tomorrow I will haunt you with my naked ass rubbing up and down your precious bat."

"Let's get some sleep since tomorrow is going to be fun."

They went out the next morning walking towards the parking lot where Liam had left them the night before.

James walked into the lot looking around and realized it was only 7 in the morning and they would need to wait three more hours for Liam. He held out a slight hope Liam would come back late in the night and park in the parking lot but that was not the case. James walked back into the woods and opened up his roll device.

"Not there." James said.

"Damn, guess he really did go out partying. Should we send him a message?"

"Yeah, what do you want it to say?"

"Tell him to meet me here and you're going to walk to town to scope out the bar."

"Okay, so I am walking all the way back to town just to wait a few hours until she shows up?"

"Yes, it is part of your characters veteran history. Let me see that sleeping bag."

Za zipped the sleeping bag closed looking over at James grinning ripped a small hole in the end a person's feet would go. Then he unzipped it and put it over James' head. Za tore it under James' waist and turned the bag so the zipper side would be in the middle of James' chest. James caught on to what he was doing and unsheathed his rubber covered fingers on his left hand. He tore out the right side next to his shoulder and pushed his hand straight through on the left.

"So, now I look like a crazy homeless guy. What next?" James asked.

"Hand over the skelly hand, and let's try to bag up the stump on the end to hide your elbow magnet. Hey you wearin' socks?"

"Yeah, I'm wearing socks. Skelly hand I almost forgot about that. Good one. So you want me to put my sock over my arm."

"Your right sock."

"Ok, since it is your mission. Be careful with my arm. What are you going to put it in?"

James opened up his can of chewing tobacco and placed a pinch in his mouth and disconnected his arm handing it to Za. Za had a plastic bag he found off the side of the road which he put James' left platinum arm in. James pointed to his gun belt looking up at Za, Za shook his head yes and James gave him his gun belt also.

"My roll device is on there so don't crush it." James said.

"Check this out I will keep it right here."

Za took the opened gun belt and wrapped it around his right bicep and buckled it. The gun belt fit tightly onto Za's massive arm. He moved it up, down, and around to show nothing would fall out. The yellow plastic bag with James' arm was more questionable as it deteriorated with small holes in the bottom.

"Can you please roll my arm up in what is left of the sleeping bag and put it in the truck when Liam gets here." James pleaded.

Za wrapped the arm up in the leftover sleeping bag then as he was kneeling down grabbed a handful of wet mud from a small runoff water stream. He threw the mud on James' face and chest, coating him with mud. James wiped the mud off of his face with his right hand and flung it on the ground.

"Asshole, what the hell?!" James yelled.

"Now you look like you've been living in the woods. Scram, we will meet you after you go get Nevaeh from the bar."

"I don't have any gear!"

"Take one of these pins and you should be good Liam will be waiting outside. Then we just zip down the road call a chopper and get paid."

James carefully pressed the pin into the rubber of his

right shoe. Za shook both his hands at James shooing him away to start going. James started back walking through the woods towards the camp where the twins were at. Za stepped in front of him to stop him.

"Man, use the road. Try to stay where they won't see you." Za said.

James walked back onto the road and began his walk back into town. He began trying to wipe some of the mud off before it could completely cake on and dry. All he had on him was his muddy running shoes, blue jeans, black shirt, half can of chew in his right pocket, and a ten dollar bill. His jeans and shirt were getting dirtier and dirtier as the mud dried. Mud caked into his hair hardening as the sun baked it on.

Once in town he located the bar Liam had told them about in the truck. It was a brick building in the middle of a few shops. Very much a dive bar that opened at 10 am with some low painted glass windows in the front and a metal back door. James was in town at 9:45 am with a few minutes to walk around and look at possible escape routes. A cop saw him looking into the windows of some of the other businesses and slowed down his cruiser.

"Do you need help with something?" The officer asked.

"Nope, just waiting for the bar to open."

"Alright you just stay out of trouble." The officer said, rolling his car window back up and driving across the street to watch James.

James waited until exactly 10 am and gave the doors a push but the bar was still locked up. He walked around the block and noticed the cop car drove around following him around the building. As soon as he got to the door of the bar once again he tried it and it was open. It was dimly lit with only a few lights on over the bar. The short bright blue haired bartender stared at James for a few minutes.

"Do you have a bathroom?" James asked.

"Restroom is for paying customers only." She snarled at him.

James reached across his mud covered body and put his dirty ten dollar bill on the counter.

"Beer."

She nodded her head towards the back of the building where the bathroom was. It was a small bathroom with a urinal and a stall with an out of service sign hanging on the door. White tiles on the floor were a grimy yellow and brown tint and the wood paneling coated with graphitti. The mirror had been scratched up with graphitti all over it. James turned on the sink and for the first few seconds brown water came pouring out. He cupped his right hand and made an attempt to wash the mud out of his hair.

Massive chunks of mud plopped into the sink and he stopped washing his hair when it felt almost normal. James quickly washed his face the best he could with his hand, in an attempt to use the soap dispenser he discovered it was empty. He reached for the metal box that held the paper towels to discover it was also empty. Dripping wet from the top of his head down to his neck all he could do is try and wipe the water off with his hand.

After being in the bathroom for ten minutes he headed back to where he placed his ten dollar bill. The dank aroma of old spilled dried liquor filled his nostrils and he could see someone was sitting where he placed his bill. The guy was drinking a beer when he looked over and saw James wearing his torn up mud covered homemade jacket with no sleeves. James walked up to the bar to talk to the bartender at the far end next to the restroom.

"Where is my beer?" James asked.

"Down there." She nodded at the guy drinking at the other end.

"Where is my change?"

"You didn't specify which beer so I gave you a ten dollar one."

James shook his head and walked down to the guy drinking his beer trying to stay calm.

"Excuse me sir, I believe you are drinking my beer." James said.

"What the hell happened to you? It looks like you were dragged behind a tractor while asleep in your sleeping bag."

"Something like that happened. Beer?" James said sternly.

"Well you can have this one, but the bottle is empty."

"Damnit."

"No need to swear it is my birthday." The guy said.

"Well, happy birthday to you."

"Hey, grab this guy another beer and put it on my tab."

"Alright Harvey, here you go." The bartender said, handing James another beer.

The guy at the bar was skinny with pale skin wearing blue jeans and a plain dark green polo shirt. He was also wearing small sunglasses with blue tinted lenses. James grabbed the beer and sat down next to the guy. They both reached over to shake hands.

"James Hawthorne."

"Harvey Gould."

"Thank you, Harvey."

"No problem. Now that I take a look at you it looks like you are wearing some piss pour disguise. The only time I ever saw something so pitiful was when I was in Vietnam." Harvey said.

"So, you're a Vet?"

"Yep twenty years in, retired from the military and moved out here with big dreams. Now I live in a trailer down the street and come down here every day to drink away my problems."

"You said it was your birthday? What about friends or family?"

"My only true friends have moved away or died. As for family, I was an orphan so no family. I have been diagnosed with mild schizophrenia from severe PTSD. All I do is just pop a pill in the morning and at night and bam good to go again. The main drawback is I become withdrawn and don't actively seek to do the things I ever intend to do."

"Wow, from the War?" James asked.

"I guess, with no parents there was no way to tell if it was genetic or what. So here I sit babbling my stories to anyone who will listen. What about you? What's your story with the sleeping bag and mud?" Harvey replied.

"You probably have heard of bigfoot or sasquatch at some point in your life right? So, my genetically enhanced friend who is a bigfoot threw mud on me after making me this vest out of a sleeping bag."

"Here they say I am the crazy one. Go on tell me more of your story."

James carried on telling Harvey his story for the next three hours. He told him about losing his parents to 9/11 and his brother dying later on in the military. James also told him about meeting Za for the first time in the trailer park. He carried on telling him everything up to that point. James was careful to only drink three beers and alternate to his Yak green between them.

"Hey it is almost one. The girl you're supposed to apprehend should be here anytime right?" Harvey asked.

The bartender was down at the far end of the bar mixing drinks and placing them in styrofoam cups with lids. She wasn't paying attention to the conversation James and Harvey were having and would only walk over to them when Harvey would wave. Just as Harvey was about to go into one of his own stories a tall muscular Indonesian girl entered the building.

Nevaeh walked past the two sitting towards the door down to her friend the bartender to pick up her drinks. She was wearing skin tight grey yoga pants and a white t-shirt with the sleeves cutoff with a black sports bra underneath. Nevaeh had a flattop hair cut spiked with green dyed hair tips. Harvey nudged James' leg for him to look over, but James already knew she was there. Za wanted him to tell her how amazingly beautiful she was and how he was a military Veteran in need of some help. The only problem was it didn't happen the way Za had scripted it to James.

"Hey, say something to her." Harvey said.

"Just wait, one second until she starts to walk back." James whispered to Harvey.

Nevaeh gave the bartender a hug and started to head towards the door.

"Hello there, would you care for a drink?" James asked, tipping his beer bottle towards her.

She glanced at them both, assessing them both to not be an immediate threat. Placing her two drinks and two styrofoam food containers on the counter she sat down. Nevaeh stared at both of them with her bright green eyes. Reaching over James she grabbed the fullest looking bottle on the table and took a big gulp. Soon after she began heaving and retching trying to spit out what she swallowed. Nevaeh had just chugged on James chewing tobacco spit bottle.

"I'll kill you!!" She howled.

Nevaeh grabbed James by the muddy sleeping bag and threw him from the right side of Harvey over six feet through the pub's painted window. Glass crashed everywhere around and into James. He stayed laying on the ground when she came walking out of the bar with her food and drinks. Nevaeh stopped for a moment and threw up on the sidewalk next to James.

James had a massive piece of glass sticking out of his right calve and a piece of glass sticking out of his right forearm. Along with a gash to the top of his head bleeding all over the sidewalk, meanwhile Liam parked across the street tapping the steering wheel singing along to a techno pop song. Nevaeh gazed back into the bar watching as her friend was calling the police and an ambulance.

"Is he dead?" Asked the bartender.

"I, I.. am not sure." Nevaeh said, still heaving.

James waited until she threw up again and grabbed the pin he had placed into the rubber sole of his shoe. When she came back over he leaned up as far as he could and stuck it in her right thigh. She sat down immediately almost on top of James. He forced himself up, trying to grab onto the bricks of the building. Harvey came out and put his arm under James left side and helped him to stand.

Liam pulled the truck around from across the street to directly in front of them. He got out and opened the back door to load her up. She was still sitting in the same spot where James had stuck her with the pin.

"Nevaeh get up and get in the truck!" James barked.

She got up and began walking like a zombie to the truck throwing up on herself as she walked. Liam took over helping James from Harvey.

"Nevaeh sit down on the bed and stay still!" James barked again.

She sat down still dribbling vomit out of her mouth. Liam got James loaded up in the truck and they took off down the road. James was beginning to drift in and out of consciousness when they stopped in an open farm field. A chopper had already landed and loaded up Tristan. Nevaeh was then cuffed by one of the guys from the chopper and loaded up as well. A medic from the chopper removed the glass from James' arm and leg, leaving Liam to stitch him up.

"Boy, you look like a big pile of.."

"Don't say it Liam, I know shit." James said.

"I am reformed and trying to avoid foul language thank you very much. I was gonna say dog dew dew."

"Just finish sewing me up and let's get out of here."

Liam stitched up James' head first and went on to his arm and leg. Then Liam drove them to a park so James could take a shower before wrapping his stitches with sterile bandages. James was beat up but felt good about getting two in to make up for the failed last recovery. Liam gave James the other half of the sleeping bag with his left arm and luckily all the parts were still in it. James re-attached his left arm flexing his fingers again smiling.

"Liam where is Za? And where is my gun belt with Rust?"

"Well, I dropped Za off at the transport station. You two are not going to be Recovery agents. Sad you two would screw it up so bad."

James stared at the ground and put both of his hands on his head beginning to kneel down.

"Nah, I'm just foolin'. He is on a train going to Montana on his first solo mission. Your gun belt is right here under the bed." Liam said.

"Where is my gun?"

"You mean Rust? Well, can I keep her. Please, it is the only woman I ever had such feelings for."

"No. What about your gun isn't it the same or similar?"

"Almost exactly the same. Just yours has the iron coating to make it rusty. Actually it was the gun I first used before I picked up this dark beauty. I guess they didn't have any new guns for you to pick from. Did they? Or did you go last and no one wanted that one?"

"Yes, I went last and no one wanted Rust. Now where is it?" James asked again, getting irritated.

"Okay, let me go get her I just wanted to show you something cool since you have to have the ocular implant to use these." Liam said, walking back to the passenger side of the truck.

Liam opened up the glove box and retrieved the hand cannon known as Rust.

"Okay, now take my gun here. Do you see the colored lasery beam thingy?" Liam said.

"Yes."

"Now hold Rust in your other hand."

"Whoa, Liam this is really badass. I see two beams. Now, can I keep yours?"

"Negative, Little Liam is all mine. Hey something they never told me and it took me six years to find out is this, here hand me my gun back."

"What is that?"

"Put your finger over the target thingy for ten seconds. Now try and aim at something."

The optical targeting had switched from a straight fire mode to a ricochet mode. Ricochet mode as Liam explains will give the calculated ricochet for four ricochets. The ricochet mode is not perfect, because it calculates off a solid surface assuming all surfaces are impenetrable. James held his finger over the end of the gun switching it back to normal.

"Just don't shoot at a stop sign and expect it to bounce back at a target or you will look like a dummy." Liam said.

"Cool, thanks for showing me that."

"Okay, I will talk to you soon and hope you survive all your missions. You have all your stuff so off with you. I miss you already and wish someday you would be my boyfriend."

"Forget it Liam, never gonna happen. Get out of here I will call a cab."

"Oh and before I leave I have sent you a price breakdown and how much available funds you have. Whenever you need money go to a bank and give them your account number or use it on an ATM, no card required. The screen will not do anything until you enter your 16 digit code, then like magic your money appears. I suggest keeping 10k on you at all times in case you have to bribe someone. Happy trails my lovely and don't hesitate to call." Liam said, tearfully getting back into his truck and driving away.

CHAPTER 15
LEAVING THE STATION

Reba got up sliding the metal chair she was sitting in backwards. Shaking her head in disbelief she walked around James and took out another cigarette. The coffee cup she was using was packed with crushed cigarette butts and James' own coffee cup was full to the brim with tobacco spit. Reba pointed at James then pointed to the chair furrowing her brow.

"Ya'll shit is so unbelievable. If I wasn't seeing the metal arm thing then I would have said your bat shit crazy." Reba said.

"Well there it is." James said, hunching over the table and sitting back into the chair.

"Well, look at that almost eleven thirty. Ain't nothin' else I need to do here. The only question I have is how much do you actually make? After you answer that you can get your ass to sleep."

James grabbed his roll device out of his pocket and untwisted the caps on each end. Placing each of the ends on the table, squinting at the screen, then turning to hand the device to Reba. In Reba's hands the screen felt like aluminum foil. Black on the backside with nothing but a few wear scratches and scuffs, the front was a brightly lit up screen with a typed message.

* * *

'Retrieval Reward Breakdown (in USD):

$400,000 - Max Payout (Not ever gonna fuckin' happen so get over it)

-Minus all of this bullshit

-$35,000 for Helicopter extraction (You're going to almost always need this)

-$250,000 for cleanup (Only if you make a really shitty mess)

-$200,000 for dead (you also will need a chopper so another 35k on top of this shit stain)

- $0.00 Expired Recovery timer (Watch the clock next to your bounty or get shit on)

- P.S. James I will miss our time together, and no more cussin' I am a changed man - Liam

* * *

Reba handed the rectangular screen back over to James and he rolled it back up and twisted the ends back onto it. James leaned back over the table and stood up again after only sitting for a brief moment. Reba rubbed her eyes and grabbed the handle of the door, but stopped before pushing it down to open it.

"Your arm has to go with me back down to evidence. Put it on the table and I will put it away in your backpack. Also anything else you have on you." She said, looking over her shoulder.

James placed his left arm on the table and detached it and watched as Reba placed it back into his backpack. The roll device was already sitting on table when it buzzed with a mild sound and vibration. Reba grabbed it and placed it in the bag along with two empty Yak tins. James took what was left of his cash out of his pockets, placing it in the backpack as well. Reba put the backpack over her right shoulder and opened up the door waving James out of the room.

James headed back down the stairs with Reba behind him. He walked into the holding cell and sat down on the bed. Reba closed the door behind him shutting the lights off before she went back upstairs. The backpack was placed back in the evidence locker with James' gun, gun belt, and ammo.

The morning came swiftly with a clanging on the cell door. It was Hector knocking on the bars with a baton. He pushed the leg shackles with a hand chain hand cuffs and a leather belt through the bars. James put the leg shackles on his legs and briefly struggled to pull the hand cuff around his right wrist. The belt was still loose and was taking longer than Hector wanted to wait so he opened up the cell door.

James leaned up tall and allowed Hector to buckle and tighten the leather belt attaching all the shackles together. Hector also tightened the ankle cuffs and wrist cuff down to be tight enough to be uncomfortable. Stepping back out of the cell and standing to the wall at the rear Hector pointed the baton towards the stairs.

"Let's go, FBI is waiting to take you far away from here." Hector said.

They walked through the department heading towards the front door with only a few glimpses coming from the other officers. It was the busiest James had seen it since being there the past few days. As they walked outside down the front steps a black SUV was waiting with the engine running. The driver never got out of the vehicle and Hector opened the door shoving James into the back seat.

As the SUV pulled away the driver glanced over his shoulder looking hard at James. The driver had deep scars on his cheeks and forehead going into his eyebrows. He also had broad shoulders and jet black hair with pale skin. It took James a few minutes to realize who it was as they drove down the road away from the police station.

"Jim? Jim Berthlow?"

"Yes, James it is me."

"How has it been? Looks like your nose is okay."

"It is a prosthetic attached with tiny magnets."

"Alright then, where are you taking me to?"

"Wherever you want to go within ten miles of here, those were my orders."

"Go up the road and turn right onto the freeway up here. There is a truck stop two exits up."

"Sure thing."

James was getting nervous, the man that tried to kill him and he scarred for life was going to try and finish the job. Reaching his left arm back over his head James retracted his left forearm and hand back onto his elbow. Ripping of fabric followed by an explosion of cash filled the rear of the SUV. Jim swerved the vehicle slightly as James pulled his silicone finger covering off of his left index finger with his teeth. James leaned as far forward as he could on his knees behind Jim's seat placing his finger at Jim's throat.

"So, you're here to try and finish me off for what happened to your face? Well, I have news for you asshole, you are going to die right now." James said sternly.

"Wait, wait, I am not here to kill you, look here the cuff keys are attached to the ignition. I was going to un-cuff you when we stopped. I know you don't believe me so let me pull over."

"Keep going. Stop at the truck stop." James said, keeping his index finger pressed on Jim's throat.

They got to the truck stop and James had them park in the back. His finger was making small droplets of blood come out of Jim's neck. As they stopped Jim took out the ignition keys with his right hand and put his palm flat with the keys on his finger. Slowly Jim moved his arm with his palm flat facing the front of the SUV towards his shoulder. James waited for a moment trying to figure out if he was telling the truth or if it was a trick.

"Please Mr. Hawthorne, I am only hired as a driver nothing else. What happened in the past is done with. I have accepted it. It was my fault for what happened to my face and no one elses. Please. pleas.."

"Shut up and give me the key to the cuffs, left hand next to your neck."

Jim moved his right arm across his body to the left, placing the keys next to James' left hand. James removed his index finger from Jim's neck and took the keys quickly and unlocked his right wrist, his ankles and removed the belt. As he was finishing removing the leather belt for the shackles Jim jumped out of the SUV. James scrambled to the rear retrieving his revolver out of the gun belt already loaded with eight shots.

After sitting in the SUV for over ten minutes James noticed Jim was not coming back anytime soon. James put on his gun belt, holstered Rust, and crammed his hoodie from the back of the SUV into his shredded backpack. He exited the SUV slowly throwing the backpack onto his back and began heading towards the truck stop convenience store. Jim had parked away from everyone else towards the rear entrance of the truck stop 300 yards from the convenience store.

The truck stop had a considerable canopy covering for passenger vehicles to fuel up close to the convenience store on the entrance side, and a second larger higher canopy on the rear side of the building for semi-trucks to fuel up at. Both the canopy and the store were all painted yellow with red pin stripes, the store was a rectangular building with advertisements for deals on beer, cigarettes, soda, and food.

A double door opened with a whoosh and a ding as James entered the building.

James saw a bulky figure dressed like a Federal agent with jet black hair and pale skin run from behind a semi-trailer and out to the SUV. The SUV started up and peeled out as it left the parking lot getting back on the freeway. James could feel someone staring at him, but made his way to the counter to get some items from the clerk. Before he could get up to the clerk a slight tug at the back of his shirt had him spinning around reaching for his gun.

"Hey sweetness, long time. Give your sweet daddy a hug."

It was Liam tugging at his shirt. He appeared slightly older with some grey hairs showing on his flat top haircut. Liam stood for a few seconds with his arms out before James gave him a brief hug and pat on the back. Liam was wearing his olive green military outfit with black elbow length velvet gloves. Liam still felt and appeared just as strong as the day they met with the exception of some grey hairs.

"So, what are you doing here?" James asked.

"I tried to call you late last night but you didn't answer. We have a big meeting over at the refinery down the road to try to find out who is killing off our team."

"What? You have to be kidding. Za said we had a meeting but I thought it was for just us two." James said.

"Oh, dear you don't know. I..I am so sorry."

"Sorry for what Liam. You aren't making any sense."

"Go ahead and get your stuff and get a shower too, I will be at my truck over in the rear waiting."

Liam pointed out where his truck was parked back by the semi-trucks in the back of the lot. James walked up to the cashier and bought six rolls of Yak, and a few tokens for the showers next to the restrooms. As Liam was walking out of the door James ran after him. James caught up to Liam as he was nearly all the way to his armored truck.

"Hey you have to tell me what is going on?" James pleaded.

"Someone took out Devon, Samuel, Barbara, and Steve. This all happened in the past month with the most recent happening just before you got into town."

"Who was the most recent? Where did it happen?"

"Last question first, it happened at the old oil refinery where you were going to meet Za. I am very sorry like I said before James."

James stomach was getting tight inside and he could barely speak.

"Who was it?" Was all James could bare to whisper out.

"Za, James, Za is gone. Some kids were over at the refinery sneaking out to drink some alcohol when they came across him. They took some pictures with their phones and called the cops. Our people got there in time to confiscate the phones and make sure the cops didn't say anything."

"Tell me you are pulling my leg with some sort of sick joke."

"Really I wish I was, I have the photos and can show you, but just go take a shower and let it sink in for now. I have cried for the past few nights after I found out and didn't believe it until I got the photos from intelligence sent over to me."

James stared at the ground and turned back towards the convenience store. Liam didn't try to follow James back into the store and was beginning to cry as James was walking away. Everything became dull as James made his way to the shower. He placed his, backpack, clothes and gun belt in a locker and put tokens in the shower. Once the cold water hit his skin he didn't shiver or move all he could feel was the warm stream of tears move down his cheeks.

The shower stopped after ten minutes requiring more

tokens for more water. James stood in the shower with no water running for half an hour sobbing to himself. Then a knock came at the shower door. It was the clerk from the register demanding he get out or put more tokens in the shower. James stepped out of the shower and walked to his locker with his gear. The locker had a latching mechanism and a hole for a lock to be placed.

James had put his gear in the locker without locking it before entering the shower. He was numb and not paying attention to what he was doing. However, when he was standing naked in front of his locker he noticed a lock was on the door. Some type of combination lock with a green dial was stopping him from getting his gear. A voice from the far side of the rear of the lockers began to call out.

"Soo, you want the green light code for what is in tha locker? Doo ya? You will have to do somethin for mee." The voice called out.

A pale white guy 7 feet tall was slinking around the corner wearing overalls with no shirt covered in pimpled arms with faded tattoos. The guy was mountainous but not in the best shape. He was a person whom used size to forcefully take what he wanted even if he was built like a beer keg with hoses for arms. James took his finger tip coverings off his left hand and let them drop to the ground. Without hesitation James made his left hand into a flat number five.

James threw his hand overhand into the guys forehead where it stuck for ten seconds as the guy made some "cha, cha" sounds and dropped to the ground. The guy had a middle finger sticking into the top of his forehead followed by a ring finger sticking into the top of his brow at the beginning of his nose, and finally a pinky pining the tip of his nose down to his upper lip. James did not say anything or look at the guy, he retracted his hand and rinsed it off in the sink.

Still walking around the locker area naked James took a boot knife off of the big dead guy and placed it between the lock and locker latch. James clenched his left fist and hammered down on the lock and it popped open. The knife dropped to the ground and James got changed leaving the knife on the ground. James dragged the guy into the shower and deposited forty five minutes worth of tokens into the shower. Then he wiped the floor with some paper hand towels to clean up the blood on the ground.

James held his emotions in as he left the convenience store and walked out across the paved lot to Liam's truck. He dodged around several semi-trucks and trailers finding Liam crying into his steering wheel. A loud knock at the door of the truck caught Liam's attention and he sniffled, looking over at James standing outside. Liam opened the door to step out of the truck, but James pointed to the passenger side and walked around the front of the truck to the passenger door.

Liam scrambled over the middle of the cab to open the door and let James climb in. They glanced at each other and took in a deep breath together. James stared out into the trailer parked in front of them and Liam sniffled. Liam looked over at James to ask him a question, but stopped and stared back forward sniffling.

"Do you know who did it?" James asked, still staring forward.

"No, and I have no idea who would have even tried."

"Need a cleanup crew for shower 4 inside."

"Okay, how bad?"

"One dead."

"You want me to call it in for you?" Liam asked.

"We have a little time, besides your voice is quivering. I will call it in."

Liam was wearing a leather necklace band with a green

bead the size of a quarter on it. He handed another one to James to put on. James glanced at it and placed it on the dash of the truck. James pulled out his roll device and made the cleanup call to have the body in the shower taken care of. As the call for the cleanup crew went out all he could hear was an outgoing ringing chime with no answer for over three minutes.

"Weird, they usually answer right away." James said.

"Well honey, you know they are tied to the Term squad. Let me give Amir a call and find out what is going on."

Liam opened up his own roll device and made a call to the commander of the Termination squad. It was the same buzzing ringing with no answer at the other end. Then he tried a few other members of the Termination squad in different areas and still got no answer. They glanced at each other and shrugged.

"Where are they at?" James asked.

"Maybe they have a meeting? They might not be able to answer right now. Let me send them all a message and see if I get a response."

"Let me call Hank and see if he knows anything."

James called Hank a level 2 enhanced that was part of the Recovery squad. The device rang for a few minutes but to their surprise Hank answered.

"Hey James, long time since I talked to you." Hank said.

James put the device on speaker so Liam could hear.

"Hank, I am here with Liam and we are trying to get through to the cleanup crew. Do you know if they are available?" James asked.

"They haven't responded to my message from three days ago, and no one on the Termination squad has either. If it isn't an immediate cleanup, I guess you could run from it for now. At least that's what I had to do. I'm in the back of a truck headin' out there to Texas for this meeting."

"Thanks Hank." Both Liam and James said.

"Wait, one more thing. Did you receive a new communication necklace with a green bead on it?" James asked.

"Yeah, eyeball sized marble."

"See you later Hank." James said.

"Bye."

The device clicked off from the call and James sat back in the seat and stared over at Liam.

"Shall we go?" Liam asked.

"Just go a few miles up the road to the next rest stop."

"My lord, I am gettin' chills. Should we run away? Something bad is goin' on."

"Let's just move up the road away from here."

CHAPTER 16
ASKING FOR HELP

The truck rumbled to life as Liam turned the key on the ignition. They headed out onto the freeway making their way to the next rest area. Liam parked at the furthest spot away from any onlookers. James took his sweater off and rolled it into a ball with the necklace inside of it. Liam took his off and handed it to James to put in the sweater.

"What time is the meeting?" James asked.

"1700 hour on the dot. The message was very specific. You need to check your messages."

"They didn't send me that one. Look."

James handed his open roll device over to Liam and the message was not there.

"Well they sent it a few days ago."

"Look at the time stamp on the message on yours. It is dated and timed the day I got here. Someone must have assumed I would be gone as well."

Liam opened his mouth to talk then shut it with a confused look on his face. James opened the door to the truck and stepped out stretching his back with his arms up in the air. It was bright, sunny, and cool outside with no clouds in the sky. The rest area was sheltered by trees blocking the sight of the highway. James peeled open a can of fresh Yak wintergreen and put an ample pinch between his lower lip below his teeth.

"What's the plan now James? It's 10:45 in the am." Liam asked, as he climbed out of the truck.

"We ask the police for help."

"I think you lost your sweetness. We are strictly not to be involved with public officers."

"I mean a police officer in particular. Detective Reba Wells."

"You spilled beans to a cop? You are supposed to keep quiet about all this you damn fool."

"I was stuck at the station for a lot longer than usual and did it as a backup plan if something happened. She should be at the station still processing stuff from a recent homicide."

"Sweetie did you kill some people you weren't supposed to?"

James spit on the ground and stared back into the truck at Liam and shook his head "No."

"Some people attacked me and ended up dead a little after our fight. It wasn't me because I saw them drive off. Do you have any cups or a water bottle?" James asked.

"Nope, go grab a bottle out of the trash can to spit in and let's get a move on."

James went to the recycling can and grabbed an empty water bottle. He wiped the top of it with his shirt and walked back to Liam's truck. He climbed back in and they left the rest stop heading back towards the police station. Clouds were slowly growing in the sky above them when the sound of thunder in the distance made a crashing sound.

"Thought it would be sunny today." James said.

"Rain this afternoon into the late evening. I have some rain coats in my glove box you could wear. Strawberry is my favorite."

James opened the glove box and it was stuffed full of different flavored condoms.

"Damn Liam." James laughed.

They both laughed for a little while until they got to the police station. Now it was time to become serious about what happened at the oil refinery. Za was gone and they were going against everything they were ever told to do. Liam parked in a guest parking spot in the front of the station waving at passing officers. James ducked down in the seat trying to hide himself from being recognized.

"Honey, does this mean I will be going in to find this lady?" Liam asked.

"Yes, I was only released this morning and I am pretty sure showing my face will put me in trouble with the local law."

"Okay, you should go wait in the back. Cover up your arm and here put this on while I walk you to the back." Liam said, making his hand into a fist and pointing his thumb to the back of the cab.

James covered his left arm with his hoodie and was about to put the mask Liam had handed him on before stopping to sniff it. A used Gimp mask with a lot of wear marks on it was what Liam had handed him. James took the necklaces out of his hoodie and put it on instead, with the hood over his head tucking his left hand into the left pocket. He placed the necklaces into his right pocket throwing the mask back into Liam's lap.

"Not today party boy. Open up the back of this tank." James said.

"Almost gotcha with my sweet black honey mask."

They both got out and walked to the rear of the truck

and James stood next to the bed as Liam closed the back of the truck. Liam made his way to the steps of the station wearing his Army green fatigues with elbow length brown leopard print gloves on. He appeared very much to be a military person except for the gloves. Liam stopped at a desk with a brawny plaque on the front that read "Information."

A skinny pale guy with blonde hair was rustling through papers, and stamping on some of them. The guy was wearing a navy blue police uniform looking down the whole time focused on his paper work. Liam knocked on the desk and the guy looked up surprised for an instant.

"Is detective Wells in?" Liam asked.

"Yes, may I ask who you are?"

"Liam Harper, and yes she is expecting me."

"One second."

The guy grabbed a phone from the desk and hit an auto desk dial number. He looked away and murmured to the voice on the other end of the phone. Then he pointed to the back of the station where the detective office was.

"Down there to the right." The guy said.

Liam walked away down to the detective office where Reba was sitting behind a desk on the right of the room and an empty desk on the left. There were two chairs in front of her desk and the room smelt like old cheeseburgers and an ash tray. Reba glanced quickly up at Liam with disbelief before grabbing her firearm and placing it on the top of the desk.

"Hello Miss Wells. We have a mutual acquaintance waiting to see if you are willing to help us out." Liam said.

"Call me Reba. Is this about James? He ain't gone from here for more than a few hours and he is causin' trouble again?"

"We are in an extremely weird situation for ourselves and could really use your help."

"He told me someone would come from the military to give me a lobotomy and destroy all evidence of him being here."

"Sounds like he may have fibbed a little. All we do when someone is in this situation is send a letter congratulating you on apprehending a dangerous fugitive wanted by the U.S. Marshalls service and ask for any evidence gathered on crimes committed."

"So, no memory wiping or magic submission pins to take me away."

"We have the pins, but they are not for that. Too damned expensive to waste. Will you help us?"

Reba stood up and put her gun back into its holster and shook her head "no." Liam got up and began to walk back to the door to leave.

"Wait, meet me at the motel we picked James up at in 15 minutes. I will bring everything I have." Reba said.

"Thank you ma'am."

Liam walked out of the police station towards the door and fired up the truck. James was still in the back looking at the shirt printing machine in the rear of the truck. The screen printing machine on the desk was ample enough to print on one shirt at a time and had a separate spray stencil kit attached to the side of it.

"Reba said to meet at the motel they nabbed you at." Liam said, over his right shoulder.

"It is just up the street. So, you are doing airbrush shirts now?" James asked through the square hole to the cab of the truck.

"Oh no, I am not that good I just spray a little color around the pictures to make them pop a little more. I see your print doesn't look as pretty as it once did. I have an extra shirt you can buy and print a design on if you would like."

James' shirt was still dark black but the rock band logo was peeling off and faded. Liam printed the shirt for him over five years ago as a gift for making it five years as a Recovery agent. James pulled out the fresh black t-shirt from the drawer attached to the desk. He began to lay it out on top of the printer. The printer was an expensive setup that would press down on the shirt and spray it with vinyl ink. James grabbed a piece of cardboard out from the drawer to place inside the shirt, so it would not spray the inside of the shirt with ink.

Liam had shown James how the machine worked a dozen times and even had him print designs for other team members as requested. It was quick to print but took about an hour for an image to set after printing on the shirt. There was an old laptop covered in overspray from Liam using the airbrush and the laptop as a guide. James launched into the shirt design program and connected the laptop to the screen printer via a USB cable.

"Alrighty, you must be buying the shirt, if you're firing up the equipment. Where do we have to go?" Liam asked, over his right shoulder.

"Turn right out of the police station and about five miles down the road there is a motel."

Liam left the station and headed down the road to the motel. The shirt printing machine fired to life when James turned it on, making loud clunking sounds as the printer head moved back and forth. As they pulled into the motel parking lot the truck bounced up and down going over the potholes in the parking lot. The printer finished printing and started a countdown timer on a small digital timer on the front of the printer. It read "59" in red double digits and would only move down in minute increments.

"Honey we are here." Liam said.

CHAPTER 17
THE MOTEL

The building was an "L" shape with the office at the short front side of the parking lot on the left and the rest of the building continued on the length of the parking lot. A gravel pot hole filled parking lot was how the owner of the motel controlled people from speeding in his parking lot. A vertical florescent green vacancy sign was painted on a piece of particle board sitting on the outside of the window to the office. It was a faded tan stucco building with a red tile roof with missing roof tiles and cracked stucco all over.

Directly across the street from the motel was the bar James was attacked at. The bar was a stark contrast to the dingy motel. It was a square building with a black metal roof, whitewashed brick, actual florescent lighted signs, and black doors with diamond plate on the bottom of each door. The parking lot was also much nicer with black sealed asphalt and parking lines that appeared to be repainted weekly.

James was giving Liam the rundown of what happened the night he was arrested. He told him about being attacked by three well trained individuals. Then he told him they drove off very much alive and when the police brought him back to the police station he found out there was one more person than before. A dead city council member was there with the other three dead guys. Then a dark navy blue car pulled into the lot as James and Liam where trying to figure out why the city council guy was there in the first place.

Reba stepped out of the unmarked police car and walked into the office of the motel room. James and Liam could see she was talking to a young girl working at the counter of the motel. An unmistakable bronze flash of a badge had gotten Reba a key for a motel room. Reba exited the motel office and walked over to Liam's truck.

"Well, hi there, we need to go talk up in the room. It should be familiar to James. Can you both give me a hand with this stuff?" Reba asked, pointing to boxes in the trunk of her car.

Liam and James both grabbed an office box each and followed Reba up to room 617. The motel owner thought it would be clever to have high number rooms when the building only has 40 rooms. Rooms in the six hundred range are the top floor and rooms in the five hundred range are on the bottom floor. The room was the third from the end, boarded up window and a recently repaired door frame.

There was no police tape or anything to indicate a crime had ever occurred in the room besides a boarded up window. The room was clean and tidy with fresh linens and apple scented wall plugins. Reba had them place the boxes on the bed and turned all the lights in the room on. Reba opened up one of the boxes and handed a file to Liam to read.

"City Council Man John Norbit, blah, blah, blah, ooh here we go. Cause of death, homicide, by let me see, gunshot wound to the chest. Looks like it says 9mm bullet was removed from his arterial artery of his heart. Ok, Miss Reba, this shows me there is no way in hells bells James could have done this." Liam said.

"I just want to know why he was even left there?" James asked.

"Not left, murdered over in the parking lot of the bar across the street. The other three look like they were killed and moved, but the blood on the ground where he was found indicates he was killed on the spot." Reba said.

"So, ma'am it was a wrong place wrong time deally? That is what it sounds like to me." Liam said.

Reba shook her head "no" and grabbed another file from the same box. It had pictures of the city council man John Norbit with one of the others James had fought.

"Hey, that's the refrigerator guy that was talking my ear off in the bar." James said.

"Air Conditioning guy, you dum dum. It looks like he was a hired tough guy Mr. Norbit used to get what he wanted and would often return the favor by giving this idiot contracts to perform HVAC work on city buildings for double the cost. They would also makeup issues and repairs to systems that didn't exist just to exploit the cities funds." Reba said.

Reba was reaching in the box to hand another file to Liam when he slapped it out of her hand.

"Enough ma'am just get to the point! We have a very tight schedule today and I am on day 5 of a no caffeine cleanse!" Liam shouted.

Reba put the files back and pulled out some evidence bags from the other boxes on the bed. There was a 9mm handgun and some spent brass shell casings in one of the bags. The gun was a half metal half polymer black handgun. It was the same type of gun Reba and most of the other officers at the department would have been issued. The gun was made to be exactly what law enforcement would need, easy to maintain, durable, and rugged.

Another bag had a bunch of tiny fibers stuck to a piece of clear tape. The final evidence bag was some clear pieces of tape with finger charcoaled prints on them. Liam picked up the bag with the gun and looked it over without opening it then handed it over to James to look at.

"This gun is very clean." James said.

"It isn't the gun that is the weird part it's the brass shell casings. They are perfectly clean inside and out. We tested them for powder and they were completely clean." Reba said.

Liam was holding the finger prints up to the light in the motel room. He sat down on the bed next to all the evidence and became pale. The thumb print had a distinct flat surface with three "+++" symbols going vertical the length of the thumb.

"Was this thumb print pulled from the top of the slide of the gun?" Liam asked.

"Why, yes it was. It was the only good print we could pull from the gun. The gun was..." Reba began before Liam interrupted.

"Sitting in the middle of the four men?"

"Yes, so does it mean somethin'?" She asked.

"It is a calling card of someone I brought in a year ago. This one was a weird one too. He was an Alabama boy enhanced to level 1 and spent 15 years in the military as a covert hitman. When I went to retrieve him he was sitting on a park bench waiting to go. No fight or anything. I pin stuck him and loaded him up. A new gun and a solid print left on the barrel was a calling card he left to let someone know he was there. He should still be in getting reconditioned. If someone runs away and they have not been in active combat they end up with a one year trip to be reconditioned, and if someone has been in active combat they are required to be in for two years." Liam explained.

"Maybe he got good behavior or somethin' like that." Reba said.

"This setup is extremely strict with the process Reba, and if they do not complete it they are killed. Hell if they run away for a second time they are automatically assigned to the Termination squad." James said.

James pulled out his roll device and nudged Liam's foot with his hand.

"Send me the file on that guy." James said.

"One moment dear, what the hell's bells is going on here!" Liam shouted looking at his roll device.

The screen on Liam's device went blue then green and shutoff. Liam pointed the screen towards James and his did the same thing.

"Maybe ya'll just forgot to charge up." Reba said.

They both shook their heads "no" and rolled up their devices and put them away.

"Well at least you remember who he is. What was his name?" Reba asked.

"Robert, Randle, Ronnie, maybe Donnie, or Danny, umm sorry this one slips my mind since it wasn't very eventful. He did like to go to cheap buffet bars at 3pm exactly. Do not ask me how my brain runs since I remember the most mundane things." Liam said.

"Ok, should we go after this guy? We have a meeting later will we have time to make it back? What time is it anyway?" James asked.

"Yes. Yes. 1300." Liam said quickly.

"How'd ya know the time so fast? Some sort of clock implant?" Reba asked.

James and Liam glanced at each other and broke out laughing. Liam fell into the bed laughing while James slowly pointed to the clock on the counter directly behind her. James didn't realize the clock was there until the point he asked the question. Liam was always the more observant type, he drilled into James and Za to pay attention to the little things in their environment.

"Hoo, haw, that was a good one. Ma'am the clock is right behind you. The only thing I have ever seen tell time better than looking at a clock was a rooster." Liam said.

"So right now all we have is a big guy that eats at buffet restaurants. Unless ya'll know of some other way to find him let me know now." Reba said sternly.

James stared at Reba and Liam pointing his left index finger up and raising his eyebrows signaling to them to give him a moment. He rushed through the door and ran down the concrete stairs to the back of the building. An empty dirt lot with a few tumble weeds blowing by was all he saw. Then he turned and ran back around the building back up the stairs into the room.

"Well, my damn bike is gone." James said.

"You had a bicycle stolen?" Liam asked.

"Yes, Liam I traveled across the country in less than 3 days on a bicycle." James said sarcastically.

James gave the make, model, color, license plate number, and unique feature information to Reba so she could broadcast to all the units. She pulled out a yellow phone sized device and made radio contact to the dispatcher for the other officers in the unit. Reba also asked to have them let her know if they see the motorcycle to contact her and not make contact.

"So, black cruiser bike with drag handle bars. Should not be any of those in Texas. Honey there is little to no chance they will see the bike." Liam said.

"I am sure adding look for a big guy is also going to make it appear faster." James said, poking fun at himself.

Reba's radio buzzed with voices and one was the dispatcher asking for her.

"Reba, Officer Ortiz says she has seen one with a big guy going to the same restaurant for the past two days." The dispatcher said.

"Which restaurant?" Reba asked, clicking the button on the radio.

The radio buzzed and blipped back with the dispatcher. "Samson's Homemade Buffet."

They left the motel room and headed back to their vehicles. Reba gave them directions to where the restaurant was and how far to go. It was 7 miles away up the interstate tucked away in a strip mall. The distance was close enough to allow them time to make up a plan for how to handle the situation. It also was early enough for them to have some lunch at the same restaurant.

CHAPTER 18
THE RESTAURANT

Reba followed behind Liam and James in her unmarked police vehicle to the restaurant. It was a standalone building in the middle of a shopping center. There were a few cars parked out front of the restaurant and a black cruiser motorcycle parked on the sidewalk near the entrance of the restaurant. The building was a square building with dark grey painted brick with lavish windows and a green tile roof. There was a broad white painted wooden sign above the entrance with "Samson's Buffet," painted in red.

The plan they had all agreed on before leaving the motel was James would go make contact with the unknown level 1 and if anything went wrong Reba and Liam would be there for backup. Liam parked in the shopping center parking lot away from the restaurant to remain less obvious. James left his gun belt with his gun in Liam's truck. Reba parked next to Liam's truck and Liam got in Reba's patrol car.

James put on his black hoodie covering his arm and started walking to the restaurant across the shopping center parking lot as Reba and Liam drove up and parked at the restaurant. By the time James was at the restaurant Reba and Liam were already seated. It was a dimly lit building with bright lights over the buffet trays of food. It smelled of a combination of fried chicken and cooked onions.

One thing they hadn't thought of with the buffet was they would have to pay before eating. Reba and Liam obviously had cash to pay, but James left his cash in his backpack and had no way to pay for a twelve dollar buffet. James took a quick glance around and could see Liam and Reba sitting near a window, but couldn't see the level 1 guy. Liam made a sly pointing motion over his shoulder to around the corner where James could not see.

It was obvious the guy was there in the restaurant, but getting around the corner without paying created an obstacle they hadn't planned for. James walked up to the counter where there was no one standing at the moment to accept payment. There was a sign on the register "Restroom for Customers Only! No exceptions!" James looked around and saw a girl coming back from Reba and Liam's table. She was the only one working the front of the building. James had only seen the motorcycle and two other cars parked outside of the building, besides Reba's patrol car.

"Excuse me miss." James said.

"Welcome to Samson's Buffet twelve dollars all day for all you can eat." The girl said, like a programmed robot.

"I was just walking by and saw a guy outside keying up a blue compact car outside." James said.

"Really?" She asked.

"Yep, really. Some guy is carving it up right now." James said.

"Shit, give me a minute I will be right back." She said running to the kitchen area of the building.

James made his way past Reba and Liam's table around the corner where the level 1 guy was sitting with three empty plates of food and two other plates he was starting in on. The guy had a long brown beard and long brown hair. He was scruffy compared to the rest of the level 1 guys James had brought in. Still the guy was as big as someone that spent a lifetime in the gym taking steroids. He was slightly taller than James and was wearing a green camo t-shirt with holes and threads coming off of it.

As James walked up to the table the guy's brown eyes glanced up at him as he shoveled food into his mouth. The guy stopped eating and sat back in his chair carefully looking over James. The table was sitting on a pole bolted to the ground with a solid compacted wood composite top. James grabbed the chair pushed in across the table from the guy and sat down at the table with the guy.

"Took ya long nuff." The guy said.

"Who are you and why did you kill the guys outside of the bar?" James was trying to be vague while asking questions.

"Yer boy Liam over there took me to the shed last year. Ya know that? Of course ya do. Name given to me is Curtis. Curtis Goodwin. You must be Mr. Hawthorne." Curtis said.

"How do you know who I am?"

"Know who ya protectin' and know who ya killin'."

James leaned forward in his chair not taking his eyes off of Curtis for a moment.

"Mr. Hawthorne, are ya an arm wrestler? I myself find it to be very satisfying. Whatcha say give it a go and I tell you everythin' been goin' on? Some things you will never guess been goin' on. Choose left or right. If I win ya leave me be. I haven' no quarrel with ya just know that." Curtis said.

James pulled his chair in and put his left hand up with his elbow on the table. Curtis slowly leaned forward bending his elbow inward flexing his left bicep ripping his shirt as his massive muscles pushed the shirt beyond its limit. Their hands touched when Curtis moved backwards quickly and looked closer at James' arm.

"Take ya sweatshirt off so I can make sure you ain't using some sorta hydraulics." Curtis said.

James took his sweatshirt off and showed Curtis no hydraulic attachments to his arm. James even put a fork between his forearm bones and moved it back in forth to show there was nothing hidden. Curtis leaned back in quickly with his left hand up ready to arm wrestle James and see him go away. James moved in slowly and grasped Curtis' hand with his left hand and looked up at Curtis.

"On a count a three." Curtis said.

James nodded back at Curtis.

"One..Two..Three"

Curtis moved so quick James' forearm was bending backwards and his knuckles on his hand almost touched the table. Curtis letup a little to smile when James decided it was the moment he would make his own move. James released his arm at the elbow for a millisecond turning his elbow down towards the table. He retracted his arm in a whipping motion his arm re-attached pulling Curtis' arm back with it.

Curtis' forearm snapped in half with skin tearing away and two pointed bones sticking out of it. The bones in his arm oozed clear fluid followed by blood from the rest of the arm dribbling out in a pool onto the table. The table split open where Curtis' hand and James' reattaching arm contacted it. James let go of Curtis' hand and sat back in his chair.

Scrambling for his pants pocket Curtis tore into the velcro pocket on his right thigh pulling out a syringe with a silver liquid. He ripped off the safety cap with his mouth and spit it onto the table injecting the liquid metal material into his left bicep with blood beginning to pool out of his left arm. Shortly after injecting the liquid his left arm stopped bleeding completely followed by a metallic foam coming from the wound.

James sat back watching as the amputation worthy injury seemed to heal in a matter of seconds. Curtis calmly placed the safety cap back on the syringe using both his hands and placed it back into his pocket. The table was covered in blood, food, and some of Curtis' own bone marrow. The restaurant staff was running around the corner when Liam stopped them, he showed them a broken plate and from what James could see they accepted his explanation and went away.

Curtis again fumbled around in the pocket on his pants on his thigh this time on his left side. He brought out a flip cell phone and pushed an autodial button on it to make a phone call. James rubbed the back of his head with his left hand, realizing he wiped blood and food on the back of his head reached for a napkin. Curtis tossed him a few packs of wet hand wipes and handed James the phone.

"Hello Curtis, did you take care of the business we discussed? I need to know my asset is safe." The voice said.

"If you mean try and have me killed? Then he failed and I am coming for you next."

"Haa, is this James? You were always the one that got away. Damn it is good to hear your voice."

"Who is this?"

"Amir, you dumb ass. I wasn't trying to have you killed. If I was I would be there myself. Curtis was there to make sure you are protected since we are under attack."

"Hey Amir, I kinda broke Curtis' arm. What the hell is going on?"

"Well, Curtis has seen much worse so I am sure he will be okay. I cannot tell you over the phone but he does have some documents you can use. Sorry I can't explain more. The files he has have everything I know up until today."

The phone abruptly hung up and James stared up at Curtis as he was reaching for something under his chair. He retrieved two notebooks and two file folders from under his chair. He leaned forward to hand it to James shaking his head back and forth.

"Whelp, guess ya win. Never thought ya had an arm like that. Ya know those goons at the motel when you got here were hired to kill ya. Ya'll is welcome for me taken care of things. Here take this." Curtis said.

"What is up with the head shake?"

"Amir bet me I would do this job for free if ya could beat me in arm wrestling contest. If I won I would be paid double and keep yer bike. I was gonna give up the files to ya anyways, but I never counted on your arm bein' able to do that."

"What is up with the syringe filled with what looks like mercury?"

"Bingo, it is mercury. I am 65 years old but filled with first edition nano robots. They power up with heat caused by some reaction to mercury. It's like the mercury is food they eat to fix me up. Except the mercury leaves me feeling run down a few hours later. It is like a whole pot of coffee all at once with a hard crash."

"Okay, well, thank you."

James stood up grabbing the files off of the table turning to walk away from Curtis when he remembered something at the last second.

"Keys for my bike. I noticed it wasn't hot wired so you must have put in a new ignition." James said.

"Ya'll is smart. Are you sure you don't want me to watch it for a lil' while for ya?"

James shook his head back and forth sticking his left

hand out towards Curtis, he begrudgingly handed the new keys over to James. Liam and Reba stood up beginning to walk over to Curtis and James. Curtis stood up suddenly and made a dash out the back door setting off the buildings emergency alarm. Liam was about to give chase when James grabbed his arm to stop him.

"Liam he is not against us. We have some stuff here to look over from Amir." James said.

Liam stared up at James with tearful eyes and said "Amir?"

One of the restaurant staff members was running around the corner to find out what set off the alarm. They were more concerned with someone running off with some extra dessert to pay attention to Reba, Liam and James leaving the restaurant. James had his hoodie draped over his left arm as they briskly walked out of the restaurant.

"We need to setup in your truck somewhere that isn't a shopping mall." James said.

"There is a park a few streets over we could go to." Reba said.

"We could just setup at Reba's house. It is about a mile away from here." James said.

"How'd ya know. Oh right you read over files on us." Reba said.

"Files? Honey what did you tell this poor woman? We don't carry files. He probably looked up your social media info and was able to find out your addresses due to it being public information. Files! Ha." Liam said.

"But how'd he know.." Reba stopped and punched James in the arm.

"Well, I used to be a PC support tech and most people leave information out they believe is private out in the open for the public. The whole day before I went to the bar waiting for Za I looked up the local police department.

Found public information for your department listed online and practiced the addresses for anyone that was a detective in my head. Guess I was bored." James said.

They had all agreed the park was slightly better than the shopping mall and drove out to the park. Both Liam and Reba parked at the furthest spots away from the park in the parking lot. Liam expanded his armored trucks pop outs and they setup a workstation with all the files and notebooks from Amir.

James came into the park shortly behind them on his motorcycle. He parked it across two handicapped spaces near a restroom at the park. James had come to the decision his motorcycle would be safer in police impound then left in front of a restaurant. He had Reba report it to the parking unit to have it impounded.

CHAPTER 19
SOMETHING FOUL

While James, Reba, and Liam were getting their makeshift workstation setup something was happening on the other side of town. Two enormous black semi-trucks with trailers pulled into the oil refinery. They parked one in front of the other in a single file line inside one of the refineries enormous warehouses. There was a driver and passenger in the front of each of the trucks.

The driver of the lead truck got out to open up the trailer when a sharp hot pain hit him in the right shoulder followed by darkness. Shortly after the driver of the rear truck jumped out and attempted to run away only to have his face crushed through the back of his skull by a brass knuckled fist. Both of the passengers were level 1 enhanced and were supposed to ensure the drivers did not know what they were transporting.

One of the passengers was Jim Berthlow whom was picked up from the same truck stop he dropped James off at earlier. The other was Harry Wheeston, with a pair of brass knuckles and gargantuan stature. Jim had a bowie knife which he used to stick into the drivers shoulder then stick into the left temple of the driver's head. Both were the same height, build, and shoe size. The only difference was Jim was pale skinned with jet black hair and Harry was very dark skinned with light curly hair.

Neither one talked while they went and opened up their own respective truck trailers. First they opened up the back of the trailer to reveal a flat metal wall with a keyboard panel affixed to the lower left of the panel. The keyboard had full letter and numbers set up in a QWERTY pattern. Both typed into the keyboard and both truck trailers opened up on the right with the side doors rolling upwards, a metal ramp extended from underneath of the opened sides of the trailers.

A small figure with a size-able grey head wearing a metallic black jumpsuit climbed around one of the boxes in the rear truck looking to make sure it was safe. The truck in the front had another small figure with a grey head sipping on a flask of whiskey wearing a child's monster truck shirt and blue sweatpants. Fred was the one in the truck in the front. The other was unknown to everyone except Fred, and Fred didn't say a word.

Jim and Harry grabbed pallet jacks and emptied each trucks 8 pallets worth of equipment into the empty warehouse. Four of the pallets from the truck Fred was in were the newly upgraded Walter. One box retained the upper body, followed by the lower body, two legs broken down into multiple parts, and two arms broken down into multiple parts. Jim opened up the four pallets for Fred and Jim had placed all the parts on the ground.

Fred pointed to each part and had Jim line them up as Fred would click on buttons on a remote. The separated parts of the giant robot would whirl around as he tapped a button. Jim would slide an arm up into place and Fred would lock them into place, and this was the same with all the disconnected parts.

The other Zeta Reticuli was called Ivan, and was piecing together his own robot with the help of Harry. Ivan's machine was a mechanical giant suit with a cockpit similar to a jet facing vertically down instead of horizontal. Squared shoulders with a massive chain gun for a right arm and a gigantic flame thrower for the left. The shoulders contained short range missiles with target tracking capability, and was painted in a dark green. Ivan's machine was only similar to Walter, because it was the same height and had legs.

After each machine was built they began unloading the other equipment they had brought. They had constructed two recovery tanks and added the small metal balls containing the nano-bots. Two computer consoles were set next to each tank and connected power with a commercial generator that was in the warehouse building. Fred knew about the generator because he had sent someone in advance to investigate the building as a potential meeting site.

Just as they had finished getting the tanks setup Harry and Jim stripped off their clothing. Jim and Harry both received an injection of a chemical concoction from Ivan and shortly after began to feel the effects. Their bones felt like they were burning from the inside going out to their skin. The skin on Jim's cheeks began to bubble burning away from the inside, Harry's forehead was peeling away starting to drip down his face. Both of them began screaming and convulsing as their skin was burned away.

After they both had passed out from the extreme pain Walter picked them up and put each one in their own recovery tank. Fred began to run a surgical protocol with the nano-bots on one machine and Ivan did the same on the other machine. Walter dropped four metal hoses 3 feet in length that were the same size as garden hose into each of the tanks. Fred directed the nano-bots to connect two hoses to the top of Jim's skull above his ears then down to above his shoulder blade on each side. Ivan ran the same exact procedure on Harry.

Walter then placed a metal diamond shaped device 7 inches long with the top width of 10 inches into each tank also dropping eight titanium screws into each tank. The diamond shaped device had two holes on the front upper corners one across from each other and an opening the size of a golf ball on the front of the device in the middle. Ivan and Fred set the devices at the upper sternum of Jim and Harry's chest, screwing them down into sternum and rib bone.

Jim was moving in the tank as Fred did not administer any pain sedatives like Ivan was doing for Harry. Instead Fred had Walter reach into the tank and clamp down onto his legs and head holding him down. Next the two remaining hoses were connected to the front of the diamond shaped plate on the front of each of their chests. The other part of the hose was placed between the lower ribs directly into the lungs on each side.

Ivan quickly ran over and dropped an orange ball into the opening on Harry's chest as he pushed upward out of the tank gasping for air. Fred took another sip of whiskey as Jim was beginning to drown in his own blood. After a long few seconds Fred casually reached into the tank and placed the same type of orange ball into Jim's chest device.

The recovery tanks are good for recovery of anyone with un-altered DNA for repairs, but when they are used with someone with altered DNA interesting things happen. Fred had Walter release Jim from his grasp as Jim wriggled around in agony in the tank Fred began the recovery sequence. Ivan did the same thing with much less movement from Harry since he was using the anesthetics feature of the device.

Skin was being regenerated on both Jim and Harry's bodies as the orange ball inserted into their chest plate was dissolved into an aerosol fed directly into their lungs. The aersol increased the amount of blood in the body by double making Jim and Harry's muscles max out for the duration on the inhaled orange ball which last over two days. The tank Jim was in began to make new nerves for his missing nose when he came up out of the tank due to pain from having all of his skin regenerated with fresh nerve endings.

Ivan and Fred shutdown both tanks and watched as the small metal balls climbed out of Jim and Harrys mouths and other orifices. The injection given before the surgery was to prevent organ failure caused by the nano-machines trying to correct the larger organs of an enhanced. An enlarged heart was what they all had to keep up with the extra muscle mass, but they never knew why most of them did not live past 50. The danger of an organ such as the heart being shrunk back down ensured an agonizing death in the tank with blood not flowing to the proper portions, as well as cardiac arrest looming over a smaller heart.

Harry was sitting up looking at his arms when he noticed his right hand felt fused at the wrist as well as his fingers. Looking closer where his hand was there was a cream colored horn with black razor sharp edges coming to a point. His left arm felt normal except for a cylindrical 4 inch horn sticking out of the end of his elbow with the same colorings as his right hand. Harry also noticed his skin was now a satin white with thick callus skin.

Ivan brought a mirror over for Harry to take a better look at himself. Revealing he had only had a an extra bone layer over his forehead and two smaller 2 inch horns protruding from the top of his cheek bones. Harry's eyes were both blood shot red with no difference in vision. The titanium tubes were still extending out of his body, but the diamond shaped piece of metal was all but absorbed by skin except for the opening to insert more orange balls to increase blood in the body. Skin and horns caused by excessive bone growth was another side effect of an enhanced using a recovery tank to repair a damaged body.

Fred walked away from Jim and was too busy getting Walter his suit on to help Jim. Ivan ran over with the mirror showing Jim his new body. Jim was still missing his nose but now had another layer of bone over his forehead and upper cheek not covered by skin. His skin was the same satin white as Harry's and his diamond shaped metal device was also absorbed except for the opening on the front which was currently closed. The only other abnormality Jim had was fifty small half inch horns on top of his head that looked like spiked thick hair.

The last crate from the lead truck was being carried over to Harry and Jim by Walter. Two cow carcasses starting to rot from not being properly stored. Jim and Harry still naked rushed over devouring the meat without hesitation revealing something neither one had noticed at first. Their teeth were now double rowed razors for consuming meat. A few of Jim's teeth came off when biting into the bone of the cow but were replaced by teeth from the second row. Their teeth were now able to regrow at a rapid rate.

After they had finished the first carcass a clicking sound could be heard from above them in the rafters of the warehouse. A loud shriek followed by a crashing sound shaking the ground came rushing toward the crate of meat. Demonic beast with the same white satin skin came running over to feed on the meat.

The creature was 9 feet tall towering over both Jim and Harry with both of its arms fused into razor sharp bone horns extending behind the monster's elbows. The horns extended three feet back from the elbow and six feet forward from the elbow. This monster was galloping with its scythe arms towards them. Thick black fur covering small portions of its white body with no ears, nose, or skin on its cheeks. The creature's teeth were a round spiked bullet shape similar to a crocodiles.

Jim took a step back while Harry began to feed on the second cow. The creature looked over shrieking at Harry to move away from the cow. Harry stood his ground and made an attempt to attack the creature. It quickly stood up leaning back scissoring its arms slicing Harry in half then settling back down walking on its spike arms towards Jim.

Monstrous creature gave him a quick glance and looked back at Harry's wriggling corpse and began to eat Harrys head. Jim grabbed one of the legs of the cow and backed away slowly eating away from this other monster. The creature spit out the metal pieces recently implanted into Harry's body leaving nothing else. Going back and finishing the bones of the cow Jim and Harry could not eat and the other portion of the cow left in the crate.

Walter gave Jim a duffle bag with black fatigue pants, socks, boots, and a bullet resistant cloak. Jim began to dress himself as the creature with the scythe bladed arms moved towards Ivan. The creature made a teeth chattering sound beginning to hiss at Ivan, letting out a loud shriek and lunging at Ivan. Then freezing up a foot within reaching Ivan seething in pain screeching arching its back up and down in pain. The creature turned over slowly using its bladed arms as braces and disappeared back into the darkness.

Ivan handed Jim what appeared to be a circular watch with an elastic band and pointed to the direction the creature went then pointed to the watch. A deterrent device to stop the creature from attacking anyone wearing the watch. The creature was placed in the building two weeks before Fred, Ivan, and Jim had arrived.

The creature was a former level 2 thought to have been killed many years ago by the Russian military. Being dead for several hours before Ivan, acting as an assistant to the Russian military brought the creature back to life in its current state. No one actually knows who the creature used to be since most level two enhanced work only in the most deep cover operations. Re-animation as well as transformation came at a significant cost.

After being brought back, unable to speak or even communicate indicating severe brain damage from the procedure. The creature only acted on primal instincts and was implanted with a safety device between its lower C6 and C7 neck vertebrae. The device sends out two spikes via a miniature solenoid to the nerves in the creature's neck creating a shocking pain throughout the body.

In the Russian military they called the creature the Nozh or Chopper in English. The Nozh was only used in extreme situations to completely decimate an area. It was kept to whatever area it was supposed to be in using a GPS system to give a virtual wall using the device in its neck. Since the creature does not have hands it had no way of removing the device or ever escaping.

Ivan tapped on the watch Jim was wearing to turn it on and walked back over to his mechanical suit taking Jim by the hand after he had put on his clothes. Ivan simply pointed to a 4 foot long wood box loaded with eight short range missiles. Then Ivan pointed to his mechanical suit to have Jim load the missiles into the box shoulders.

Jim carried two missiles over as Ivan popped the shoulder plates open from inside of the suit. Carefully he slid each missile into place one by one until the shoulder mounted missiles were all fully loaded. Then Ivan using the giant mechanical robotic suit pointed the gun arm towards another crate containing ammunition. Jim nodded and pulled out a crate marked with 25x218mmSR with bullet boxes made to directly attach underneath the arm.

Each bullet was huge and the 500 round magazine attaching under the gatling gun arm almost touched onto the ground until Ivan rotated the magazine holder on the right arm horizontal allowing for another bulky magazine to be attached. Ivan once again rotated the arm and Jim attached another giant magazine to the arm. The arm had three magazines attached to it giving the appearance of a propeller.

Before Ivan could point with the left arm Jim had already grabbed two 4 foot tall 3 foot round containers with fuel in them for the flame throwing arm. As Jim placed the containers in place they hissed filling up empty space in the arms pipes. After attaching the final container Ivan pointed the flame throwing arm over the empty space of the warehouse. The warehouse lit up with bright flames shooting from Ivan's robotic creation almost touching the walls 50 yards away.

Time approached 3pm, Ivan hopped down out of his suit, and began helping Jim and Fred clean up empty boxes. Fred wore one of the new green beaded necklaces walking over to Jim and handing him a piece of paper. The paper stated what Fred wanted Jim to read when all the remaining recovery agents had shown up later in the day.

CHAPTER 20
GOOD NEWS?

James sat across from Liam on a chair as Liam sat on the edge of his bed with a fold down table between them. There were the files and folders laid out with Reba standing next to the door. Liam thumbed through the file folders looking for anything useful. Reba's radio chattered something in the background. She clicked it off and stood closer to the table, then her phone made a message ding, Reba took a glance and started to appear a little uneasy.

In front of them laid a pile of large full page pictures with numbers on them in the first folder Liam opened up. The next folder had two pieces of typed on paper, with something typed on them that was blacked out by a marker. Two notebooks a black and green one, both filled out completely by hand. The first notebook from a General Semenov hand written in Russian. Strike two, it had seemed then Liam glanced at the green one hand written in English by Amir with numbers referencing pictures.

"Well, where to start? Either of you know Russian?" Liam asked.

"Sorry, I got to go. Just got a call about a possible homicide at a truck stop down the road." Reba said.

"Let's start with Amir's notebook and go from there. Reba it was me if you are wondering. Hurry back." James said.

"What are you...never mind I need to go. I will try to be back in an hour. It is 3 in the pm now so don't ya'll go anywhere until I come back." Reba said.

Reba stepped down out of Liam's truck and hit her siren as soon as she left the parking lot of the park. James grabbed the picture folder while Liam held the green notebook in his hands. James laid out the pictures across the table to take a look at what each one had.

"Oh, sure I will read a story to my lovely as he shows the pictures." Liam said smugly.

"If you insist."

Liam started to read the notebook from Amir out loud as James sat back in the chair waiting for a picture number.

If you are reading this notebook then something bad is going to happen if it hasn't already. Please do not assume anything you have seen is what actually is going on. Mysterious workings are going on.

"Okay, I've heard enough let's skip to the pictures and what they are section." James said, looking down at the pictures.

"My dear, you don't like my reading?"

"No, Liam we have less than two hours to figure out what is going on so..you know let's speed this shit up."

Liam thumbed through the notebook a few pages and found the first one with a number for a picture. Picture number 1103 was of a helicopter crash with body parts everywhere with a level 2 holding an antiaircraft gun. Noted to be a Russian made weapon used on top of Russian ships to shoot surface to air missiles. The weapon was modified to be used with a giant trigger to allow something that could pick up 700 pounds easily. The crew was one of Amir's from two years ago that were all killed.

"I remember hearing they had a rotor malfunction in the chopper, but the picture says otherwise." Liam said.

"Wow, it looks like something fishy is going on. Next picture."

Once again Liam thumbed through the notebook and found the corresponding number of 1789 for the next picture. In the picture was a large metal briefcase being handed to two guys in military gear by Fred. The military gear they were wearing was Russian with noted Russian aircraft behind them. There were only two pictures left on the table to review with Liam halfway through the notebook.

Going through the notebook Liam found the last two pictures were of the same time, but in two different regions. 1609-1 was a picture of Fred in his Lab working on something with Russian markings. The other picture 1609-2 was another alien similar to Fred working on another machine with Russian markings. On the back of picture 1609-1 were GPS coordinates indicating Fred was in a secret base in Nevada and the other picture 1609-2 showed the other Zeta with GPS coordinates deep in Siberia.

"Do you see this?" James asked.

"Honey, all I see are two little grey men working on something."

"Slide the pictures together. Like this."

Liam slid the pictures with the one with Fred up diagonally to the other picture with the Russian Zeta. The two parts seemed to fit perfectly together as an arm attaching to a machine. They could not tell exactly what it was, but they were in different areas working on the same machine. As they placed the files back together they heard a knocking sound at the rear door of the truck.

Liam peered out through a small square bullet resistant window looking down he saw Reba standing. She had her arms crossed and seemed a little upset at something. Liam turned back to James as James was un-holstering his gun. Quickly Liam waved his hand down for James to put his gun away.

"It's Reba she's back." Liam said.

"Wow, has it been an hour?" James asked.

"Nope only about thirty minutes. She looks kinda angry."

Liam opened the door and Reba stood outside with her arms crossed.

"You sum-bitch you killed the guy at the gas station!" Reba hollered.

"Meee?"

"Not you Liam, Mr. Hawthorne sitting behind you." Reba sneered.

"I told you before you left. Guy was trying to rape me." James said.

"Well, we have had a few reports, but nothin' solid since most of the time men are embarrassed to admit to bein' raped. I tried to pull tapes on the store, but they were all blurred for the time you were there. What does that mean?" Reba asked.

"Another wonderful side effect from having this thing on my left arm where my elbow is. Kinda distorts a camera from seeing me." James said.

"More like blobby man. I seen video recorded of you and you turn into a blobby man. Hopefully your crazy arm doesn't give you cancer." Liam said.

"Hopefully your electric hands don't fry your dick off." James replied.

"Enough, now what did you find out." Reba said stepping back into the truck.

"Not much more than our boss alien is suspected of running off to Russia. Here you can take a look at the notebook and let me know if you notice anything else." Liam said.

Reba read through Amir's notebook while Liam and James played with the shirt printing machine. After 20 minutes Reba placed the notebook down and started going through the Russian notebook with her phone. Reba was trying to translate what was written in the note book using a translation application on her phone. After a few more minutes Reba dropped both notebooks on the table knocking on the side of the table to grab Liam and James' attention.

"So, your friend Amir says you are being tracked by your cigar phones, which you probably already know. He also mentions you should not have any private conversations around the phone as it could be recording everything you say even turned off." Reba said.

"Well, good thing we left them up in the cab in the locked glove box then." James said.

"Hello, we already know all this stuff. Anything else miss detective." Liam sneered.

"Well did ya'll consider he might be warning you of being targeted by a satellite weapon? Written down in bold in the notebook and had the satellite number attached. Some sort of direct heat laser. Invisible until you see the person next to you spontaneously combust. Did ya'll guys even read the whole notebook?" Reba asked.

"We got the gist of it and went from there. So, what could you figure out from the Russian notebook?" James asked back.

"Seems they have been playin' more with re-animation

of soldiers for the past thirty years with some mixed results. Most of what I could gather was they were able to re-animate with a lot of drawbacks making whatever they worked on previously obsolete." Reba said.

"Russian zombie soldiers, would be kind of cool to see." James said.

"Helllss no. I will not deal with zombies, those are one of my phobias." Liam said.

"Relax the notebook said they needed far too much food and would actually die again after three months for random reasons. Heart failure was the most common. Plus they required expensive mechanical support to stay alive." Reba said.

"We have a zombie army, but at a cost of trillion dollars to make just one and they die after a few months. Why wouldn't you want that?" James asked sarcastically.

"Honey you make me laugh. No zombies, good now was there anything else?" Liam asked.

"Just showing the same thing Amir was saying with an American alien creature working with a Russian alien creature." Reba said.

"This confirms Amir was right about them working together, but why would they be working together?" James asked.

Reba and Liam glanced at each other and shrugged. No one knew exactly why Fred was working with another Zeta. Both James and Liam knew Zeta Reticuli where limited in numbers currently on Earth and were not supposed to conspire against other countries. James glanced at Liam and back over to Reba nodding to tell her something.

"Go ahead hun. You can tell her. Not like anyone would believe any of this anyways." Liam said.

"So, we told you about how outer space aliens exist and are on Earth. Well, they have some strict rules imposed on those working and staying on the planet. They are space refugees from a few thousand years ago and set out rules after the destruction of some human civilizations early on. Currently they reside on one of either Saturn or Jupiter's moons. I am sorry I don't remember which one. To keep up with resource trading they trade knowledge by having some of their own raised here.

There are about five hundred living on Earth and they are kind of their outcasts kids. Instead of throwing one of theirs into a jail cell they simply execute the offender and send the children to Earth to be raised by some secret Government agency. They allocate which Government gets the younglings by the amount of resources they trade. Believe it or not the United States is third for receiving young aliens.

One of the main advantages of having them is they have an extremely high intellect and can help any government survive. So, they have placed rules to stop what we believe is happening from becoming a nuclear war started by Zeta Reticuli. Rule number one is no conspiring with others from other countries for any reason. Rule number two is no involvement in chemical warfare. Rule number three is no involvement in germ warfare. Finally rule number four is no involvement in nuclear warfare."

"What happens when they break a rule?" Reba asked.

James and Liam glanced at each other shrugged then looked back at Reba.

"We have no idea how they even enforce these supposed rules since they have not been broken in over a hundred years. They must have had some sort of enforcement in the past, but now we have no idea since they have been playing nice for such a long time." Liam said.

Liam removed his gloves and began loading up his gun and speed loaders placing them on his belt. James took a brief moment checking over his own gun and speed loaders making sure every single one had a bullet in it. Reba was staring at Liam looking at his black translucent forearms in a trance.

"Stare any longer and I will have to charge you." Liam said.

"I..I am sorry, I never have seen anything like that. Liam your arms look amazing." Reba said.

Liam's left arm began to glow a neon blue as he slowly reached his arm out behind James. Too busy checking his ammo to pay attention to Liam, James did not see what was about to happen. Liam simply touched James' right shoulder and he went down onto the bed. A high voltage shock jolted his body freezing up his muscles causing him to collapse. Reba started to giggle as James jumped back up after a short while standing on the far side of the bed away from Liam.

"Asshole! Great, now I have to wait thirty minutes for my fucking left arm!" James shouted.

"Had to show what my gentle touch can do." Liam said slighly.

"Wow, can you control how much shock your arms put out?" Reba asked.

"I don't know exactly how much, but playing with a volt meter a small jolt like you just saw is around 30,000 volts. A shocker as I like to call them is up to 100,000 volts and 10 amps. They told me I could kill a dinosaur if I ever needed to." Liam said.

James and Liam finished looking over their gear with James grabbing his freshly printed shirt with some extra airbrush done by Liam. James put on his new black shirt with the word "Pain" printed in large red lettering across his chest. Liam had added some red airbrush to make it appear like it was splatter stamped onto the shirt. It was time for them to leave to their meeting to find out if any of what Amir was saying was true or if it was a simple mistake.

Liam put both of the new leather strapped necklaces with green beads in a metal box under the bed in the back of his truck and gave both his and James' roll devices to Reba. Reba placed the devices in the trunk of her patrol car. They had agreed Reba would park her car outside of the oil refinery and find a ride back to the station with another officer. This was to throw off anyone trying to GPS track them as they would be in the meeting location while the devices would show they were outside.

"Okay time to move out. Reba, give us two hours after you drop off your car then come back by the refinery. There shouldn't be any trouble." James said.

CHAPTER 21
THE MEETING

The rain was beginning to come down hard pounding on the roof of Liam's truck as they drove through the open gate to the refinery. They were not sure where to go until they saw the tail lights of a car circling the entrance to a humongous warehouse, being parked outside. A total of six cars including Liam's rusty armored truck parked outside of the building. Three of the cars were flashy sports cars with the other two being lavish black SUV's.

Out of the sporty car they followed in a man with a red hair flat top got out and began to run inside. Liam and James got out stepping into the puddle filed parking lot being soaked by the down pour of rain. As they ran in behind the guy with red hair he stopped after getting inside and turned back at James and Liam.

"James!? Is that you. You're still alive?" the guy asked.

James stared at him with the wheels in his brain slowly starting to turn.

"It's me, Miles. How have you been. I had to go back to working in the Reform jail after posting a bad time fighting that damned machine. Been a Recovery Agent for about two years now." Miles said.

James stared at him about to speak.

"How nice honey, but this one is mine. Come on now, we have a meeting. Chit chat can wait." Liam said.

"Rright well I will talk to you after." Miles said.

There were two semi-trucks with trailers parked one in front of the other in the open building. The building smelled of old oil, spilt gasoline, and something else toxic. It was a brightly illuminated room with lights hanging 20 feet over head. They only saw eight other agents in the room with them, which meant half the team was either gone or didn't show up.

Everyone was gathered in a circle chatting it up shaking hands and telling old war stories. James and Liam headed over to the group with everyone in a good mood. Four were level 2 enhanced towering over the rest of the group. The total left was ten including James and Liam, one level one women and one level 1 guy were looking around for some of the other members of the group by poking their heads out of the circle and looking around.

"Well shit, only ten left. There is somethin' really bad goin' on. All these people chattering away like everything is okay." Liam whispered to James.

James looked around at everyone beginning to become irritated at everyone carrying on like nothing is happening.

"Shut the fuck up! Za is Dead! Something is going on and we should not..." James started to yell when a squeal from a megaphone interrupted him.

Everyone turned around to see a white figure with what appeared to be a white skull mask and black pants standing on the top of the rear of the first truck trailer. Walter walked around from behind the trailer carrying Fred on his turned up palms. The appearance of a mini-figure being carried like a dear kid's toy always seemed a bit funny to James. Looking closer at the guy with the white mask it was clearer it was his protruding skull over his forehead with no nose, and some weird tubes sticking out of him.

"Today marks the first day in a day of change! We all can unite to become something more! Most of you are already enhanced and I ask if you want to be better than you are now!" The Creature with the skull face bellowed through a megaphone briefly pausing looking around the room.

"I used to be known by some of you as Jim Berthlow, now I have become more than a meek low level enhanced soldier. Now I am stronger, beyond the grasp of any conception of death! Join me! I ask you step forward and join me!" Jim bellowed into the megaphone.

Everyone stood around looking at each other dumbfounded by what this pale white former figure of a man was saying. Standing below Jim on the right Fred was waving for someone to come over from behind the truck trailer. To the left of Fred and Walter was what looked like a fighter jet cockpit with legs and weapons for arms with boxed shoulders. Another Zeta Reticuli alien came out between the rear of the first truck trailer.

It was wearing a military green jumpsuit with a Russian hammer and sickle printed in red on the left of its jumpsuit. The same hammer and sickle crossing symbol was painted on the left side of the airplane with legs. As the alien walked out it stood in front of the robotic thing to the left of Fred and Walter indicating it was his machine.

"Ivan, is the fellow down here joining us in destroying the Zeta Reticuli to obtain their technology! It would mean we could be beyond gods with this technology on a level of complexity beyond what any of our most brilliant scientist understand. How? You may ask will we achieve this? By going beyond what they know for physical enhancements and attacking them when they do not expect it! So, now who will join us on this mission!" Jim howled through the megaphone.

Jim took a few steps back on the top of the truck trailer waiting for anyone to step forward. After four minutes of uncertainty one person stepped forward slowly walking up towards Fred and Ivan. A shriek followed by a spray of misting blood into the air erupted from the guy whom stepped forward. It was Miles stepping forward, only to be sliced into four pieces in an instant by some giant dusty white creature with long scythe arms.

"Nozh, smelt weakness on this one! Now I ask those who are strong to step forward!" Jim hollered without the megaphone.

The creature known as Nozh was crunching on Miles bones devouring him with its demonic appearance. James tapped Liam on the arm and he glanced over at him and they both nodded at each other. Before they could make out what they were going to do Jim began pointing over to Fred. All Fred did was point at the beaded necklace to indicate he would communicate through the telepathic necklace.

As soon as Fred pressed the button on the green bead on his necklace deafening explosions occurred simultaneously. Everyone wearing a green bead necklace had their neck either blown open or had been completely removed of their heads. James and Liam had left their necklaces in Liam's truck under the bed and two others had not worn theirs.

Alyson Whitmoore didn't trust the convenient change to necklace color at the last minute and Hank the level 2 enhanced they talked to earlier was simply wearing his blue necklace instead of the new green one. Hank forgot which one to wear and picked the blue one out of color preference which ended up keeping him alive for the time being.

After Fred released the button on his necklace a

booming blast of rapid gunfire came from James, Liam, Alyson, and Hank. James blew Ivan's head apart like a ripe pineapple being thrown at a wall while Liam fired away at Jim standing on the truck. Alyson and Hank opened fire at Fred and Walter with no luck since Walter swiftly turned his back to the opening gunfire protecting Fred as bullets ricocheted off of Walters back. Jim stumbled backwards falling off of the trailer with the Nozh creature screeching as it began after Hank.

Alyson, Liam, and James ran out the door as the creature sliced Hank from shoulder to stomach in half biting at Hank's head with its protruding cylindrical teeth. Liam pointed to his truck for them to seek refuge, but it was in flames from the explosion occurring in the box under the bed with both his and James' necklaces. Alyson pointed to the rear of the building and they began to run past a humongous closed roll up door where the semi-trucks had entered.

Just after they made it past the door it tore open with Walters' mannequin head peering around. James fired three rounds at the monstrous robots head hitting it twice making the head explode leaving the two cameras it had for eyes dangling loosely by wires. The giant robot ripped out its two cameras it had for eyes, where its head was, and tore open its shirt at the top of its chest revealing a massive baseball size camera lens. It began after them followed by Fred in Ivan's mech suit around the corner of the building.

Alyson slid under a row of enormous pipes behind the building while James and Liam led the robot down behind the building. Walter appeared to struggle to locate them running into pipes and following something invisible to Liam and James. It smashed the ground with both of its fists sending pieces of concrete flying into the air ten feet behind

James and Liam. They rushed up a metal ladder running towards another building with broken out windows.

Walter was smashing the metal ladder behind them as it tried to crawl after them, its massive weight caused it to fall back to the ground. As they made their way to the door of the building they found the door was locked. It was a solid metal door with deadbolt holding it closed. James grabbed the door with his left hand then released his hand with a solid grip on the push down handle, James jumped back over the edge of the platform retracting his body back to his arm trying to leverage his falling weight against the door.

The handle held for a brief moment then exploded off with James falling only a few feet to the ground with the handle still grasped in his left hand. James threw the handle back up to Liam at the door. Liam used the end of the handle to pry the deadbolt open from inside of the door. Walter was making his way towards James still smashing around missing James by ten feet.

Piercing loud explosions erupted behind Walter as bowling ball sized holes ripped through the giant robots body. A whirring sound could be heard after the robot collapsed forward almost landing on top of James. Fred was firing the jet robots mini-gun, Walters massive size was blocking his view of who was hiding in front of him. Since Fred saw Walter having no success at killing them he thought he would take over.

Liam opened fire on Fred in the mechanical jet suit to draw his attention away from James. Fred turned the robots gun turret upwards and fired at Liam as he fled back into the open door way, blasting holes into the brick building. James ran up to the cockpit firing bullets at it trying to crack the ballistic glass. All it did was waste ammo ricocheting bullets way from it. Fred smiled and began to turn the giant gun back towards James.

The rain was heavy, as the loud revving engine of a large SUV being driven at a high rate of speed came to a crashing stop into the back of Fred in the mechanical suit. Fred was jolted forward forcing the robot onto its face trapping Fred inside. Alyson jumped out of the back of the SUV and scrambled up the makeshift ladder made by the remains of the old ladder and the roof of the SUV.

James had rolled away just in time to avoid being crushed by Fred and climbed up after Alyson. They ran towards the bullet riddled door Liam went through to find him with only a few scrapes from diving behind a desk in the room. It appeared to be an old guard room for the building with some old file cabinets a chair and a desk. The room was small, dark, and riddled with gigantic bullet holes.

"Hey guys, what do you say we go kill the monster in the warehouse and that son of a bitch Jim Berthlow?" Alyson asked.

"What about Fred?" Liam asked.

"Leave him he will be stuck for a while with the rain. There is another door on the side of the building we could go through." Alyson said.

"Fred is stuck look at him try to struggle to push that thing to stand, probably overloaded with ammo. Let's go." James said.

The mechanical suit Fred was in was whining and whirring as he tried to use the arms to force it to stand. Having fully loaded shoulder missiles overloaded the capacity for the weaponized arms to lift the robot up from a face down position. James opened up a fresh can of Yak chew and placed what he thought might be his last dip in his lip and threw the rest of the can out to the open.

As they made their way to the door James stood back with his gun up as Alyson opened the door and Liam covered next to James. They could see into the building from the door, the creature was still crunching on Hanks giant level 2 body. Looking around going in slowly they did not see Jim anywhere in the building. James and Liam both set the sights on their guns to ricochet mode and had planned at trying to disable the creature by shooting it in the eyes.

James led them in slipping behind the semi-trucks with Liam and Alyson close behind. The Nozh was directly in front of them 20 feet from the trucks with 10 feet to the back wall behind them, the trucks were parked too close to go between them. Liam pointed to James and under the rear of the front trailer, then he pointed to Alyson to the rear of the truck on the end. Finally he pointed to himself then to the front of the lead truck.

The hand signaling meant to them James was to go straight on at the Nozh while Liam went to the left with Alyson closing in on the right. Liam pointed his hand up in the air with his right index finger quickly snapping his wrist signaling them to go. James crouched under the first truck's trailer belly crawling with his eyes and gun pointed towards the Nozh. The Nozh only lifted its head clicking its teeth briefly while they made their way towards it.

Alyson and Liam paused at their perspective ends until James was out and up on his feet. James swiftly began walking towards the Nozh with a green laser beam he could only see pointing at the monster's head. Liam had his own green laser beam he was able to see coming off of his gun also pointed at the Nozh's head. As they got within ten feet of the Nozh creature it gazed up hissing at them protecting its' meal.

They all stopped for a brief moment when Liam yelled out, "Fire!"

A barrage of armor piercing .44 magnum rounds fired

out at the creature with the bullets sticking to it like thumb tacks. As soon as they began firing the Nozh had closed its eyes with an inner eyelid turning its dried out powdery white skinned head sniffing the air. They continued to reload firing rapidly until it screeched out loudly leaping into the air swinging its left sickle blade arm up into the air straight down into the top of James' right ankle.

Now James was pinned to the concrete by the Nozh's bladed arm it still had its eyes closed as James collapsed to his back in pain still trying to kill the monster with his gun. The Nozh swung its right bladed arm over where James was once standing then lifted its arm up to rip James in half. Liam leapt from the left of the creature with glowing blue arms grasping the Nozh's left leg.

"Grrzzaahgg.." Howled the Nozh.

Pale white creature covered in blood and entrails seized up beginning to fall backwards with James still pinned to the concrete. Suddenly a whipping sound came from behind them as the Nozh's body was exploding in chunks by something from the back of the building. The Nozh's arm was blown off with the left bladed arm still pinning James to the concrete floor.

Lights in the room began to flicker as the whipping sound continued ripping through the wall behind the semis. The sound was growing louder as the whipping sound of an aircraft gatling gun moved from the center of the room left then right, in an up and down zig zag. Alyson recognized the sound and ran for the hole in the roll up door made by Walter, diving through the opening before the whipping of the large caliber bullets went where she was standing.

Now the building was carved open in the front and back by the bullets of the aircraft gun. The lights went out completely leaving Liam and James in complete darkness with the sound of the emptied gun whirring followed by compressed gas being sparked into a small flame. Fred had exhausted all the ammo from the gun turning to the flame thrower to burn out anyone left alive. The left arm of the mechanical suit lit a vast flame engulfing what was left of the semi-trucks and trailers.

After setting the trucks on fire they burbled bursting into flames with black diesel smoke. Fred briefly paused stepping in through where the wall was in the mechanical suit. James was not hit by any of the bullets fired through the building. Liam was grazed on the thigh before laying down on his belly on the floor. Even though Liam was only grazed a three inch chunk of his right thigh was gone.

The top of the warehouse began to sway in the wind with rain dribbling into the building. Alyson remembered someone mentioning demolitions in their last mission to flush out a hiding level 2. She knocked out the driver side window of the first car she came up to. It was some flashy sports car with dark tinted windows. The glass cracked leaving the tinting film intact as she pushed a hole in the glass with the barrel of her gun large enough to reach her arm in and trigger the automatic lock.

Unlocking the car all she found was a few boxes of ammo and a change of clothes. The next vehicle she checked was a lavish black SUV like she had driven into Fred with earlier. It had ballistic glass windows, making it harder to break into she tried ferociously to break the glass with no luck. Then she tried the door handle finding it was unlocked. Alyson found a few bricks of plastic explosive along with a simple digital timer.

To be sure she knew how the timer worked she played with it for a quick moment while it was not plugged into the explosive. Alyson figured out the timer had to be set then started by pressing a separate button on the explosive. She got two bricks setup with one minute on one followed by two minutes on another. The two minute timer one she was going to keep tucked under her shirt in case it came down to having to sacrifice herself.

As Fred made his way closer to where the trucks were parked he stopped for a moment surveying the scene of destruction. Two half eaten bodies laid on the ground with five other dead on the ground in different locations in front of the burning trucks. Two figures were moving on the ground in front of him as he stood waiting.

Jim went leaping out from behind Fred with his powder white skin, thick skull face, and hoses sticking out of his head. As he approached James holding Za's bat in his left arm dragging it on the ground as he got closer. Jim lifted the 300 pound bat with little effort making and upward swing at James left arm. James was laying pinned on the ground facing away from Jim making him an easy target.

A quick clinking sound was made as James' left metal forearm bent from the force of the bat striking it. James quickly began firing over his shoulder at the monstrous Jim standing behind him. Each shot made contact sticking to Jim's body and face like thumb tacks with little effect. Jim reached down as James emptied his trusted Rust into the shark toothed monster.

"You won't be needing this." Jim said.

Jim crushed James' right arm with his foot breaking the bones in his forearm ripping Rust from his right hand. Jim had lowered his left arm dropping the top of the bat on the ground while still grasping it. Jim kneeled down as he tossed Rust out into the rain through the opening in the front of the building. Liam grasped the end of the bat with his hands sending a massive shock of electricity through the bat causing Jim to stumble backwards.

Liam began firing his own gun at Jim as he was stumbling backwards, trying for a fatal headshot. He hit Jim with three shots to the face before Jim smashed the bat on Liam's legs crushing both his knees then kicking him out of the building into the rain. Liam slid across a muddy field into a small hill outside of the building. Jim dropped the bat kneeling down and stepped over James as he wrapped James' shirt in his hands beginning to lift him up slowly.

The ripping pain of James' foot being torn open by the Nozh blade that had pinned him to the ground was immense. James' left arm had already straightened itself out again and he was trying to claw at Jim's arm with no luck. It was like clawing at a solid oak tree with a dull spoon. Jim's skin was so thick he only noticed James clawing madly when he pulled him in closer.

"Keep tryin' you worm. Your little metal hand will not help you." Jim said.

"Ha, you would never be able to beat me one on one." James said, trying to force Jim to release him.

James was being held in the air now by Jim facing the front of the building away from where Fred was standing in his mechanical suit. The left arm of the suit had a small blue fire burning with the building being lit up by the burning trucks. James made out a shadowy figure moving in the darkness towards the right side of Fred. It was Alyson, slipping in behind Fred's right side placing something on his side. James was hoping it was an explosive as she got it placed James knew he had to keep Jim from turning around.

"You know you are lucky you can't smell anything. It smells like a bloody shit filled room out here. By the way, in case you were wondering you smell like microwaved rotten fish. Maybe we should start calling you a Shit Fis..."

Jim moved his left hand from James' shirt to over his mouth to shut him up. James could feel the crushing pressure over his mouth as Jim began squeezing harder. Jim pulled James in closer to his face squeezing harder on

James' mouth. A crunching loud pop sound rang through James' ears as Jim crushed James' jaw with his hand. A bloody chewing tobacco ooze began to flow through Jim's fingers before he realized James was stalling for something.

"Why are you trying to stall? Your friend is probably dead and there is no one else around." Jim sneered.

James was very close to Jim's face as he turned his head looking back towards Fred. Something slipped away from Fred's side as he glanced back.

"Fred that bitch stuck som....."

James stuck his middle finger on his left platinum hand deep into Jim's left eye. As Jim's vision had gone to half of what it was he dropped James to the ground. James had completely released his arm allowing for the tip of his finger to remain in Jim's eye socket. Jim spun around about to scream when a concussive blast filled the room.

Alyson had successfully placed the plastic explosive on Fred's side while he eagerly watched James being tortured. She started the 1 minute and 2 minute timers at the same time before coming around the corner of the building. Alyson carefully slipped the plastic explosive on the right hip of the mechanical suit when James first saw her. By the time James saw her half the time of the timer was gone leaving 30 seconds to stick the explosive to the mechanical suit and run.

After she finally got it to stick to the robot suit she found Jim had finally turned seeing her with 19 seconds left on the timer. Alyson ran away as fast as she could to the rear of the facility dropping the second brick of plastic explosive she attached to herself on one of the many pipes running through the refinery. Fred could see Jim was trying to tell him something but by that time it was too late.

In slow motion the blast threw Fred to his left as his right side exploded. Following the explosion on his right side the tanks ruptured on his left flamethrower arm causing the missiles packed in the each shoulder to explode. The concussion of the blast knocked down the swaying building roof throwing James and Jim out into the rain with burning bodies everywhere. James was knocked back into blackness by the explosion laying on his back in the mud with rain pouring down over him.

CHAPTER 22
TIME TO GO HOME

A steady beeping sound was ringing in James' ear as he slowly cracked his eyes open to a white panel ceiling with fluorescent lights. His throat was sore and it was hard to move around in what felt to be a hard bed. A lady wearing scrubs and a hospital face mask was standing next to him at the side of the bed. She had dark blue scrubs with dark brown curly hair and olive skin. James could see I.V. lines running into his right arm and feel what he guessed would be a catheter between his legs.

"Hello there, don't try to move. Let me get Dr. Robertson in here to fill you in on what we have done for you." The Nurse said.

"mmmhh." James tried to talk.

"Don't try to speak either, your muscles are weak and it might be a little bit before they start feeling better." She said, stepping out of the room.

After 20 minutes the Doctor walked into the room wearing a medical face mask. The Doctor was a short guy with dark skin and greying black hair. James felt like an eight hundred pound blanket was covering his body. Dr. Robertson pulled the sheet covering James off and began poking his legs with a pen then moved to his left foot skipping his right foot. The Doctor shined a pen light in his eyes, then checked in his ears with an ear light, and finally pried open his mouth shining the same light.

"So, Mr. Hawthorne you were in a tornado at your home. You probably don't remember much but this is what happened. You have had multiple lacerations, contusions, some skull fractures, and your right foot was cut open badly and we had to amputate it. Also you had suffered multiple facial fractures causing us to have to wire your jaw shut for a 4 week period. You are lucky to be alive after this. You were in a coma for two months followed by one medically induced coma to help prevent seizures." Dr. Robertson stated, then stepped out of the room.

James was feeling weak and could not wrap his mind around the idea of a tornado being the cause of his injuries. He tried to move his fingers on his right hand and they felt like they were held in place by an invisible stone. Trying to move his mouth felt like someone had their hand under his jaw holding it in place. James attempted to move his legs and it still felt like the 800 pound blanket was on top of them. The nurse came back in the room watching his eyes moving around to the parts of his body he was trying to move.

"Take it easy, it will take some time to gain your strength back. You've been out of it for a while and your muscles will have to wake up slowly." The nurse said.

James was down to 153 pounds from his 220 before the claimed tornado accident had occurred. The nurse put a mirror over his face and he could see his short hair with multiple surgical scars across his head and a smaller jaw. He only had his right canine tooth and a premolar on the left side left in his mouth. James ended up staying in the hospital for another month to gaining his motor skills and speech back.

After his discharge from the hospital he was up to 160 pounds and could maneuver around with crutches. For the past month he had been wearing a red hoodie, a flip flop, and sweatpants from the hospital's lost and found that had been there for a few years. They had told him he was in Kentucky and even given him a drivers license they claimed to have recovered from his clothes after the tornado.

The hospital arranged a transport to take him back to his address on his license. A hospital transport car took him back to the trailer park he was at when the tornado had happened. It was a drive down unfamiliar roads he did not recognize all the way to the park.

The trailer park was not one of the several nicer ones the medical car had passed, but a rundown park with a convenience store setup in front of it. James got out of the car with the assistance of the driver realizing he did not have a key for his supposed trailer. He took his crutches swinging himself down the driveway to the park managers office. James knocked on the door and heard a shuffling coming towards the door slowly. A tall balding grey haired black guy answered the door.

"Yep, whatcha want?" He asked.

"Sorry to bother you but I need to grab a spare key for my trailer if you have one?" James asked.

"Which number are ya livin' in? Need an ID also."

"Number seventeen."

"Whelp let me take a look. Well, look here you will be owing four months back rent and six months back on utilities. So, twelve hundred in an hour and it'll be good or I will be throwin' yer ass out on the street."

James nodded in acceptance of the terms to paying the guy 1200 dollars while he was given the key to his trailer.

None of it felt familiar to him as he cruised back with his crutches swinging his single foot forward. James unlocked the door finding it difficult to push open with something in the way. Clothes and paper debris were all over in front of the door along with a torn apart small couch and flipped mattress in the bedroom. All signs pointed to someone had been in the trailer looking for something while he was gone.

One of the pieces of clothes on the ground was a moth chewed through green t-shirt and some jeans. James stepped into the trailer closing the door he sat down on the pile of clothes and put the shirt and jeans on. Trying to stand up James tripped over a couch cushion finding a left tennis shoe on the ground next to it. He put the single shoe on his foot tying the lace on the shoe slowly with his only hand.

As he made his way around the trashed trailer he found the back window was open where someone had come into the trailer looking for something. James knew if there was anything of value in the trailer it had already been taken. Besides the trailer being turned upside down the walls were ripped open with most of the copper wiring ripped out.

James figured he would have to leave, grabbing a plastic bag he found placing some extra clothes in it. Things seemed too weird to be true, but every time he tried to remember what had happened his head hurt. Especially when trying to recall anything from before his stay at the hospital. There was a phone planted on the counter in the kitchen slash living area seemingly untouched. It began ringing all of a sudden when James was getting ready to leave the trailer.

"Hello?" James said juggling his crutches.

"Hi, honey they told me you left the hospital today. I hope you are okay." A woman's voice said.

"Who is this?"

"Don't tell me you don't recognize your own mother's voice. Anyway we have a cab coming to pick you up to take you to the airport in about 20 minutes so you can come home. The taxi will pick you up from the store outside of the park."

"Alright."

"Bye honey, see you tonight."

The feeling the person on the phone was not his mom was overwhelming, as was the possibility it was indeed his mother. James knew he had some pretty severe trauma from the tornado and they told him some dreams during the coma could feel real. Separating reality from the dreams made him complacent to whatever someone had told him. As James made his way through the trailer park about to leave a kid on a bicycle stopped him.

"Hey dude, need a fix?" The kid questioned, flashing a small bag of white crystals.

"How old are you? 9? Go home kid and knock it off with that stuff." James said, trying to brush the kid off.

"I'm eelevann dude, you know you need some. Look at your mouth. You got the smashed mouth. You know you want some." The kid kept insisting.

"No, thank you bud. I had an accident. Not into anything like that."

The kid changed his tactics.

"Well you know it helps with pain, and helps you feel stronger."

"Scram kid, I have to go."

"Fuck you!" The kid screamed as a couple of guys walked up from the back of the park.

"You harassin' my little friend here." The first guy said.

"What's your problem buddy." The second guy said.

Both were the drug dealers of the park known as the Brine brothers and were not to be crossed. They were wiry white young guys wearing oversized white hoodies with gold chains and red backwards facing baseball caps with two noticeable handguns tucked in the waist bands of their baggy pants. James thought they appeared comically like 90's gangster wannabes trying to act tougher than they actually were.

"No problem here, I am just running.."

James tried to say as one of them violently shoved him over to the ground knocking him onto his back. The first guy jumped up in the air after shoving him with his fist in the air to try and drive a punch to James' head. James lifted his right crutch up as hard as he could nailing the guy between the legs with the blunt foot of the crutch. The guy keeled over with his waist band gun sliding onto the ground next to James' right arm.

The second brother had his gun already drawn onto James, but was still in a temporary shock watching his brother fall over. James fired twice rapidly hitting the standing brother in the chest dropping him to the ground. The other brother next to James hit James in the hand with his own crutch knocking the gun away. This time the first brother had the upper hand and was holding the crutch overhead ready to beat James with it.

As the standing Brine brother was about to swing the crutch at James a loud crashing boom rang out from behind them. The remaining Brine brothers face exploded shooting out blood and brain matter all over James as the brother dropped to the ground. Then a tall dark skinned woman wearing a tank top, tight blue jeans, hi-top shoes, and neon green hair stepped over them and fired another cracking boom at the head of the brother James had shot.

"Hi James, it's been a little while." She said.

"Who!?" James was confused.

"Alyson Whitmoore, they told me you might be a little

messed in the head. Alright here is the deal you can come with me and we can finish off some stuff, or you can go hop in the taxi at the store and go pretend to live with your mom."

"What are you talking about?" James asked.

"Come with me or stay wondering who you are."

"I think I will go with you, things seem to not make any sense to me here. Can you help me understand what is going on?"

"I can do better than that! Leave your crutches here and your bag of crap. Roll onto your belly and bridge your body with your arms and legs like a cat."

James rolled onto his belly bracing himself up on his knees with his right arm as Alyson scooped him up over her left shoulder. The kid was sitting on his bike less than fifty feet away in shock of what he had seen. Tears began to run down his eyes as he tried to decide what he should do in the moment.

"Hey boy, go home to your mom and tell her you love her!" Alyson shouted to the kid.

He got off of his bicycle walking it back to his house crying heavily and sniffling as he went.

"You good James?" Alyson asked.

"As good as I can be."

Alyson was walking out of the park with James over her shoulder when the Trailer park managers' door burst open. A booming crack exploded the guys chest open followed by another as his body was falling down bursting the top of his head open. The semi-automatic .44 magnum Alyson was carrying silently went back into its sheath. Alyson did not even buckle when firing still carrying James on her left shoulder while she fired from her right side.

"Hey, he was the manager not some drug dealing asshole." James said.

"Orders are if you agreed to go then I will be allowed to remove any obstacles in the way. Besides he is just some Russian spy anyway, he would have killed you in two weeks if they didn't find out what they wanted."

The park was oddly quiet as they walked out and the sound of sirens going by didn't happen as expected. Alyson put James in the front seat of her black SUV parked outside of the convenience store. As the SUV fired to life a police scanner popped on blipping about loose horses and a minor fender bender. Nothing about shots fired in the trailer park or a possible homicide. They drove down the road for forty five minutes turning into a Military base.

Alyson rolled her window down at the gate as the guard approached the car and another guard was looking at an extending mirror checking the bottom of the vehicle. The radio in the guard shack buzzed as the guard was at the window of Alyson's SUV. The guard promptly turned around and answered the phone.

"Yes Sir!" was shouted by the guard.

The gate opened as they waved Alyson into the base past the barracks towards an empty hangar. She parked the SUV in the empty hangar in the back right corner and went to pick James up carrying him once again over her left shoulder. Alyson knocked at on the back wall the front of the SUV was almost touching. A hidden ramp appeared the length of the back wall going down into a hidden room the size of the hangar above it.

Fluorescent lighting flooded the room below the hangar with grey cement flooring and walls with a white ceiling. There was a set of monitors to their right showing the perimeter as well as the interior of the hangar. Someone transporting material above on the road outside the hangar triggered a motion sensor causing one of the monitors to beep. Alyson walked down the ramp carrying James over her shoulder into the room.

Towards the middle of the room was a metal folding table with a tool box on top of it. Next to the table was what James thought was a metal bathtub. It seemed familiar to him, but his head ached as he tried to remember where he saw it before. There were four metal chairs next to the table and two other people in the room he knew, but at the same time didn't know. They walked on and were quickly greeted by a woman wearing a long Doctor's coat. Alyson dropped James down into a metal chair next to the table.

"Hello James, it has been a long time. You probably remember me as Doctor Garcia. Now I go by Doctor Nasser. Anyway, how are you feeling?" Dr. Nasser asked.

"Other than looking like a meth head and feeling like my brain is trying to leap through the front of my skull, I'm good."

"Here we are again, this time being on my team is essential for your survival." The guy standing just to the right of the Doctor said.

"I feel like I know you, but I can't...Errghh! My head, why can't I remember!" James yelled out.

"We will try to help, my wife will have you back on your feet and make you better. Trust me." The guy said.

The guy had bulbous muscular looking arms under a long sleeve military green spandex shirt with a black bullet proof vest covering his torso. He was wearing black cargo pants with well-worn black combat boots. Something was weird about his hands, they had black metal knuckles with pieces of metal covering tubes for his fingers. Looking closer his arms had odd ridges running up and down under his shirt.

"Did you remember something? I only ask since you seem to be staring at my hands." The guy said.

"Are you a robot?" James asked.

"Not quite yet. Strip down so we can start." The guy said.

"Don't worry James it just makes it easier to work on your body to fix your injuries in the tank." Dr. Nasser assured him.

James looked up and around at them before starting to undress himself slowly. He was able to pull his shirt off with little effort with one hand, but he toppled over onto the ground trying to untie his shoe on his left foot. The others rushed over to help, but he waved them away as he was able to wiggle his shoe off and pull his pants off on the ground. Then he looked up ready to climb into the tank they were going to put him in.

"James you have to fully undress." Dr. Nasser said.

Slowly he slid his underwear off and with help from Alyson to stand got to the edge of the tank.

"One second let met activate the oxygen so it doesn't feel like your drowning. Now when you go in hold your breath for ten seconds then breathe normally." Dr. Nasser said.

The tank was humming with bb sized metallic beads three feet deep and ten feet long. It was five feet wide with hoses and cables attached to the outside being fed with different small tanks on the back side. James was being cradled by Alyson as she slowly lower him in and pulled her arms away. He started to count in his head holding his breath. Then felt a burning pain at the bottom of his right leg where his foot once connected to it.

Burning pain was growing outward from his leg then his bones began burning throughout his entire body. As the burning started to go away, his head started throbbing then began burning all the way through the base of his neck then down his back. Slowly all the burning inside was going away as his muscles began to burn through his entire body down to where his right foot once was.

James had been in the tank for twenty minutes as Dr. Nasser sent nano repair bots to the areas of his body injured by the fight with Fred and Jim. He would thrash in the tank back and forth as she kept the targeting damaged areas of his body. Then it all stopped and he could feel a cooling menthol sensation through his body. James began to feel himself being pushed up slowly by the beads in the tank to the surface.

"Well, how do you feel?" Dr. Nasser asked.

"You married Amir?" James quipped.

"He's back and just as charming as ever. Now move your ass out of there we have work to do." Amir said.

"Heyyy! Heyy! I can feel my foot. You grew my foot back!" James yelled, excitedly.

Amir handed James a set of jeans, underwear, new combat boots, and a partially torn t-shirt with the word pain printed on it. James put the clothes on and got up standing once again on two feet. The tank was able to replicate his foot from data saved on a thumb drive Dr. Garcia had taken before leaving the training center. Walking around again James felt like he was more energetic than before he went into the tank. Touching his teeth again with his tongue made him smile.

"Sorry, the information I had was pretty old so I had to attempt a full body rebuild for you. It seems to have worked." Dr. Nasser said surprised.

"Wait, what!? You didn't know if this would work? Old data like how old?"

"Just from the last time you were in one of the tanks about ten years ago. This is the first time I have ever attempted something like this on a full body repair. It was going to be our only shot at getting your brain re-jogged." Dr. Nasser said.

"Listen to me James, the Russians are also after you and

me trying to find out what happened to their Zeta. Since I was busy getting covered in my co-workers blood I didn't see exactly what happened to the other one." Alyson said.

"I blew its creepy little head open all over the place. It was dead pretty early on." James said.

"Well that is good, knowing he is no longer a threat and bad since the Russian's believe he is being hidden. I will go make some calls and see what we can do." Amir said, walking away.

A pinging sound was coming from one of the monitors alerting them someone was coming towards the garage. They all looked towards the monitors seeing Liam getting out of a massive military truck parking next to Alyson's SUV. Dr. Nasser pressed a button next to the monitor and it began to make a brief audio screech.

"Hold on Liam, we're coming up." She said.

They all headed out of the underground bunker to the surface with James being the last one out. Liam saw James and began to become emotional, crying as he reached over and gave him a strong hug. Alyson went over to the truck Liam was driving and started talking to someone sitting in the back of the truck. Dr. Nasser and Amir got into the SUV Alyson had driven into the building and left without saying anything. Liam pulled himself back wiping tears of joy from his cheek looking over James still holding onto his shoulders.

"Ohh Hun, I am so glad to see you in one piece. You look a little fitter and younger too. What's your secret?" Liam said sniffling.

"They threw me in the regen tank and this is how I turned out. Who is in the truck?" James asked.

"Mr. Curtis Goodwin is with us on our new mission."

"Huh, why? What new mission?"

"We are a five person team now. Didn't Amir tell you?

Oh, I guess not, he must have rushed off again. Well, we have been tasked with bringing in Jim Berthlow, Fred, and anyone else they are associating with. Ideally alive but they say dead is okay as long as we don't blow up the bodies."

"How is Fred still alive, or even Jim? What happened after the explosion?" James asked, puzzled.

"It is one of those weird things Honey, I was kicked outside with both my legs broken and luckily I slid into a ditch keeping my delightful self-alive. As I came too from going unconscious I saw Jim's screaming burning body push you out in the explosion. The robot suit Fred was wearing was missing the jet fighter middle thingy when they investigated the burnt out remains."

"So they could be dead?"

"Could be, won't cut it we have to find out for sure. Plus the Russians think we stole their little gray man."

James could hear shifting around going on in the truck as Alyson walked over to talk to James and Liam. Curtis appeared like an unkempt long hair biker carrying a tool box jumping down from the back of the truck. He walked up to James handing him the tool box. James opened up the box and found polished platinum metal pieces being held in place with a grey foam.

"Hey Ya, I found this and cleaned it up for ya." Curtis said.

Twenty eight pieces of various sizes of platinum laid in the box almost calling to James, he stuck his left elbow over the box. The pieces re-assembled his left arm into its former platinum prosthetic. James clenched his hand opening and closing his fist looking at the single missing fingertip. The missing finger tip on his middle finger was last seen stabbing into Jim Berthlow's eyeball.

"Well, let's go get these fuckers." James said, looking up at everyone.

CHAPTER 23
BACK TO ABNORMAL?

Looking out of the building the heat from the pavement whisked into the air giving it a watered down reflection. James had gotten all of his tools back except for his gun and the tip of his finger. Wearing a gun-belt over an untucked t-shirt with holes, blood stains, and small tares, James did not appear to be a trained field agent. He was ready to go, hopeful Amir was going to come back with his gun. Everyone waited for over 20 minutes for Amir to return. He came back in a black SUV without his wife and a panicked look on his face.

"We have to go, now! No time for me to explain we have to move out of here!" Amir shouted with a panic in his voice.

No one said anything back they all hopped into the SUV with Amir as he made his way to the gate at the front of the Military base. Amir stopped to the right of the gate and got out of the SUV walking over to the gate guard. They seemed to exchange a few words as Amir handed the keys to the black SUV to the guard, hurrying back. Amir opened the driver side door only to stick his head inside looking around at everyone.

"We have to go out of here. Go three miles out west and

meet at the Motel with three boarded up windows in a row. You will know it when you see it. We are about to be chased by the local law enforcement. Just do as I say and go now!" Amir said, still panicked slamming his hand on the roof.

Curtis, Amir, James, Alyson, and Liam split off running in different directions, after the first mile they were near city streets with allies they could disappear into. Sirens and screeching tires could be heard along with shouting as the police closed in on Curtis. Helicopter blades chopping at the air over head could be heard above them. Alyson ran into a clothing store and bought a beanie and an overcoat to conceal herself.

Amir ran onto a city bus taking him slowly closer to the motel as the bus stopped at every street corner. Liam ran into James at a convenience store as James was buying three cans of Yak wintergreen and a basic blue baseball cap. There was a problem at the register when James realized he had absolutely no cash on him. James pushed the cans to the side with the hat acting like he was going to his car to grab his wallet. Liam left the convenience store before James dropping a fifty dollar bill on the ground as he left.

James grabbed the bill and bought his hat and Yak leaving a different crossing direction than Liam. Running down the street a city bus with Amir on it passed behind James, and Alyson came up to the parking lot of the motel. As Liam crossed the street to the motel a police car flew behind him as he stepped onto the curb of the parking lot. Another police car's brakes squealed as it slid to a stop at the entrance to the parking lot of the motel. James was watching from the alley across the street hiding in the shadows.

Amir got off the bus a few hundred feet from where James was standing, also stopping to watch what was happening with the cop car at the motel. The passenger door for the police car opened up as the driver hunkered down not to be seen. The cars lights and sirens were going wild as the cars motor began to rev up to redline with the car door being slammed closed. A figure was standing as the car went down the road crashing a few blocks away.

It was Curtis smiling as he jogged over to Alyson and Liam both grabbing onto their holstered guns. Taking their hands off their guns James and Amir ran across the street as Amir waved everyone over to a round sewer drain cover in the corner of the motel parking lot. Amir flipped the cover up like a coin in the air grabbing the spinning lid while everyone went down a metal ladder.

"So, is that a fake manhole cover? Since they weigh almost 250 pounds to stop people from climbing into underground areas they aren't supposed to." James asked.

"Go ahead and lift it up." Amir said, looking down at James pulling the lid closed with a loud clang.

"Whoa, check this place out. It's like an underground apartment." Curtis said.

The room underground was the size of the motel and parking lot above with 15 foot ceilings. It was wide open with couches, chairs, wall-mounted TV screens, freestanding clothing racks with clothes, guns mounted up covering one of the walls, ammo boxes in every corner, and a simple shower curtain rod with a curtain to cover the only toilet in the room. Cinderblocks painted white with concrete flooring was the only color to the room. Four hanging fluorescent lights lit up the room with one of them buzzing and flickering.

"Wow Amir, is this where you live?" James asked.

"It is just one of many of the secret bunkers my team has in case anything like this happens." Amir said.

"Umm..Amir you gotta explain the "like this" part. What did you do to have the boyz in blue to chase us? Unpaid parkin' tickets would be my first guess." Liam asked.

"And what about your wife? You left her behind?" Alyson asked.

"She is safe, at least safer than we are. Everyone take a seat and I will explain." Amir said.

James sat down on the far left side of the couch with Alyson next to him, Liam and Curtis sat down on the right side with everyone slightly nudging each other on the couch. Amir stood a few feet in front of everyone getting ready to explain what was going on. As Amir was readying to give his statement James began to pop open a can of Yak wintergreen placing a plug in his lower lip. Just as he went to close the can with his left hand his needle sharp finger tips pierced the can open.

"Shit, sorry." James said.

"Stop you're getting it everywhere!" Alyson yelled.

"Here take this and this." Amir said sternly, handing James a plastic cup and a small trash can.

"What a waste. Damnit. Did anyone happen to pick up the finger caps for these?" James said, moving his fingers on his left hand.

Alyson handed him an evidence bag with his rubber finger tips in it. James put four of them on leaving the middle one in the bag placing it in his front jean pocket.

"Thank you." James said.

"Are you done!?" Amir snarled.

"I think so, carry on." James said, sitting back on the couch.

"So, as some of you know the Russians were watching James to find out if he had any new info on their missing Zeta. When I left you earlier I went to tell them it was confirmed dead. Which leaves us with a plus since they told me they would not interfere with our investigation of our Zeta known as Fred." Amir said.

"Cool, so we are off the hook with them now. Right?" Alyson asked.

"Not exactly, they are giving us a week to prove Fred is handled, with hard evidence of his death or having him turned over to them. Since our Government would never allow us to turn him over killing him will be our only option. We are going to need to pick up some recording gear to send video to the Russians. Myself, Curtis, and Alyson will carry the body camera gear which will upload live to both the US and Russian secret video servers."

"Whoa.. whoa." James said.

"What is it now James? Do you have a problem with this? Both you and Liam have issues with delicate electronics. That is why it has to be us three." Amir said.

"No, just getting a killer buzz. First time I have had chew in over three months. Sorry." James said.

"Both squads have been officially dissolved after the incident in Texas. I am the only living member of the Termination squad as you may or may not know. While James was sitting in the holding cell in Texas the two helicopters my crew used were shot out of the air by anti-aircraft weapons leaving me with damaged legs and one arm completely sheared off. That is when I called Curtis to give you the documents he gave you in Texas." Amir said.

"Looks like they fixed ya good enough for now. Ain't gonna get them parts from the auto part store are ya?" Curtis asked.

"No, I guess not. I was out of everything for a month with members of my squad slowly dying on hospital beds next to me. Dr. Garcia only recently discovered a recovery tank and found out all the others had been destroyed by Fred. Lucky for James we were able to use it before being kicked off the base." Amir said.

"James hun, just so you know the move to eliminate the Recovery and Termination squad was made after the number crunchers found it was cheaper to use robots instead. It makes me sick. The remaining enhanced were supposed to be implanted explosive chips to eliminate the need to have us chase them down. All except Curtis of course." Liam said.

"Why not Curtis, and how in the hell did he sneak out of the Remediation jail after a month?" James asked.

"Well I am retired, and ya know it was an extra money type job. I been getting paid for a long time to just go to jail and do an assessment of how things is handled." Curtis said.

"I was wondering the same thing but never got the chance to ask. Please tell me I did good on the ass exam." Liam said.

"Damnit Liam, you're making me laugh so hard. Not an ass exam an assessment, besides all you did was pick him up from a bench. I think he means he assess the Jail not you, ya goof." Alyson said.

"Okay now everyone settle down, I have some other things you need to know. Our accounts have all been emptied by Fred to fund whatever the hell he is doing. Some more good news is my contact told me we had only a few minutes to leave the base earlier as we are all being charged for capital murders and conspiracy. They are going to charge us all with the deaths of our squads since Fred technically does not exist to the world and we are easy scape goats. On the other side of the coin if we can upload the video to our Government the charges will be cleared. Another helping of shit to add to this pile is we are not going to receive a break from our own government. One last thing a note from evidence gathered at the scene in Texas was left stuck into the gate after our Government took over. It simply said "Ya'll forgot somethin'."" Amir said.

"So, on the run with no money, wanted for death

sentence crimes, and probably going on a suicide mission with no chance of survival? Like I said earlier let's go get these fuckers!" James shouted.

"Plan is to grab some gear to locate Fredo and go back to Texas for any clues he left there?" Curtis asked.

"Yes, exactly. James and Liam will go to Texas and Alyson, myself, and Curtis will acquire the tracking gear outside of Bermuda. Someone Curtis has ties with will be helping us out." Amir said.

"Well, did anyone happen to pick up my gun Rust?" James asked.

"Rust? You mean your meteor gun?" Amir asked back.

"Meteor gun? What are you talking about?"

"Your gun, like my two shorter barreled revolvers is made out a piece of meteorite with steel alloy inner barrel and internal parts. Liam has the exact same gun as you, how did you not figure this out?" Amir asked.

"Ha..hahahahaaha..I told him it was camouflage and he needed to rub it all over himself. It has been my longest running joke. He even calls it "Rust" since he never tried to clean or oil the outside of it. Here take a look at mine honey." Liam attempted to hand his gun to James.

James pushed Liam's gun away and stood up.

"Hell, he probably doesn't even know about why he isn't deaf from firing with no ear protection on either." Amir said.

"So, no one got my gun? What hearing loss my ears are fine." James grumbled.

"Nope, I would have grabbed it if it was in the evidence. Did they not explain the ear web thing to you back at training? You are making a stupid face, so they basically altered our ear drums with tiny hairs in a web pattern. Keeps us from losing our hearing. You really never shot a gun before all of this? Don't give me that stupid look." Alyson said.

"How the hell are we going to get out of here and

shouldn't we load up on some of these rifles?" James asked, a little lost in some of the new revelations.

"We are going to split up, plus carrying a rifle is an easy way to get picked up by law enforcement. There are two older model sedans I had my wife buy a few weeks ago, and we parked them behind the motel. The monitors show a live feed of outside and we will make a move here soon when the police move out. They have already checked the motel and looks like we will be leaving soon enough. There is a paper map in the glove box of each car leading to a private airstrip. Everyone try to sleep and we will sneak out early." Amir said.

Amir pulled out some old Army surplus cots from behind the couch they were sitting on and the men let Alyson sleep on the couch. Not because she was a woman, but because she had already called dibs on it. They all got a few hours of sleep before Amir startled everyone awake by banging his hand on a metal ammo box. They all began to stand up shuffling around and began to load up on handgun ammo. James had loaded his speed loaders with no gun while Curtis took a cushion from the couch stuffing a .308 rifle into it.

"One thing before we go we need a team name. I was thinking the Home and Garden Crew. Starring Amir Nasser the Garden Hose, James Hawthorne the Metal Rake, Liam Harper the Battery Charger, Curtis Goodwin the Yard Critter, and finally Alyson Whitmoore the Bad Ass." Alyson said, smirking.

"We can discuss this later, it's go time." Amir said.

Amir climbed up the metal rung ladder first popping the manhole cover open allowing the others to run around the motel then closing the manhole cover. One of the sedans was a small four door with silver paint and a dented front fender. The other sedan wasn't a sedan but a small hatchback mostly red with different colored front fenders missing its front bumper. Amir, Curtis, and Alyson got into the silver car driving away cautiously, while James and Liam got into the hatchback. Liam drove as James navigated them four miles down to the airfield.

Two small prop passenger planes were in the hangar Amir had led them to. Amir started up the first plane right away ready to take off with Alyson and Curtis. Liam climbed into the other plane with James, as they followed Amir up and out of the runway. Amir had left instructions in the plane if they needed to land on another airfield with coded names and flight clearances. Liam appeared comfortable flying the small plane while James felt a little worried about Liam's flight skills.

"So, how do we know we are going to Texas? There is no GPS in this thing. How do you know how to fly an airplane?" James asked.

"Oh, honey don't you worry. I have flown a few times in the military and also dated a few guys with planes in my days on this Earth. It is pretty easy we fly low and follow the interstate south west to where we need to go. Once we see a major city we can alter direction." Liam replied.

"Okay, we should be there in a few hours then?"

"Yep, a whole lot less hours than driving. Make yourself comfortable and don't wet your pants."

CHAPTER 24
RETURN TO TEXAS

Liam was able to successfully navigate them to a landing strip ten miles from where the police station James was interrogated. They left the plane in an open hangar trying to figure out how to contact anyone they may know in the area. Both James and Liam did not possess any type of phone or communication device. They left the airport and jumped onto the back of a stopped semi at a stop sign standing on the under rung safety bar on the trailer, gripping onto the rear door opening bars.

"Well, if we don't get attention for carrying guns then going on the freeway will definitely get us plenty of attention!" James yelled over to Liam.

"Just enjoy yourself we might not make it out of this one! Besides guns in Texas don't matter. Whoo hoo!" Liam shouted as they went out onto the freeway.

The truck was heading south the direction they wanted to go when a police cruiser flashed its lights behind the truck causing the driver to pull over on the freeway. As soon as the truck stopped James and Liam stood still on the back of the truck like statues. Liam and James slowly climbed down as the cop began to scream over the loud speaker in his car.

"Get down on the fucking ground, hands out over your heads. Don't move!"

"What? Sorry I can't hear you! James go left!" Liam yelled.

James ran left towards the police cruiser's passenger door and as he got to the door a loud bang rang out. Liam fired his gun through the cruisers windshield smashing the officers badge into his bullet proof vest. Ducking down at the passenger door James slowly peeked his head up as Liam pulled the cop from the car. The cop went to grab his gun when Liam sent a mild shock through the cop's body leaving him motionless and tensed up on the ground. Liam backed the cruiser up quickly then gassed the car forward around the disabled cop heading towards the police station where Reba was.

"Unit Forty Seven, what is your status?" The radio buzzed.

"Code 4." Liam said over the radio.

"Unit Forty Seven what is your call sign?" The radio buzzed again.

Liam put his right hand on the radio and gave a quick blue blast of electricity to the radio causing it to smoke and spark. James had never seen this side of Liam and he was beginning to like it. Most of the time Liam was very low key easy going, but something had changed.

"Oh my, I am giving into some of my aggressive tendencies. Please don't get the wrong impression." Liam said apologetically.

"Ha, I was wondering when the gloves were going to come off. Nice job Liam. Turn right up here we are almost there."

They shared a quick smile then laughed at the situation

as they pulled the cop car with a bullet hole through the windshield into the police station. Liam even parked in one of the reserved handicapped spots in the front of the station. The car they had stolen so happened to be a state trooper and was not one of the cars at the station. James and Liam ran into the station asking the guy at the front desk to talk to a detective. Just as they began to ask for a detective James recognized one of the officers sitting off to the side with an arm brace.

"Hector!" James yelled.

Hector walked over looking at James with his metal arm as if he had seen a ghost. James and Liam stepped over to talk to Hector. He was solemn for a brief moment not talking waving for them to follow him with his good arm. Hector led them to Sam's office where a slimmer figure sitting behind a desk wearing a clean light blue button up shirt, with a dark brown tie, and a clean shaven face was staring at them.

Liam and James stepped into the office still standing as Hector closed the door behind them. It looked a little like Sam, but so much had changed about his appearance from the last time James had seen him. Liam glanced at James expecting him to start talking to the guy, but James' brain was still trying to figure out who the guy was.

"Sam?" James asked.

"Yes, it is me Mr. Hawthorne if I do recall. Well, you look like you are doing pretty well, aside from a ripped up shirt." Sam said.

"Well, here is the thing Sam we really need to talk to Reba. Is she out or somewhere else about?"

"Reba moved to Dallas shortly after the explosion at the oil refinery. She was gone when I finally was able to come back two weeks ago."

"God Damnit, Sam if you are fucking with me!"

"Do not use the Lords name in vain in my office! The only reason I am not throwing you into a cage or puttin' a bullet in your head is because of this here cross I wear on my neck. I should thank you for what you did."

"What are you talking about?"

"Yeah, I wanna know too." Liam said.

"You see, when you busted up my face I suffered what would've been a fatal heart attack. If I wasn't rushed to the hospital I would've died. After I woke up from surgery the doc said I would be dead in a week if it wasn't for being rushed to the hospital with my face busted up. Also having my jaw wired shut for two months helped with my weight loss. Naturally I believe you are just a mischievous worker of God and you saved me."

"Weird." James and Liam said at the same time.

"Did Reba happen to leave anything here like a note or something in her log book here for me?" James asked.

"She did leave a box here with something you might want." Sam said.

Sam picked up a white file box sitting in the corner of his office and went to put it down on his desk. The box made a thud as it slipped out of his hands above the table. Sliding the lid off of the box Sam pulled out Rust. He placed it on the desk and put the empty box back in the corner of his office.

"I thought it was some sort of wooden toy gun until I picked it up. Thing is for sure heavier than it looks. All she left me was a note on top of the box saying to please make sure James Hawthorne gets this. Not sure if it works or not since it looks like a solid piece of rusted iron." Sam said.

James took his rusty revolver into his right hand holding the hammer halfway back and fanning the cylinder with his left hand moving it up to his ear. He took a pen off of Sam's desk and pressed it as far into the barrel as he could. Then he turned the barrel down on the desk and smashed it down three times with the pen, a barrel shaped wad of dirt came out of it. With his right hand he unlatched the cylinder flicking his wrist in a lighting quick motion loaded eight rounds of .44 with his left hand.

"Whelp, guess it is clean enough." James said.

"I've never seen a gun like that one. Where did you get it?" Sam asked.

"Same place I got this." James said, lifting his left hand into the air.

"Excuse me, also the same place I got these." Liam said, putting his translucent black hands in the air making them glow with electricity.

"Come on Liam we need to go."

"One last thing, you look a lot younger than before we met, how is that possible?" Sam asked.

"Simple, nano-reconstruction of my cellular body using my preserved DNA matrix." James replied.

James stepped out of the door first with Liam right behind him they went outside to find the car they had driven to the station was gone. For a moment they thought they would need to steal another police cruiser. Hector came around with a set of keys and placed them into Liam's right hand.

"Please go and don't ever come back." Hector said pleadingly.

They ran down the steps of the station looking for a car for a brief moment when James saw it. Parked on the street in a fire zone was his motorcycle. Liam smiled looking at James for a brief moment.

"Can I drive it?" Liam asked.

"Damn, how many times has this thing had the ignition changed? No, give me the keys."

"Where am I gonna sit honey, there is no back seat?"

James took the keys starting the motorcycle up as it rumbled to life he pulled the rear fender off and flipped it over locking it in place behind his seat upside down. The extra wide tire on the back of the cruiser made the flipped over fender into a wide enough seat for a passenger. It was an all blacked out cruiser with only a headlight for lights. It was the only vehicle he had ever purchased in his entire time as a recovery agent. The bike had a tricked out 200 plus rear wheel horsepower motor, bigger brakes, turn down short exhaust pipes, drag bars, and some custom wheels.

"What is your gas mileage on this testosterone piggy!?" Liam yelled over the sound of the bike.

"Ninety miles, if I am lucky. Good news for us is it looks like we have a full tank for now!" James yelled back.

James sat on the bike as Liam awkwardly maneuvered behind him and they headed towards the oil refinery. As soon as they got to the refinery they couldn't believe what they were seeing. The whole refinery was gone and a vast parking lot was in place of the fence and the warehouse they battled Fred in. Behind the parking lot they saw the entire refinery was torn down to an empty dirt lot with a sign for a future construction site of some automobile manufacturer.

They had decided it would be best to head back to the plane since there was nothing else left there for them. Once they got back to the airport they realized Amir did not leave anyway to communicate with them. Liam decided to fuel up the plane while James turned the two way radio on to listen for something from Amir. It was getting dark on their second day with only five days left to stop Fred or face attacks from the Russians.

Liam got the plane fueled up and they sat on the ground outside as James spit on the ground the radio buzzed with a familiar voice.

"Please don't spit on my plane." Amir said, from the radio.

Liam grasped the radio. "Where are we supposed to meet up?"

"Sit tight for the next 20 minutes we will pick you up. Over and out."

Liam put the radio microphone back on the radio and rummaged around the small interior of the plane. He found one MRE pack and split it with James since they had not eaten since the night before. As they finished their meal they could hear a loud explosion over head as a black aircraft approached in the distance. The craft came down the runway stopping outside of the hangar they were sitting in.

"I sure do hope they had a more productive day than we did. Of course I did get my gun back but we have nothing else to go on." James said.

"Looks like we are about to find out, get ready just in case it isn't them." Liam said, taking his gun out.

CHAPTER 25
GREY DAY

As Amir flew south east with Liam and James going south west there was a growing concern over the place they were going. Curtis was the only one to know where to go leaving him to switch with Amir mid-flight. Alyson sat in a fold down seat behind the co-pilot, she was now less cramped up since Amir switched with Curtis. The main worry was Curtis did not have the best memory since the mercury powered nano-bots in his system often would distort his reality.

"How are you doing back there Alyson?" Amir asked.

"As good as I can do. You know the guy flying this plane told me last night he thought the walls were melting in the bunker and he needed some ice from the couch to stop it?"

Curtis grinned as the plane weaved back and forth in the air, dodging invisible traffic in the air. Alyson gripped her seatbelt tightly as nervous sweat beaded down her face. Amir shut his eyes waiting until they got to where they were going. After a few hours the slightly erratic flight became erratic as the plane nose-dived towards the ocean before pulling up flying straight again.

"The fuuck are you doing Curtis!" Amir screamed.

Curtis didn't react and kept going straight focused on where he was going. Alyson was tensed up gripping her seat belt breathing in and out heavily trying to calm herself. As soon as Alyson had got herself settled again the instruments in the small plane began beeping faster and faster. The gauges spun giving no bearing as a dense white fog built up around them. Amir was now beginning to panic as Curtis put on a pair of sunglasses he had hanging from his shirt collar.

The plane made what felt like a pull upward then began to dive straight down towards the ocean. Amir and Alyson braced for impact the best they could as they seemed to be destined to die at this moment. Just before the plane was at the ocean surface Amir could see a small circle of seagulls sitting perfectly still on the water's surface as the plane barreled down on them.

Curtis remaining calm was pulling the throttle back, and at the instant they were to hit the surface of the water, the plane was landing on a runway surface. There were no hangars just an open runway with rolling green hills behind it. As the plane eased to a stop both Alyson and Amir took in a deep breath. Alyson flung the door open as fast as she could with Amir behind her. Curtis casually stepped out looking around he grabbed a rock and started to talk to it.

"Hey Marco, it's Curtis ya know the favor you be owe'n me, well I really need it now." Curtis said, talking to the rock.

A small figure came out from behind them waving its right arm in the air from forty feet away. When the figure got closer it looked like a little person standing three and a half feet tall wearing a light yellow polo shirt, khaki slacks, and brown dress shoes. The figure was bald with dark sun tanned skin and bright blue eyes.

"Curtis you can stop talking to rocks, come on over here

and climb in my car. Let us all go back to my place so we can talk." Marco said.

"Marco ya look a little different. Did ya get sick or somethin'?" Curtis asked.

"We don't got time for your shit Curtis, we should go with him if he can help us. Remember we are fighting the clock on this." Alyson said.

Amir stared at Alyson admiring her commitment to keeping them on track and not letting Curtis ramble on as he was known to do. They followed Marco away from the plane back the way he came and ran into a solid object in front of them. Marco's car was covered in a screen material with several cameras being used to make the car appear invisible. Clicking a key lock in his hand Marco's massive boat sized sedan was now visible. They got in heading towards what appeared to be the grass going towards one of the hills.

As they got to the grass it began to turn from grass to a white fog then an open road leading to a small town with small houses. Marco parked in his driveway waving for everyone to follow him into his house. The house was a single story building with an average doorway, counter tops, appliances, and door handles moved much lower for a smaller person's convenience.

Marco removed a silver necklace he was wearing around his neck and his appearance faded as it changed. His skin turned from dark tan to a dark grey, his fingers changed from five to four elongated fingers, his head was relatively bigger, ears on the side of his head faded away into holes on the side of his head, and his eyes changed to an oval shape sitting diagonally on his face. The clothes he was wearing did not change, and his facial features remained.

"Ahh, now this is better. The disguise gives me a

headache after about an hour. Seeing no one jumping to run out the door is a good sign." Marco said.

"How come you aren't chattering your teeth, or soundin' like a guy with a lisp?" Alyson asked.

"I am a second generation Zeta and it is kind of similar to someone from another country being second generation. My parents sounded like chatterboxes making chattering sounds and hissing. It is a terrifying language in comparison to the ones here on Earth." Marco said.

"Marco we have a short time frame and Curtis over there going through your fridge said you could help." Amir said.

Curtis was carrying two armfuls of food to the counter behind the fridge making himself at home eating everything Marco had.

"Ya got any mayo?" Curtis asked.

"No, disgusting stuff. There are some bread rolls fresh made in the cabinet next to the fridge. Make enough for everyone." Marco said.

"Marco we need to stop Fred and his insane plan!" Alyson yelled.

"Alright here is what I can tell you. Since Fred has not proven to be a viable threat to the Zetas on Titan. It is similar to police saying they cannot arrest someone if they are not actively committing a crime. Even though we have proof he is dangerous here, they don't believe he has the means to propel his group into outer space, let alone Saturn's moon. It is much easier to ignore him until he does something to disrupt trade or actually does attempt a direct attack." Marco said.

Marco grabbed a coffee mug off the counter swirling it around in his hands looking into the liquid in the cup. Curtis made some simple sandwiches out of bread rolls, meat, cheese, and mustard. Amir stood crossing his arms next to Alyson as Curtis handed out sandwiches to everyone. Marco was still swirling the coffee mug around when Amir threw his sandwich at Marco knocking him over.

"I've been a patient person my whole life, even as I was being dismembered in Afghanistan. Now for the first time in my life I've lost all of my patience. Now all I have is this..." Amir said, drawing both of his guns on Marco.

As Amir began to level his guns on Marco his arms began to tremble as the guns appeared to become heavier in his hands. Suddenly as Amir slowly got his guns to finally level his arms dropped down to his sides dropping both of his revolvers to the ground. His once slightly bent knees locked forcing him to a complete standing upward position. Amir's heels slide together with his arms straight down at his sides frozen.

"So, it does work." Marco said.

"What the hell is this? I can't move!" Amir shouted.

"As an avid inventor of weapons for the Military I added a final touch to each of my inventions. I placed a coded inhibitor in each one of my creations before production on any of them began. The inhibitor was simple enough to tell everyone it was a necessary component so each and every unit carried it. No one knows what the part is or what it does except for me."

"Release me!!"

"You know I will after you cool off for a few minutes and let me go over some of the details of what you and your small group are facing."

Marco pulled out a chair sitting at his kitchen table waving for Alyson and Curtis to follow him. They sat around the square four chair table with Marco at the back facing Amir so he could hear what he had to say. Curtis grabbed Amir's sandwich and started to eat it while Marco lifted his left hand into the air. He pointed to a bracelet he was wearing on his wrist with several charms on it. The bracelet was four rows wide with a dozen charms going around each row.

"Do you know what these are?" Marco asked, looking at Amir.

"Ha, ha, ha, those is from yer kids cereal collection." Curtis chuckled.

"No, Curtis these are not charms. They are inhibitors for each of my 46 creations and two of my fathers. He only thought about doing inhibitors on his last two creations." Marco said.

"Alright we get it you control your toys, now can we move on. Is there a part where we get help?" Alyson asked.

"One moment Alyson, Curtis try and strike me."

"Are ya sure?"

Marco nodded in approval as Curtis stood up and went to swing his fist at Marcos head with a right hook. Marco went flailing onto the ground as Curtis' punch connected knocking him out cold. Alyson jumped up to help Marco as Curtis began to turn grey and seizure on the floor next to Marco. Curtis' muscles were tensed up and he was flailing his body on the ground like a fish. Alyson splashed cold water on Marco's face waking him up. A little dazed Marco finally got up and walked back to his chair trying to figure out what happened.

"Well, I guess it took a little longer for that one to kick in. Curtis was part of the second creation I invented. First I will turn his inhibitor off then I will turn yours off Amir." Marco said, slightly shaken.

Marco simply ran his right hand over the bracelet turning the inhibitors off allowing for Curtis and Amir to move again. Curtis had vomited out the sandwich he ate all over the floor, he stood up slowly staggering his way back to the chair he was sitting in. Amir kneeled down and picked up both of his revolvers, holstering them, walked over and sat in the empty seat at the table.

"Ya told me to hit ya, now I'm hungry all over again." Curtis said.

"As you are all aware I have retired from inventing things, not much of a creator anymore. It has been about ten years since I retired. Since retirement has bored me, I decided I would keep an eye on my creations. I have had great success with tracking all of my creations and recently a few of my creations were stolen from a secret storage location. It has been about five months and I have not been able to triangulate where these 30 creations have gone. I have a strong feeling they are something you will encounter. There is something I have here to show you." Marco said.

Marco walked over to his fridge and brought back four beer cans. It did not seem like an appropriate time to drink a beer. Marco popped the beer tab open tossing it to Curtis to catch. As Curtis attempted to catch the can it bounced off of his chest and he began to seize again flopping himself back onto the ground. Amir stood up immediately with his arms straight down at his sides again unable to move.

"Temporary inhibitors disguised as beer cans. I think these may come in handy especially if my creations are in Fred's hands. They only work for thirty seconds so use them wisely."

Curtis picked himself up from the floor for a second time and Amir sat back down as Marco gave them a six pack of inhibitor cans. Marco also slid a pack of cigarettes across the table to Curtis. Alyson was given a duffle bag with .44 magnum ammo as well from Marco. Each item appeared ordinary use to them with nothing appearing to stand out.

"So, ya think I'm a smoker?" Curtis asked.

"No, there are twelve self-injectable syringes in there filled with a mix I worked on to try to stop you from having such bad side effects from injecting poisonous metal into your veins. You will only need to take one shot a week and they will power your nano-bots for that time. The ammunition I have given you will shoot the same as similar grain magnum ammo, but the bullets if shot into something they stick into will heat and explode. I believe it is similar to a small plastic explosive blast. They have not been tested in the field yet, so hopefully they get the job done." Marco said.

"The inhibitor cans knock out people like Amir and Curtis, so what use do we have for them?" Alyson asked.

"About six months ago a few of my old creations were sold to an unknown buyer, we can only assume is Fred. They are each sonar detecting with heat vision cameras setup with long range rifles to snipe out any threat set within their internal parameters. Each one of those cans sitting on the table have a 2460 foot range." Marco replied.

"So, how many did he buy? Also what will these cans do if James goes to throw one?" Amir asked.

"James? Oh, you mean Mr. Hawthorne. Nothing will happen to him since his invention pre-dates anything I have created. Fred purchased seven or eight of the bots. I don't know exactly how many he got. Since they were stolen and resold to him. They only have a half mile range so you may have only a slight challenge." Marco said.

They all glanced at each other uneasy with the challenges presented to them. Curtis stood up and began loading up on sandwiches, taking a paper bag full with him. Alyson began to speak then stood looking out one of the windows in the house. Amir sat back in his seat calculating a plan of attack in his head.

"How? I mean how the fuck do we do this?" Alyson said, pounding her fist on the window frame.

"Well, I did mention they use sonar so it is quite easy to disrupt their system from a distance of slightly over a half a mile away with one of these cans. Closing in and disabling them is another challenge. Make sure you keep track of your time since 30 seconds is all you have." Marco said.

"Alright I have a plan, let's move out of here and gather our other two crew members." Amir said.

Amir stood up ready to head for the door when Marco grabbed him by the hand leading him to the stairs in the back of the house. The others followed to the stairs leading up to the roof of the house where a vehicle similar to a stealth triangle bomber was. It was all black with an upper and lower portion separated by an invisible field. It looked like two flat triangles floating a few feet from each other still attached by an invisible force.

"You can take my drone. There is enough room for eight people inside of it. The upper section is what you could consider the motor to be and the lower section is the cargo storage area. This ship is an Earth built Zeta drone given to me by my father. It is completely undetectable by any current form of human system. I will fly you where you need to go. Look into the dome in the middle and talk to it. I will be able to see you here on my screen. I almost forgot, here are your cameras to carry in to show both the United States and Russia you are innocent." Marco stated.

They were each handed a pin the size of thumb tack with a little backing protector to pin to their clothing. Alyson stuck hers into the jacket she was wearing as Amir pinned his through the middle of his gun belt. Then it was Curtis' turn and he stuck his into his forehead smiling as Alyson and Amir both shook their heads in disapproval. Curtis pulled the pin from his forehead sticking it through his left ear instead, pinning it in place with the small metal backstop.

"Hand the cameras back to me. Here I will put them on these headbands. Alyson you can give these out to everyone to wear. Amir I have some two way inner ear radios you can use." Marco said, taking the pin cameras and sticking them into black headbands and handing them back with the earpiece radios.

"Cool, I always wanted to fly in a slice o' pizza." Curtis said.

A platform angled down allowing them to board the drone ship Marco was having them enter. Eight seats with harnesses were circling a metal ball in the middle of the ship. A white light was coming from the floor and ceiling almost blinding if it was stared at too long. They sat around the orb buckling in as the ships platform closed. There was no landing gear and it hummed gently with no indication of propulsion noise.

"We need to go to a location in Texas where James and Liam are. I am not sure exactly where it is, but they landed there a few hours ago in a small personal aircraft." Amir said, talking to the orb.

"Oh, I got them here. You have someone in the American Government looking out for you. These two could have been caught pretty easily if someone was using the back door system to look. Hold on you should be there in 4." Marco said.

"Can I speak to them on the planes radio?" Amir asked.

"Go ahead, I will set it to the frequency. All set go ahead and speak I will stay quiet." Marco said.

The orb went from a metal glowing ball into a clear overhead image of James and Liam. Amir could see Liam messing with the radio as James was leaning to spit on the tire of the plane.

"Please don't spit on my plane." Amir said, speaking into the orb.

Liam grasped the radio. "Where are we supposed to meet up?"

"Sit tight for the next 20 minutes we will pick you up. Over and out."

There was no sensation of movement from inside of the drone. No feeling of shifting, acceleration, directional change, or anything to indicate they had even left Marco's house. The only indication they had moved was the door opening to James and Liam standing outside of an airplane hangar with their mouths opened in awe with guns drawn.

"Get in Idiots! We have places to go!" Alyson shouted.

James and Liam climbed into the strange looking flying machine with a round orb in the middle of a circle of seats with Amir and Curtis buckled into five point harnesses. Alyson sat down next to Amir in an open seat buckling in, James and Liam sat down in two empty seats and buckled themselves in. The stair ramp door closed and a slight buzzing sound could be heard.

"So, we have about two hours of sunlight left once we land to go take out Fred. Lucky for us we are heading west and will gain some daylight." Amir said.

"It was rolling into seven here in Texas so some extra light should help. How do we know where he is?" James asked.

"A mutual friend gave us the last known location of where some military robots were delivered. These were things made only known to black ops programs and since we know of only one being that would want to purchase these bots we have to assume it is Fred." Amir said.

"Yeah, they got some boom boom bots we can't take lightly. Here have a sandwich if ya want I made some for ya guys." Curtis said.

"Hell, do we even know if he recruited anyone else besides the bots? I assume there is going to be an amazing force waiting for us." Liam said.

"Liam, don't worry we got some cool ammo and metal arm over there so we should be good." Alyson said.

The drone ship landed on a dirt road near a grove of redwood trees early in the evening. They all got out of the drone and Amir had everyone load up on the explosive ammo given to them by Marco. Alyson had to explain to James the cans were not beer cans and not to try to open them for a refreshment. Disappearing into the night sky the drone was gone flying back to where it had come from.

CHAPTER 26
DATE WITH A MONSTER

Amir gave everyone an inner ear radio to stay in radio contact with each other. Miniature camera head bands were worn by everyone to transmit everything they saw to the Russian and Americans black operations groups. The head bands were simple black stretchy bands with a bead in the middle for a camera. Once ready they began to move in an arrow pattern with 20 feet between them with Amir leading the point.

All of them had their guns drawn sweeping their coverage areas except for Curtis since he didn't remember to bring the gun he stuffed into the couch cushion. Amir tried to hand him one of his revolvers, but Curtis pushed his hand with the gun away.

Their radio's began to buzz. "James, I can't see your camera and only can barely make out your figure on the other cameras. Throw yours away, I thought this might happen. Your left arm is interfering with the camera. This can be advantageous and I would suggest you take point." The voice said.

"Who is talking?" James asked quietly.

"Sorry, it is Marco. I am not supposed to help but no one

else can hear what is being said over the radios besides me. So, I will help when I can." Marco said over the earpiece.

They all shifted positions with James moving from the right rear to the middle point with Amir moving to the right. From left to right they marched with Alyson on the left rear, Curtis middle left, James center, Amir middle right, Liam right rear. Curtis injected himself with the fluid Marco had given them while marching. On a dirt road with one direction to go they kept going up a low hill looking for any signs Fred had been in the area. They came to a metal bar gate locked on the road blocking any incoming traffic from going up the hill.

Curtis broke off from the formation sprinting far ahead of everyone after he spotted something on one of the Redwood trees a few hundred feet up the road from the gate. Everyone else moved slowly still as if nothing had changed sweeping with their handguns for any threats. Once they caught up with Curtis they could see he was talking to someone or something.

A redwood tree painted with blood had a torso chained to it with only a slowly moving head and blood stained fatigues. What was left of a person was able to talk and was talking to Curtis. It was Billy Drafter a level one James had brought in a few years ago. He wriggled and coughed out blood as he tried to talk, he was only able to burble out a few words to the group.

"Theirr alll dea.." was all Billy could say before his head slumped down.

"Curtis, where the hell is your ear piece?" Amir asked irritated.

"Tossed it, can't stand shit in my ears." Curtis said without a "Ya."

"What did he say?" Liam asked.

"Fred has been growing an army of Nozh creatures to set

loose on the Zetas. Billy here was trying to run away since Fred had killed the fifty guys he hired to help, testing his damn bots. He was able to wreck one of the trucks with a load of bots up the road before Jim caught him and did this." Curtis said.

"How come you can talk normal now?" Alyson asked.

"Must be the shot I took from Marco, I feel amped up but more clear headed than I have been in thirty plus years." Curtis said.

"We need to move off the road and try to see if we can find the truck Billy was talking about." Amir said.

They all nodded in approval except for Curtis who kept himself on the middle of the roadway. Alyson and Amir took the left side of the road as Liam and James took the right side using the trees as cover they moved at a faster pace. Liam spotted the truck on the right side of the road and Curtis ran up towards it. Alyson and Amir stayed hidden providing cover to Curtis as he approached the truck.

Curtis tore open the rear of the semi-truck trailer revealing two rows of robots hanging on rails from the roof of the trailer with one in the middle towards the rear of the trailer. There were a total of 15 robots in the trailer all were missing one key component. None of the robots had the battery packs that were supposed to be attached to their backs. Liam checked the cab and found a single bullet hole through the driver side of the windshield. Liam could see a bloodied seat with a hole through the right shoulder of the seat.

James remained at the back of the trailer looking around with Curtis for anything they could use. There was only the robots hanging in the back with nothing else in the trailer of the truck. Amir and Alyson headed back to the trailer of the truck as Liam walked slowly around the front of the truck noticing the driver side door was open with a slight trail of blood leading away up the hill. Then he saw a body fifty feet up the road lying face down.

"Shit, well there goes the plan of using the robots. What should we do now?" James asked.

"Plan B." Curtis said.

Curtis opened up the package of syringes given to him by Marco and injected all of them into his right forearm. Liam circled back to the rear of the truck as Curtis jumped out of the truck falling to his knees. They all stood back staring at Curtis as his veins began popping out and his eyes turned bloodshot red. He stood up and ran before anyone could had a chance to say anything he was past the dead truck driver.

"James! What did you tell him!?" Liam yelled.

"It wasn't James, it was crazy ass Curtis. He said somethin' about plan B and injected himself with the rest of the crap Marco gave him." Alyson said.

James took out his Yak and packed in a wad of chewing tobacco looking around at everyone as they all simultaneously exhaled. Curtis made it a few hundred feet past the truck driver when the sound of an electrical transformer exploding echoed through the redwoods. A bolt from a rail gun ripped through Curtis' right shoulder another electrical explosion followed with another bolt ripping through his left thigh. Curtis kept going until a third electrical explosion was heard with a bolt tearing through his right knee.

"What the fuck was that!?" James yelled.

"Those are rail guns being fired. I am afraid Curtis will not survive this." Marco said, through the ear piece.

"We have to help him, even if he is a weird asshole." Amir said.

"Alright my preciouses and lady let's get this thing rolling." Liam said.

"It looks like it got stuck in the soft soil." James said.

"So, disconnect the trailer and let's go!" Alyson said.

They were able to disconnect the trailer from the truck and Liam pulled away with James and Amir on the back of the truck. Alyson was running behind the truck when Liam set the cruise control to 20mph, then leapt away from the truck. James and Amir did the same jumping off the back of the truck as a it was being pelted from all sides by rail gun bolts until it went off the side of the road stuck on a redwood tree. It was dusk with the sun almost all the way down and night was closing in on them.

Suddenly the rail guns had all stopped firing as Curtis wounds were healing with the over clocked nano-bots. Curtis got up off the ground readying himself to takeoff running up the hill again when he was stopped by a figure with a skull face and hoses protruding from its head and back. The figure placed an orange ball into an opening on its chest and started to chuckle. Jim Berthlow was standing in front of Curtis with a remote in his hand, he turned off the robots to confront Curtis.

"So, you are the one trying to climb up my hill? I have not seen anyone recover like that before, but it is still far inferior to what I am." Jim said.

Curtis leapt forward quickly trying to throw right hook at Jim's face only to have his arm caught and crushed under Jim's grip. Jim tossed Curtis away on the ground leaving Curtis a few seconds to recover. This time Curtis tried to kick Jim's legs out with a powerful left swinging forward kick to the side of Jim's right leg. The bone in Curtis' shin had shattered as Jim stood un-phased by the kick. Curtis stood on one leg in extreme pain as the nano-bots tried to repair his leg.

"What in the fuck is that thing!" Amir yelled.

"It's Jim Berthlow. At least it was." James said.

"We have to try and help him." Amir said.

They were 100 yards away firing their guns at Jim whenever they had clear shots running and closing the gap between them quickly. Halting fire when Curtis would stand and firing after he would go down until they got closer and could see Jim grab a colossal metal bat off the ground next to him. James recognized the four bladed bat as Za's bat. Alyson and Amir closed in front of Jim as Liam and James circled around his back firing when they had clear shots, while constantly reloading.

"I thought these were exploding bullets. They have no effect on him." Alyson said.

Bullets were sticking to Jim's powdery white body like thumb tacks all over his body. They were less than 20 feet away when Curtis tried to throw a left uppercut but was suddenly stopped. Jim swung the giant metal club with only his left hand in a swiping motion slicing Curtis' left shoulder all the way through to his right shoulder. Blood covered the bat and Jim as Curtis' body dropped to the ground and his shoulders, arms, and upper torso fell to the ground.

"NOOOO!!!" Amir screamed.

Jim took the bat in both hands as Amir kept firing both guns then dropping his guns as Jim readied the bat on his right to make a baseball swing at Amir. As the bat swung Amir was able to place his hands out to grab it in both hands, but the force of the swing ripped both of Amir's arms off sending him spiraling to the ground. Alyson was caught by one of Amir's spinning arms knocking her to the ground. Jim put the bat over his head to crush it down on Alyson.

Liam was close enough to grab onto the tubes on Jim's back, Liam's forearms were glowing bright blue as he sent an explosive electrical charge through Jim's body. Jim tensed up frozen from the shock as James fired point blank at Jim's head. A small piece of platinum came out of Jim's left eye re-attaching to James' left hand as Liam released his electric grip. Jim fell to his knees dropping the bat and braced himself with his palms as Liam went back to send another charge through Jim's body.

Grasping onto the protruding hoses on Jim's back Liam tried to shock him again but was shaken off by Jim. James took his shirt off and rolled it up putting it over Jim's mouth like a horse bridle. Jim stood up with James on his back he grabbed the bat off the ground and went to swat James off of his back with it when Alyson shot Jim directly in the chest where the access port for the orange ball was. The bullet exploded the access port open leaving an opening in Jim's chest.

James released his entire arm onto the ground falling away from Jim backwards as Alyson grabbed James' ulna off the ground. Alyson shoved the sharp end of the metal bone into Jim's chest with a heavy thrust then let go. Liam gripped the metal bone sending an explosive shock through the opening not letting go as Jim's single right eye popped and his body began to smoke. Liam let go once again jumping backwards ready to fire his gun as Jim dropped to the ground falling forward.

"Is he?" Liam asked.

"Fuck, I hope so. Anyone got some grenades to shove up his ass?" James asked.

"How about this?" Alyson said.

Alyson shoved her gun up Jim's rectal cavity firing and entire clip as guts exploded out the front of Jim's body.

"After all this shit is hopefully over would you consider marriage?" James asked.

"Hey, can one of you assholes help me!" Amir yelled.

"Oh shit, he is still alive." Liam said.

"Over here you dickhead." Amir said.

Liam helped Amir to his feet as James held his arms up for him like they could be re-attached.

"They don't work like yours, I am not going to be much help with only two legs." Amir said.

"You can still kick? If you can still kick you are still useful. Get over yourself and let's go find the jackass behind all this." Alyson said.

James went back to Jim's corpse and pulled out his ulna from his chest reconnecting his left arm. Amir was covered in a black translucent hydraulic fluid from his arms being ripped off of his body. Alyson and Liam walked over to look over the pieces of Curtis laying on the ground, and saw a bloody liquid metal combination of body parts flung all over the dirt. It was dark now with a bright moonlit sky giving them decent vision in the night. James pulled the wad of chewing tobacco from his lip and threw it down on Jim's gaping monstrous face.

Liam looked around for the direction Jim had come from to try and locate where Fred was. Looking around all he could see was a thick grove of redwood trees coming to a crescent shape a few hundred feet behind Jim. It appeared there were trees removed from the area in a recent time period with some tracks into the dirt stopping at the center of the crescent. Suddenly Liam saw what he was looking for pointing up into the sky.

"Look up there, what is that thing?" Liam said.

"It looks like two large pyramids stuck together." James said.

"Rhombus is the shape you are trying to think of, dumb ass." Amir said.

"Hey Marco, you there? If you are what is that thing?" Alyson asked.

"Looks like a big problem. It is a ship, it spins releasing solid metal containers. When the containers crash to the ground they open up releasing whatever is packed into them. There are no records of any of these being around for over 2300 years on this planet. My people would call it a "Seeder" used to terraform planets with life. The last one used on Earth was used for destruction at the northern pole to trigger a massive sea level rise." Marco said, over the ear piece.

"So, this thing could've caused something like the destruction of Atlantis?" James asked.

"Yes, or several of Earth's more advance cultures when they got out of hand for the Zetas." Marco said.

The ship was a half mile long from tip to tip hovering at the top of the tree line horizontally. It glimmered in the moonlight not moving in the wind sitting completely still. It was broad in the center where a flash of bright light shot to the ground. The light was a white expansive laser beam focusing at the middle of the tree crescent.

"Quickly look for something resembling a garage door opener near or on Jim's body!" Marco yelled.

They looked around the ground where he was laying when Alyson found it in Jim's right pant pocket.

"Got it. Now what?" Alyson asked.

"Okay, this is very important. Hold the button down until it clicks in your hand then throw it away from you as far as you can." Marco said.

Alyson held the button down for thirty seconds until it made the click sound Marco had mentioned. She threw it down the hill seeing the hidden robotic killing machines come sprinting out of the woods to gather around it. The robots stood in a perfect circle around the device as they began beeping at the same time.

"Run away!" Marco shouted.

They all ran towards the crescent circle where the light beam was coming from when the robots beeping sped up.

Suddenly the battery packs all exploded destroying all of the robots. A blurry figure was coming down from the light above like a balloon being dropped from above. Instantly they recognized Fred wearing a skin tight black outfit with his oversized goggles.

"Get him!" Liam and James yelled at the same time.

Amir ran forward jumping shoulder first knocking Fred to the ground away from the light. Fred got up quickly scrambling back to the light beam as it changed from a white to a blue hue. Just as he reached for the light a hand grabbed his leg tossing him away again to the ground. It was Alyson drawing her gun down on him to keep him in place. Fred went to touch a button on his goggles when Alyson fired a shot to the right of him causing a small explosion. As Fred laid frozen in place Alyson reached forward taking his goggles off of his head with her gun pointed at his forehead.

"Quickly one of you needs to move into the light to board the ship!" Marco barked.

"I'll go!" James and Liam said at the same time.

James and Liam were standing shoulder to shoulder and Liam waved for James to go. Just as he was readying to run Liam placed his right hand on James' bare chest shocking him enough to knock him to the ground. James was laying on the ground with his left arm now disconnected.

Liam ran to the light, drawn up into the ship as the light dimmed and went out. James got back up surprised Liam would shock him and run ahead to the ship. The ship went up into the air making a quick westward movement aligning itself for space travel as it turned from horizontal to vertical.

All Amir, Alyson, and James could do was watch as it left them with Fred on the ground shivering with fear. James stood next to Alyson with his gun drawn on Fred, he fired one shot to the left of Fred closer than where Alyson had fired on Fred's right. Fred's arm opened up with a large gash from the explosion of the bullet.

"Which one of these fucking buttons brings him back!" James screamed at Fred pointing to the goggles.

"Itss onn auopilott." Fred chattered back.

"Liam the only way to stop the ship is to engage the metal guidance ball in the middle of the ship. It is probably glowing somewhere in front of you. If you can send a charge to it the ship will certainly explode. The other option is to see where it is going to take you, if you leave orbit we will lose communication with you." Marco said through the earpiece.

"Roger that. James, I loved you more than a brother and Alyson you were the best woman I've ever met. Amir, I will always remember how honest you were with me and loved you like a good friend. I will miss al..." Liam said, before the ship left orbit.

It was out of the atmosphere in a matter of seconds flying beyond the reach of visual and radio contact of their current devices. A flash appeared in the night sky of a distant explosion with meteor streaks coming back down in the distance. James holstered his gun and grabbed Fred aggressively from the front of his shirt with his right hand ripping Fred's shirt as he picked him up off of the ground. As soon as James had Fred up off the ground he threw him back down. Fred held both of his hands up trying to show he had given up.

"James, calm down and step back from him. We have choppers in bound and enough evidence to clear all of you. We need to bring him in for interrogation." Marco said.

James stepped back ten feet from Fred with Alyson still keeping her gun drawn onto Fred.

"Tell me Marco what will happen to him after the interrogation, will he go to prison or be executed for his crimes?" James asked.

"No, since he technically doesn't exist in the Earthlings world he will be reassigned to a different job without access to any of the tech he was using before. His knowledge is quite valuable and he will simply be monitored more closely." Marco responded.

"Hmm...That is kinda what I thought would happen." James said.

Blammm!!! James fired a single shot exploding Fred's head covering Alyson in blood and brain matter from the little monster. Amir started laughing as Alyson wiped blood and brain matter from her face, she also started laughing. James smiled with tears in his eyes as they all began to breakdown together.

The whipping of helicopter blades coming in from all sides was growing louder and louder. A small white drone dropped out of a helicopter from overhead spinning down towards them. The drone released tranquilizer darts as it spun to the ground. Amir was struck in the forehead as Alyson was struck in the thigh and James was struck in the right shoulder and left thigh. Everything went black for them as another team took over to evaluate what had happened.

CHAPTER 27
SEALED SECRET

They were awoken by a blaring overhead alarm finding themselves in individual rooms with grey concrete floors and cream colored steel doors with small slits for windows. There was a popping sound of the mechanical doors unlocking then sliding open followed by a loud clang. The room outside of the locked cells was a circle with thousands of doors making it a mile in diameter from one door to another across the room. Sunlight was shining through the roof of the circular building slowly getting darker as the roof spun closed. Only a small beam of light was shining directly in the middle of the room.

James saw Amir to his right stumbling out of his cell with a bed sheet wrapped around his leg. Amir's armless figure was getting closer to James as they both walked towards each other while walking toward the center beam of light. They saw Alyson walking from directly across the way also heading towards the beam of light. James lifted his left arm to wave only to find his arm was gone and was only waving his elbow. Amir began to chuckle at him then stopped when he realized James still has one good arm and he is missing two. James still had no shirt which didn't bother him since the room was relatively warm.

There was a broad circular table in the middle of the beam of light with two figures standing by it with three chairs. One was a short Asian woman in a black dress suit and the other was a tan bald little person wearing a black suit. On the table were three separate stacks of paper with three separate pens on top of each of them. Alyson made a hand gesture when they were closer to take them out and Amir shook his head "No."

"Amir, what is this place?" James whispered.

"It is the place you've been sending people for years. Rehabilitation for enhanced soldiers or you could also call it a prison." Amir whispered back.

"So, where do they execute the ones that fail this place?" James whispered.

"I think somewhere outside. It is somewhere in the middle of the desert. One time I visited it to better understand what the recovery group does." Amir whispered back.

"Lady and Gentlemen, I am General Misty Rail. Today we are here to discuss recent events and conditions of your release." Misty said.

Misty put her hand out signaling for them all to sit down in front of the stack of papers in front of them.

"Can I get a shirt and possibly an arm? Also who is this guy?" James asked, pointing at the guy next to her.

"That's Marco." Alyson and Amir both said at the same time.

"Marco there is no reason for your disguise here they all know enough." Misty said.

Marco twisted his wrist watch and was transformed from an image of a man in a suit to a Zeta with dark grey skin in a black suit.

"Let me just ask, what level of trouble are we in?" James asked.

"Well as for your two counterparts they are in no trouble at all, but as for you, you are in the deepest level of shit one can imagine." Misty replied.

"Killing Fred was very bad, but having him stay alive may have been worse. I am only here as a mediator and cannot help what has already been decided for each of you." Marco said.

"These documents are a hundred pages for both Alyson and Amir, but six hundred and fifty pages for James. Please take your time and read through everything on them. You can return to any cell to read or sit here and read each one. A signature will be required on the last page." Misty said.

"Ha, I guess Amir won't be signing anything." James said laughing.

"Not exactly, I brought something for him to sign with. Amir which hand do you write with?" Marco asked.

"Right." Amir responded.

Marco took out a few tools from a briefcase he had under the table and removed the damaged ends of Amir's arms in less than three minutes. In less than a minute Marco attached a crude looking metal pole on Amir's right arm with a simple twist down holding device for a pen. Amir gazed up then down shaking his head in disapproval.

"Just put the pen in my mouth and I will sign it that way." Amir said.

"I was going to mention I am left handed, but after seeing the other option, I will make do using my other hand." James said.

Alyson took her packet with her walking away to sit in one of the open cells to read the document. James sat at the table for a few minutes before walking away back to an open cell to go over all the documents pages. Amir was left with no choice but to sit at the table as Marco turned the pages for him. Amir had finished first and signed his papers, leaving out of a substantial double door with Misty escorting him. As soon as she got back to the table Alyson had also finished signing the paperwork and was on her way out of the facility.

It had been two hours since Alyson had left the facility with both Marco and General Misty Rail still standing by the table waiting for James. Marco left the facility for a brief period to retrieve a metal container with wheels that could double as a large check bag at an airport. The wheels made an echoing squealing sound as Marco rolled it towards the table. James was walking out of the cell about the same time and was back at the table.

"So, I read all the way through the punishment part and assume the rest is reasons for punishment." James said.

"Hold on Mr. Hawthorne there are about 150 more pages after the punishment section. I should know I was one of the people whom wrote the paperwork specifically for you." Misty said.

"One thing which is strange is this document is quite large and it would be almost impossible to write in one night, how long have we been here?" James asked.

"One week, you were all put into a temporary sleep so we could figure out what to do." Marco said.

"What!? So, I was in a coma for a week. Guess it isn't so bad I've been under for longer." James said.

"Not exactly a coma, we've been testing new suspended animation where your entire system slows to a crawl. I got the idea from watching a nature show about a frog which can be frozen entirely and unthawed with no harm. Instead of freezing your bodies, since humans are a little different from frogs we chemically slowed down your systems. This is the 9th successful test." Marco said bluntly.

"I can't read any more of this I have a splitting headache from lack of stimulants and need something. You can lock me up, since it is where this is all pointing too." James said.

"Locking you up, ha, you made me smile. No, we are far from just locking you up. After you took out Jim Berthlow the Russians had agreed you acted accordingly and strongly wanted to purchase you three from the United States. Then when the United States saw you do the same thing they cleared you all of any previous punishments. The only time anything controversial arose was when you shot Fred." Misty said.

"So, if I let the piece of shit live then I would be walking out of here? What about Liam? He sacrificed himself for nothing?" James asked.

Marco rolled a can of Yak wintergreen across the table to James and dumped out his cup of coffee on the ground giving it to James. Misty snatched up the can of chewing tobacco peeling the top with her thumbnail popping the top open. She tilted the can to James as he leaned forward grabbing a pinch, placing it in his lower lip. James sat back in the chair taking a deep breath in then spit into the cup Marco had dumped out.

"Liam has been recognized as a hero to the Zetas, as well as a hero to both the United States and Russia. There is some grey area where you fall into with what to do. Officially Fred never existed. We cannot imprison you for someone whom never existed." Misty said.

"With assistance of some Zetas from off this planet I tested skin samples of the Nozh creature as well as recent samples from Mr. Berthlow. They showed the powder their bodies produced was an inert fungus spore which would only react in a high nitrogen gas enriched environment." Marco said.

"So, what does that mean? They turn into mushrooms?" James asked.

"Nope, they grow in the environment and when inhaled grow into massive fungal balls in the lungs. It just so happens the environment of Saturn's moon Titan is nitrogen rich. Zetas can survive in a more nitrogen rich environment just as humans survive in an oxygen rich environment. Without going into too much anatomical detail I will say, Zetas adapted to survive in these two types of environments." Marco said.

"Fred was going to kill a bunch of Zetas? Why?" James asked.

"James, Fred was going to attempt to kill over a billion Zetas. My personal theory along with many others is to steal their advanced technology and return here with it. The Zetas are relatively peaceful since they consider everyone here less technologically advanced. I can only speculate as to why since he is not here to interrogate." Marco said.

"So, Zetas leave us alone because we are primitive creatures to them?" James asked.

"We are not considered primitive, it is just we are about a thousand years behind them on technology. They've done test with a few humans on their planet and found with the proper training with their technology humans are as proficient as they are. They trade us some resources for bits of tech information to help us advance." Misty said.

"My parents were sent here as children just as Fred was, and it is the reason he seemed to know a little bit more about the planet than most do. They believe by allowing the children of the punished to exist it will allow the Earth to advance. They are usually sent here at the age of around four Earth years. Now you try to remember how a car runs from when you were four. It just doesn't work. Fred was a rare case and was almost nine when he came here. Just as humans can grow from being small to an average size, Fred did the same. Since when he was younger he was small, even for a Zeta, they thought he was much younger than he actually was. Fred slipped through the system with a slight edge on all of us." Marco said.

"What is going to be done with me after all of this?" James asked.

"You are free to live your life as a citizen of the United States with no contact with Russia. Also you are not allowed to enter a Military base for the rest of your life. Sign the papers and you will be free to go." Misty said.

James leaned forward spitting into the cup, flipping the document to the last page he signed sloppily with his right hand. Misty closed up the document lifting it off the table walking out of the building. James began to stand up when Marco waved both of his hands in a downward motion slowly signaling James to stay sitting in the chair. After a few minutes the door to the building opened then slammed shut with a clang.

"Now Misty is gone I can tell you how I actually feel about what you did. I was a bit apprehensive about the violence, but when I realized how you saved more lives by ending a tyrant before he could get started I cried. Tears of joy, I was immediately contacted by the Zetas on Titan and after we found out about the spores they wanted to give you a hero's welcome. I told them you probably would be happier with something a little less grand." Marco said.

Marco laid the metal case on the ground waving for James to come over and look at it. First Marco handed him a six pack of beer. Then took out a machine looking similar to the machine which had ground off James left arm originally. Marco began to step towards James with the machine when James recoiled.

"Keep the arm grinder away from me!" James yelled, gripping his left elbow.

"No, no this is not the machine you think it is. Stick your left arm section out, please." Marco said.

James apprehensively stuck his left elbow out towards Marco. The machine sounded like an electric drill as it went over the control device on James left arm. It buzzed and got hot then stopped as James looked back at his left elbow it still appeared to be the same with a metal dish similar to a beer can bottom. Marco put the machine back in the case then pulled out a rectangular box three feet long by one foot wide, by one foot high. Marco opened the box placing three large platinum bars into the box.

Pressing the only button on the box it vibrated slightly then dinged like a microwave after thirty seconds. Marco opened the box showing James a new arm made from platinum. The arm did not appear different from his other arm, other than having less scratches and slightly more shiny. James grinned slightly seeing he would be able to keep his left arm.

"This arm is different than your previous one. I made sure you didn't need to carry any rubber finger tips with you as the finger tips will simply form into a dull user friendly tip when not being used in an aggressive manner. Simply flatten out your palm and the tips go from sharp to dull, or vice versa. Also, since you were successful at mastering the range of ten feet I had the distance you can disconnect your hand increased to twenty feet. Doubling your effective attacking range with this device." Marco said.

"Wow, this is awesome! Thank you Marco, I thought I was never going to have this again."

James re-attached his left arm playing with the deadly new self needling finger tip feature.

"Well, I had to retune your connection device on the end

of your arm, thus the reason for the tool I put on your arm earlier. Now the arm was my contribution, this next one you are receiving directly from the Zetas."

Marco pulled something familiar to James as it looked to be a new black gun belt with holster. The belt had six smaller holding spots for speed loaders three additional than his previous belt. It looked to be the same size as well as a thigh buckle for the gun to be more secure on his body. One main difference was it wasn't brown and worn out, it was just new. Marco handed the belt to James as he looked it over in his hands it felt similar and smelt like fresh leather. James shrugged a little in disappointment as he took the belt forcing a smile to appear happy with something as basic as a gun belt.

"Oh no, you have to put it on." Marco said.

James pulled the belt over his waist above his hips then buckled the leg strap to his right thigh.

"Now here is the other part to the belt. I figured you didn't want it oiled so I simply clear coated the outside for you so you won't become so dirty carrying it." Marco said.

Reaching into the case pulling out something heavy enough for Marco to use two hands to grasp it he handed James his familiar weapon. Rust was clear coated and had been cleaned up inside and oiled. James reached his right arm out took the bulky gun and pointed it up in the air, he pulled the hammer slightly back fanning the cylinder with his left hand. The cylinder spun smoothly until James put the hammer back in place dropping the gun into the holster.

"Wow, new gun belt and cleaned up, but still dirty looking gun. This is pretty cool." James said.

"Look down at your waist now."

Directing his eyes down to his waist there was a watery outline of the gun belt, holster, and gun. It seemed to disappear as James holstered his gun then he drew his gun out and it appeared again. James kept drawing and holstering until Marco threw a speed loader at James' head connecting with his forehead. James stopped immediately looking back up at Marco as he slid James the last few items from the case. The last items were five more speed loaders to make the total six and a black t-shirt with a white unicorn on it.

"What type of shirt is this, a unicorn shirt with a rainbow horn?" James asked confused.

"Liam had printed the shirt with intentions of wearing it, but you know what happened. It was recovered from what was left of his vehicle in Texas. Luckily I know enough people I was able to call in an old favor for it. If you do not want it, I can take it back."

"Marco, you can try to take it back, but it will not end good for you."

"This is what I thought you would say. Now with all of this out of the way, you are not a Government Agent anymore and must act only as a citizen. I did not give you any of those things you have. Your finances at this moment are....hold on, fifty seven dollars."

Marco took out a wallet from his pocket handing James the cash he had on him.

"Officially you are a regular citizen with no special privileges. Walk carefully through this world and I may contact you with some work opportunities. Now let's step out of this place it still disturbs me." Marco said.

"Why, this place is pretty dull?"

"Oh, yes you still don't know let's walk and talk."

Marco waved for James to follow him as he closed the case and began to walk out of the building.

"What happened here?" James asked.

"Fred broke into the facility and used a nerve gas agent to knock out all of them, roughly ten thousand. He kept a few out as perimeter guards until he got his robots, then killed them as you saw. The rest were loaded into containers to be exposed to the same fate as Jim. Unlike Jim they were put into a preservative sleep state the same as we used on you. They were what he was planning to destroy Titan with."

"Well, won't someone just make more enhanced?"

"The enhancing of soldiers stopped about a year ago as a shift towards better technology for current soldiers was more cost effective. Making ten thousand strong versus making an entire military strong made more sense to the higher ups. So, for now you are out of a job and broke since Fred stole everyone's funds for purchasing of black market equipment."

The sun blazed across James' eyes as Marco pushed the door open. A hairdryer hot wind blew across his face as he blinked to find his bearings. They were on a dirt road in the middle of the desert with two old large sedans outside. Marco put the case into the trunk of one of the cars and got in. Pointing out of the window Marco said.

"Take the car and head out to a place you feel safe."

As the window rolled up on Marco's vehicle a trail of dust kicked up as he drove away. James got into the car and drove for a few miles until he found a paved road. Following the dirty tire marks on the black pavement would send James the way Marco and everyone else went. James turned the opposite direction heading down his own path.

www.ingramcontent.com/pod-product-compliance
Lightning Source LLC
LaVergne TN
LVHW091109080826
845145LV00008B/1855

* 9 7 8 0 5 7 8 9 5 4 0 1 1 *